THE
BEATEN TRACK

Louise Mangos

RED DOG

UK

Published by RED DOG PRESS 2022

First Edition

Hardback ISBN 978-1-914480-63-8
Paperback ISBN 978-1-914480-61-4
Ebook ISBN 978-1-914480-62-1

This novel is dedicated to the folk encountered on my travels around the world who've let me pitch my tent in their grounds, offered me a hot meal on a cold day, a cold beer on a hot day, shared their stories round the campfire, and walked beside me on life's beaten track.

PROLOGUE

RAINDROPS SPATTER AGAINST the stiff sack that's been pulled over my head – *pop-pop-pop* – it sounds like distant gunfire. I hear the swelling rush of flooding water; we must be next to the river. The air is diminishing inside the claustrophobic space and smells of the fermented sourness of cattle feed and mouldy cardboard boxes.

You surprised the hell out of me this time.

I can't get purchase on the wet grass as you yank me by the rope into the river. I gasp with the temperature of the spring melt. My soaked boot rolls over a rock on the uneven riverbed and the flow sweeps me off my feet. Without the use of my arms, I fall into the water. I wriggle inside the sack, trying to work the rope up my arms. Cold seeps into my bones.

Two strands of the coiled rope begin to work themselves up my body. By craning my neck and reaching my hand towards my head, I am able to tear away one piece of sack from my face. You pull the rope again and I have to let go. I've managed to rip a section of the thick-layered feed sack away from one eye, and when I stare upwards, the shadowy monolith of the mountain above the farm towers over me in the dark. Cold raindrops against my eyeball make me blink.

I'm pulled down again into deep water. When I bob up, I take a gulp of air and cough violently as pieces of disintegrating paper fill my mouth. I spit them out, take another quick breath in the biting air.

Time for this stupid game to end.

I'm almost upright, but my feet no longer detect the riverbed. In the cold weightlessness, one of my arms loosens the rope a little more around my torso and I work it until the space becomes bigger. I start to kick out at all angles, hoping to find contact, to make you let go, to escape your clutch. My foot thumps against one of your limbs, but the water has dulled the impact of my boot. Instead I stop moving my legs to conserve energy.

Time has slowed, and I try to think of anything other than the oxygen my lungs are craving. We are both still under the water. I keep working my arm, and suddenly it comes free at the elbow, the rope having worked its way to my bicep.

I will not let you win. I will not let you take what rightfully belongs to me. I will fight to the end. Not mine. Yours. That you thought you could beat me is laughable.

I reach up with my hand, my fingers tangling in strands of your hair floating in the current. I clamp my hand over the front of your face, my thumb and forefinger finding the soft pits of your eyeballs. The other fingers of my hand squeeze your jaw, digging into your cheek, to force you to release the last of the air from your lungs, endeavouring to steal the last of the life from your body.

ONE

January 1988

I'VE ARRANGED TO have coffee with my best friend in the Café Tivoli on the main street in Châtel St Denis, but the waitress approaches me with a frown as I enter. Valérie has left a message saying she can't make it.

'A problem with her car she needs to fix,' the waitress says. 'She told me to look for a woman with a baby.'

I curse Valérie under my breath. She has no idea how much organisation it takes to get out of the house, and I've been looking forward to a good chat. My spare time is precious, between the turmoil of feeding and laundry, not helped by a disturbed sleep pattern and Papa's dementia.

Kai's fallen asleep. The smell of roasting coffee is alluring, so I decide to stay. Although I should be taking advantage and resting too, it feels good to be out. My brother's girlfriend, Marianne, is looking after Papa today. I feel guilty relief at being away from the house. Papa's frailty and decreasing moments of lucidity seem to have heightened my postnatal anxiety.

The café is crowded and my spirits fall as I scan the room, then lift again on spotting a free table in the corner by the window. The pram is cumbersome as I manoeuvre between seated customers. I feel inept, like a learner driver on her first lesson, bumping into the backs of chairs, causing sighs of protest and irritated glances.

Someone brushes past me. He waves his hand to placate customers who are obliged to move out of the way and he eases my passage to the table. Flushed with gratitude, I turn to thank my saviour.

'*Merci, Monsieur.*'

He tips his head, then points to the seat opposite mine.

'May I?' he asks.

I smile when I hear his accent. American, or maybe Canadian. I still can't tell, even after all those months globe-trotting with hordes of North American backpackers.

His sun-bleached hair flops over his blue eyes, and I can tell he's well-built under his linen shirt. As a single mother, my sole purpose should be to nurture my baby for these first uncertain months, so I'm a little abashed for reacting to this man's attention.

He picks up Kai's muslin that's fallen to the floor and hangs it over the handle of the pram. He leans down to peer in before sliding onto his seat.

'He's beautiful,' he says, eyeing the baby blue blanket.

Like many North American tourists, he assumes we all speak English. I smile.

'Thank you, on behalf of the baby,' I say. 'He's called Kai.'

I'm curious to see a shadow flit across his features.

'That's an interesting name,' he says.

He settles in his seat, and smiles back at me. His teeth are straight and white. Like a film star. I narrow my eyes and study his face, wondering if I've seen him on the cinema screen. He holds out his hand.

'I'm Scott,' he says. 'It's real nice to meet you.'

'Sandrine. But call me Sandy.'

His grip is strong, confident.

'Sandy…' he murmurs.

The way he says my name makes me tingle. I pull at my creased blouse and suck in my stomach, still soft from carrying Kai, wishing I'd paid more attention to some postnatal toning.

'Kai was the name of the baby's father,' I say. 'But we lost him before the little one was born.'

It isn't exactly a lie, but it feels weird saying this out loud to a stranger. Scott will probably excuse himself and take off at any moment. It isn't the first time in the past few months I've felt an overwhelming need to cry for no reason. Something to do with hormones.

But he reaches across the table and puts his hand on my arm. A Patek Philippe watch flashes at his wrist.

'Then it sounds like someone should be taking care of you,' he says.

I clear my throat, and change the subject, trying to cover my blush.

'It hasn't snowed much yet this season. Last year when I was away on my travels, they experienced the coldest temperatures on record here. What brings you to Switzerland?'

'I arrived a few months ago for work, so it looks like we've both picked the right year to be here, for the weather,' he says.

The awkward moment passes, and we continue the small talk. By the time we've finished our coffees, Kai begins to stir. I reach for my purse. Scott wants to pay, but I insist on splitting the bill. Outside the café he offers me a lift home, pointing to a black Range Rover in a parking space near the *Place d'Armes*.

I marvel at his chivalry, although it seems a bit forward. I nevertheless refuse, thinking of Kai's safety without a car seat. After we swap phone numbers, he helps me lift the pram onto the bus. He says he'll call soon. I'm sure that's the end of my Cinderella meets Prince Charming moment.

'MUST BE THE pheromones I'm giving off,' I joke with Valérie later on the phone.

'Do you fancy him?' she asks.

'He was rather lovely. Incredibly handsome. Makes a change to meet someone sophisticated and wealthy.'

'You deserve a little attention after your nightmare last year, Sand,' Valérie says, and I shiver. 'Makes a change from all those backpacking hippies.'

Valérie hums a few bars of Roy Orbison's *Pretty Woman* and mentions something about finding a rich handsome suitor to sweep me off my feet. I don't think any more of it; I'm sure Scott won't call.

TWO

BUT HE DOES call a few days later. We arrange to meet in Vevey on a market day when he says he has time off work. It's a mild winter morning. We walk along the shore of Lac Léman and through the old town while Kai wriggles in the pram, practising a new high-pitched screeching. Scott doesn't seem bothered. The bustle of the market, with accordion music filtering down the alleyways between the stalls, drowns Kai's vocals.

'How're you doing?' Scott asks.

I marvel at his calmness with Kai beginning to demand more attention in the pram.

'A little tired,' I say. An understatement. 'I think Kai's getting hungry. I need to find somewhere to feed him.'

I force a smile. In truth the smell of vegetable scraps, overripe fruit and caustic textile dye is making me feel a little ill. In my role as a new mother, I have no idea how to play out what is effectively our first date.

Scott places his hand lightly on the small of my back as we navigate our way through the crowds. When he helps guide the pram out of the way of a child on a scooter, I turn to thank him for these little kindnesses. My stomach does a flip as our eyes meet.

Away from the market, we find an empty bench on the promenade by the lake where I breastfeed Kai under a shawl.

Scott pulls the cloth across my shoulder when a gust of wind blows it away and tactfully averts his gaze. We share a bottle of apple juice and a cheese *ramequin* he bought from the bakery stall. He breaks off morsels of the small quiche and hands them to me.

'Tell me about growing up in the States,' I say.

He shrugs. 'Not much to tell. High school. College. After I graduated I got a job at a bank in Chicago. A couple of years later I was offered a contract in Geneva. I love Switzerland. It's like living in a fairy tale. All this alpine quaintness. I could see myself staying on, perhaps renewing my contract.' He pauses. 'But I don't want to talk about me. I want to find out about you.'

There are dark moments of my round-the-world journey last year I don't want to share with anyone. Grim memories that are best forgotten. I think about what I might tell him about myself.

'Where did you learn to speak English?' he continues before I get the chance to speak. 'Your accent is perfect.'

'I went to a private bilingual school. Up there. You can see it just below the forest.' I point to a turreted building on a slope above the town.

'Looks expensive.'

'An uncle of ours emigrated to Australia years ago. He made a fortune running a sheep station in Queensland. Although he had kids of his own, he set up a trust for my brother and me for our education. Probably felt guilty about leaving my father here to run the family farm.'

'Did you enjoy it?'

'We had a great childhood and the school was fun. Now I've seen more of the world, I can really appreciate that.'

'What did you do when you graduated?'

'I had okay grades, and a few offers of places at university here and in the UK. But I decided to save up to travel first. I intended to re-apply after the year off, but came back with something a little unexpected…'

I lift Kai in my arms as I say the word 'unexpected' and press my lips against his silky head.

'Where did you travel?' Scott asks.

I don't want to talk about my backpacking trip, so I remain vague about the journey, giving him a brief itinerary. When I mention America, New Zealand, Australia and Asia, a muscle ticks in his cheek. What must he think about the whims of a girl who doesn't know what to do with her life and has carelessly allowed herself to get pregnant?

'Let me drive you home,' he says.

'That's a kind offer. But I don't want to put Kai in a car without a proper baby seat. You probably think I'm being over-protective…'

'Well, my neighbour has a car seat his kid grew too big for, and I've borrowed it.'

'Are you serious?'

I warm to his thoughtfulness, and wonder what Valérie would say. Probably that Scott must really fancy me if he's prepared to go this far.

I lift Kai out of the pram and put him in the car seat. It's a Maxi Cosi, the current in-thing for yuppie parents with budgets way above my own. It looks brand new, but I don't say anything. I'm amazed he's done this for me, on the off-chance he can drive me home. I click the buckles around Kai's little body. My fatigue and guilt are forgotten in this new hopeful excitement.

I settle into the passenger seat, enjoying the smell of new leather, and stroke the polished walnut inlay of the dashboard. My brother Pierre will be jealous about me getting a ride in this modern descendent of our farm vehicles.

'Are you interested in seeing my place?' Scott asks as he starts the engine.

I press my lips together. This is going fast.

'Okay,' I say after a pause. 'Just a few minutes. I have to get the little guy home.'

We drive through the terraced vineyards above Lac Léman, with snow lying in crusty patches between the rows of gnarled dormant vines. On the outskirts of the village of Chardonne, Scott pulls up in front of a duplex apartment. It's constructed mostly of glass on the south side, taking maximum advantage of the spectacular view across the lake to the snowy French peaks.

'Holy shit!' slips out of my mouth before I can stop it.

'No cursing,' he says jokingly, turning to look at Kai asleep in the car seat.

Scott unlocks the door and with Kai still in the Maxi Cosi hanging in the crook of my elbow, we walk into a stunning modern interior. I imagine my mother tapping under my chin with her hand, and remember to close my mouth. I've just walked into the house of my dreams.

'J P Morgan is a generous company to work for,' Scott says, seeing my expression. 'They take care of everything. My personal health and welfare.'

I try not to sound eager when he asks if I want to look around. The four bedrooms are tastefully decorated in the earthy colours I love. Everything looks fresh and new. *How perfect*, I want to say, and then think it might look like I'm coming on a bit strong. I mention I need to use the bathroom. I'm surprised when he shows me to his ensuite rather than the guest bathroom, allowing me so quickly into his personal space. Perhaps he wants to prove he doesn't have anything to hide. I bite my lip as I take Kai with me, thank him and lock the door behind me. I marvel at the contrast to our cranky old pipes in the bathroom at the farm with its wonky towel rails, bath toys and piles of infant laundry in the corner. My toes curl with pleasure inside my socks as they suck up the warmth of Scott's underfloor heating and I hold the plush towel to my cheek after I've dried my hands.

I take a quick peek inside his bathroom cabinet and stare at the creams and lotions. I'm contemplating the level of his vanity when my gaze falls on a bottle of saline solution for contact lenses. I'm secretly thrilled that there is this one tiny imperfection in Scott's otherwise impeccable physique. On the top shelf is a bone fish hook, a typical tourist souvenir from New Zealand. I make a note to ask whether he'd been there, as he hadn't mentioned it when I talked about my travels. It lies next to a watch, the kind divers use. I imagine it would be rather pleasant to go scuba-diving or snorkelling on a tropical reef with this handsome American.

I close the cabinet, comb my unruly hair with my fingers, pick up Kai in the Maxi Cosi, and join Scott at the foot of the stairs.

'How long have you been in this place?' I ask.

'A couple of months. I lived in a condo in Geneva for a while until I decided to move to somewhere less urban.'

'That's a bit of a commute. You'll never use half these rooms. Unless you have family to stay. Don't you feel lost in here?'

'Would you like a tea? Coffee? Something else?' he asks, brushing off my question.

As we walk to the kitchen, I wonder not for the first time what on earth a guy like this is doing flirting with someone like me. But as I place the Maxi Cosi on the slate-tiled floor, I choose not to question his motives too closely. I surely deserve a little attention?

As I stand up, Scott holds my shoulders. He gazes into my eyes, and my heart spikes with the intensity of his look. He kisses me tentatively. I don't react immediately, and he pulls away, a little embarrassed. I grab his shirt and kiss him back. He presses his body against mine, and I feel his passion against my hip. As we draw apart, I stand on my toes to whisper 'tea, please' hoarsely in his ear.

THREE

'ARE YOU SURE about this guy, Sandrine?' Marianne asks later when I describe our day out. 'Isn't it weird he's coming on so strong? I mean, you have such a young baby.'

Scott has driven me home and dropped me off after we finished our tea. Marianne sits at the table in the farm kitchen cradling Kai in her arms while I cook dinner. It's not the first time I think the role suits her more than me. Her curtain of auburn hair falls around her face as she smiles down at Kai.

'He's so hot, Marianne, and he seems so keen. I just wish Kai was a little older. I feel so frumpy and tired right now.'

'You're a good-looking young woman, Sandrine, whether you're a mother or not. What does he do for a living? You don't want him suddenly running back to the States because his contract has finished.'

'He told me his assignment with J P Morgan could be renewed. He's sure they'd offer him a local contract if he requested it. I know you're trying to protect me—'

'I just don't want to see you get hurt.'

'I'll be fine. Don't worry. My focus is on Kai's wellbeing now.'

Marianne smiles and hugs Kai to her. I wonder whether he's making her feel broody. Since my early return from travelling I feel like I'm encroaching on Pierre and Marianne's relationship.

After Kai's arrival I've rarely been on hand to help with Papa's care, although in normal circumstances I might have moved out by now anyway, either for study or work.

'You're very kind to me, Marianne. I'm so grateful you've accepted all this.'

I turn back to the stove, and worry how the hell I'm going to support Kai and myself financially.

In the meantime, it's good to have the attention of a handsome man, no matter how fleeting it may turn out to be.

OUR COURTSHIP IS intense. We see each other almost every other day. Dinners, cinema, theatre, when Marianne can babysit. Boat trips on the lake, drives to the mountains, walks with the pram when she can't. I get the feeling Scott wants to take the relationship further, but there's the uncomfortable matter of the birth to consider. It's beyond the waiting time prescribed by the doctor, but as it would be the first time I've slept with Scott, I'm a little timid. He is lovely about it, and doesn't push me. 'I've been waiting for someone like you all my life,' is how he often puts it; he'll wait until I am ready.

He sometimes holds Kai and studies him intently. I'd like to believe if he's falling for me, he'll fall for my baby too. Adding up the positives, I know I want to give him more.

'He wants to take me to Paris!' I tell Pierre and Marianne when Scott drops me at home after a night out.

I dance around Kai who's sitting in his baby bouncer gumming his fist, waiting for his bedtime feed. He jumps at my squeal. When I kiss him on the forehead, he scrunches up his eyes as a lock of my hair tickles his nose. His mouth widens into a smile and he lets out a raucous giggle. I take it as a sign.

'And you're coming with us,' I say to him. 'I told Scott I couldn't possibly leave you behind, and he said of course you can come, little man. Can you believe it?'

'He didn't suggest you leave him with us for the weekend?' Marianne asks.

'No. He knows I couldn't leave him behind. Oh, Marianne, it's like something out of a romantic movie. Paris! A dream come true.'

'I'm guessing he wants something you haven't given him yet, hey, Sis?' Pierre says with a theatrical wink.

AFTER CHECKING INTO a spacious suite at the Plaza on the Champs Elysées, we set out on foot to discover the city. Our visit to the Louvre is abandoned when Kai begins his squealing, the sound magnified in the great halls. Scott is a gentleman, and doesn't complain about cutting short the tour.

We take a ride on a *Bâteau Mouche*. The vibration of the motor and the gentle rocking on the waters of the Seine send Kai into a deep slumber. Scott takes us to Saint Germain to buy clothes, shoes, jewellery and expensive infant outfits.

Returning to the hotel in the late afternoon, I organise a babysitter. Not wanting to be far away from Kai, I ask Scott if we can eat at the restaurant downstairs. I later find out the chef holds three Michelin stars, and tables are usually booked months in advance. Somehow Scott manages to secure a reservation anyway. We are welcomed like royalty.

The scene is set with a bottle of champagne, the sparkling art deco lights of the dining room, and every mouthful of food a sensual experience itself. Scott is initially sceptical about the tiny portions on his plate, but I know his desire for something else is replacing his appetite. And nervous excitement is blunting the edge of my own.

WE STAND AT the foot of the bed. As Scott's kisses grow bolder I know this is right. My body is reacting and I crave his touch. He takes off his shirt without removing his mouth from mine, and his chest pushes against me. This invokes a flicker of pleasure deep in my belly.

He lays me gently on the bed. Raw passion flashes in his eyes as he gazes at my body dressed in the new Chanel night shift he bought me this afternoon. My heartrate escalates. I'm glad to be horizontal, my tummy flattened by gravity. I want to look sexy for him. His muscles flex as he leans towards me. I pray my breast milk doesn't choose this moment to stain the oyster silk.

He slowly removes the garment, the material caressing my body. I lift my arms as he pulls it over my head. Throwing the shift to the floor, he kisses my neck under my ear, and moves his lips across my throat. I want him so much.

'Oh Sandy,' he breathes. 'I've waited so long for you.'

I smile, glad we can finally give ourselves to each other. He carefully enters me.

'Is it okay? Are you okay?' he asks.

I nod as his passion begins slowly and languorously. I know he is being gentle, so I encourage him as I feel my lower belly clenching with pleasure. He moves his lips from my mouth to the dip at the base of my throat. I think of Kai, sleeping soundly in his cot in the suite's sitting room next door, how much I want a normal life with love and security for him. And a fleeting thought: *Don't wake up now.*

Scott gently tugs my hair to expose more of my throat and his lips feather my skin. When I close my eyes, the vision of my baby's father – Kai senior – swims into my thoughts. A little guiltily, I sweep away his image. That time has passed. Scott and I are together now. My head falls back onto the pillow, my breath shortens.

Scott's fingers rest briefly on my collar bone, then grip my shoulder, his thumb sinking into the hollow between the clavicle and the muscle. As his grasp triggers an almost sweet pain, his hot breath whispers in my ear: 'Finally we are together.'

A shock courses through my body, a taser of memory.

Suddenly I am right back on that beach in Thailand the year before.

FOUR

June 1986

WE ARE TWO hundred feet above San Francisco Bay when I set eyes on you. I'm driving towards Sausalito across the Golden Gate Bridge, Robert Palmer's chart-topping "Addicted to Love" blaring on the radio, and there you are, half way between the two great towers. I'm drawn to your blond curls swirling in the wind. The tug of an ever-present memory. You stand stock still, and in that moment, I'm struck with the similarity your face has to the grainy black and white picture wedged into the air vent on my dash. Ma.

Your hands clutch the straps of your backpack. As I pass by, I keep staring at your image diminishing in my rear-view mirror, throwing the occasional look back to the road so I don't drift over the lanes. Your wide eyes and your open mouth make me think you've experienced a surge of terror as you glance through the mesh gaps next to the sidewalk to the waves of the Pacific white-capping into the bay below you. I can sense the fear, because I did that too, the first time I crossed the bridge on foot several weeks ago. I remember thinking Pa would have called me a sissy-boy.

Apart from the uncanny likeness to a mother I haven't seen for sixteen years, it's our first connection, that look of fear. I remember the tremble and swing of the bridge, the dizziness in my head when I thought I was about to die. I know you want to lie down to stop the swaying. But the potential embarrassment in front of surrounding witnesses, and the thought of that vertiginous drop makes you wish you could fly to the safety of solid land instead. I want to stop the car and offer you a ride, but know I would cause mayhem in the middle of the heavy freeway traffic.

Instead I park my car at Vista Point in the hope of catching sight of you. But I can't see you from the foreshortened angle of the suspension cables stacked against each other in my line of vision. I'm impatient and a little worried. I climb in my car and drive back across the bridge.

By the time I reach you, the moment has passed and you're striding along, gaze fixed ahead, your demons expunged. As I approach in the far lane, the oncoming traffic periodically blocks my line of sight. You laugh out loud, to no one in particular, most likely at the ridiculous moment of fear. And then you toss your sun-bleached curls back in the wind, exposing your slender throat. The tug of longing for my mother is replaced by something more feral, a primeval spark. In that one witnessing of your raw, wild freedom, I fall for you. It's as though you are already part of me. I've seen your moment of weakness. Your vulnerability.

And I know I have to protect you forever.

I GREW UP in a dead-end town on the dusty plains of Kansas, the Rocky Mountains a mythical temptation to the west. In the winter, the peaks seemed more attainable. I used to believe I could see them, shining on the horizon with a fresh coating of snow. In reality, I probably only saw a band of clouds in the distance.

Ma died of cancer when I was five years old. I was too young to know what was going on, though I knew she was gone. I remember crying at the funeral and for several days afterwards. A week later, Pa told me to buck up and stop my snivelling. It was time for me to be a man. At five, for Chrissakes!

I kept a photo of Ma in the draw beside my bed. Every night I took it out, touched her face, asked her to keep me safe, and said goodnight to the most beautiful woman I ever knew, to the *only* woman I ever knew.

Pa went on a drinking binge for a couple of years. I became accustomed to the back of his hand across my face. But he never met anyone new, which is a damn shame, as things might have been different for me growing up as an only child if there'd been a woman in the house.

Hitting wasn't all Pa's hands were used for.

In the darkness, he would come to my room, make me touch him, make me take him in my mouth, make me taste the salt of him, and then curse me when I wouldn't react the way he thought I should. I didn't realise the strangled pain in his voice was actually pleasure. I latched on to a brief fantasy of his torture, before it sank in that he would be back again the next night, or the night after that.

'You're damaged goods, buddy,' he'd often say. 'You'll never be good for anything. No one will ever want you.'

I had no friends, kept pretty much to myself, thinking everyone could see how unclean I was inside. I was already taller than Pa when I reached tenth grade, but by then it was too late for him to retract his actions during my childhood. Those terrible things could never be obliterated from my memory.

Pa no longer had control over me, and he knew it. His abuse changed to the verbal variety, perhaps worried I might finally fight back. I thought about it, but although I was taller than him, I was still puny and weak. He would have beaten me for sure. I never had the guts to tell anyone what he'd done to me as a kid.

I went to a local college after high school. You'd think I'd have wanted to run a million miles from that Godforsaken dust bowl, but at the time we didn't have enough money to send me out of state, and I knew I had to finish college if I had any chance of escape. But then, right after graduation, Pa sold the ranch to some big shot city ex-banker whose life ambition was to run a dude facility for stressed-out financiers. He offered more for the land than Pa could refuse.

Pa gave me a big cut of the sale of the farm. He called it a living inheritance, said he wanted to see me enjoy the money while he was still alive. At first I thought of it as a guilt payment. I almost threw his cash in his face. I wanted nothing from him. It made me feel dirty all over again. As though I was his boy whore. But then I thought refusing the money would be spiting myself, so I grabbed my share, bought a second-hand pick-up, and took off west.

When I reached Colorado, the flatlands still shimmered in my rear-view mirror. I had arrived at the mountains of my dreams, and I never wanted to look back. It felt like I hadn't travelled far enough away from my past. Rather than stopping in the place I'd half-built my hopes on for so many years, I was compelled to keep going. Once I reached the first anvils of the Rockies, I drove right up the gulley where I-70 carves into the granite, and kept going all the way to Vegas.

I HADN'T EVEN unpacked my bag, left it sitting on the bed in a grubby motel room off the main strip. I headed into the first casino I came to. It was as good a place as any to throw away Pa's dirty money.

'Hi. My name's Cindy, can I get you a drink?'

I remember frowning when the bunny girl eyed the beaker of dollar tokens at my side.

'It's free,' she whispered.

Her crimson lips matched the nails on her fingers, skilfully balancing a tray. She was the first female who'd ever shown me any attention, apart from my mother a long time ago, and I was terrified. But I'd learned to hide that shit.

'Cool. I'll have a root beer please. Just going to pump this baby for a bit,' I said, trying to sound casual as I settled onto the stool in front of a giant slot machine. I must have sounded like a juvenile fool. 'My name's Jake, by the way.'

Cindy flashed her cardboard cut-out smile and went to get my drink.

There was something like a fifty-million-to-one chance of winning the jackpot on one play of those megabuck slots, but on Good Friday 1986, when everyone else was thinking of crucifixion and death, I hit it lucky.

FIVE

SINCE ARRIVING IN San Francisco several months ago, I've been holed up at the Ritz-Carlton, surrounded by a pile of gadgets and games bought with my winnings, waiting for direction and purpose to fall into my lap. I'm now bored shitless. There's only so much Nintendo a boy can play. Seeing you is like a light turning on after years of confusing darkness. My life has meant nothing until this moment. My constant sadness is missing Mom, and my greatest joy, well, I can't think of any until now. But here you are, alive and real, like you've stepped out of that photo. I am happy for the first time.

It's not hard to follow you to the city. I've been getting used to driving back and forth over that bridge out of boredom. You ask the woman at the ferry terminal the cheapest way to get back to the Fort Mason Youth Hostel on public transport. After stopping for a milkshake in the Marina Café at Sausalito, you take a bus back to town. It's as though you're offering me an invitation to share your world. I fall in love with your voice, a soft lilt that tells me you're not American. It adds to the exoticism of you.

By the end of the following morning I've already learned to stick close to avoid losing track of you. I tail you down to Fisherman's Wharf and ride on the carriage behind yours on the tram back up Hyde Street. After only half a day I'm hooked. My mission is set in stone.

YOU'RE WAY TOO open and friendly. On the one hand, it makes my task easy, but I'm shocked at how you share your travel plans so openly with complete strangers over a coffee in a tourist café or a bowl of clam chowder on Pier 49. I want to warn you there are a lot of crazies out there. As the days progress I can't figure out how to actually approach you. You're a treasure too precious to touch. Part of me desperately wants to walk right up to you. But the longer I wait, the more terrifying that idea becomes.

I'm both excited and frightened at the ferocity of my emotions. I know if you were mine, I'd have to wrap you up somewhere safe. Remembering my mother's arms, I imagine a feeling of security. Then I'm reminded of my father, holding me with confusion each time he used my body for his pleasure, knowing this thing he was doing wasn't right.

I have to let you think you can still be free.

IT'S BEEN TOUGH moving out of the five-star hotel to the run-down establishment on North Point Street. I've become accustomed to the luxury accommodation my new-found fortune can provide.

The North Point lodgings are seedy and tired. There are probably more prostitutes in the building than travelling guests. The guy I've employed as my financial advisor would pop a pearl button on his Ralph Lauren shirt if he even took a whiff of this place.

But from the window of my room I have a great view of the main entrance of the Fort Mason youth hostel. It makes my room choice priceless, a cheap investment with high return. I haven't yet figured out how you're going to be travelling. Do you have a hire car? Are you riding the Greyhound? It's all still a guessing game.

My greatest fear is that you'll be whisked away in a taxi at any given moment, and although I have nothing else to do in my life, a need to eat, or even a simple call of nature might make me miss your next move. The pizza delivery place on the corner takes care of the first, and empty Coke bottles are often necessary for the second. I grab a few hours' sleep in the dead of night.

I can't afford to let you out of my sight.

'ARE YOU LEAVING this morning too?' I overhear you ask someone.

I'm sitting outside on the grass, a packaged sandwich at my side, knowing you're eating breakfast in the cafeteria. The window is open, and my attention is immediately sharpened. Leaving?

'*Ja*, we have the Airport Shuttle booked for eleven,' says a girl with what sounds like a German accent.

'Then we must be on the same one. I'd better go finish packing,' you say.

There's a scrape of a chair on the wooden floorboards. I grab my jacket and run back to my room. You're leaving town, and I haven't got my shit together. 11:00 am. That gives me an hour.

Back in my room, I throw my things into my pack. I keep looking out the window to make sure the shuttle bus hasn't arrived yet. I leave half my clothes lying around the room. It's no big deal. I can buy what I need later. I'm still not used to the fact I can buy anything I want. Along with a handful of credit cards, I always have cash in my pocket. A roll of greenbacks can get me anywhere.

I wait behind the bushes near the entrance to the hostel grounds. When the Express Shuttle shows up for the airport, you and five other girls load your packs and get on. The vehicle is much smaller than I expected. There's no way I can sneak on and pay my ticket without being noticed. Instead I run to my pick-up parked on North Point and throw a U-turn to slip in behind the bus and tail you to the airport. As you and the girls sort your luggage at the drop-off point outside the United terminal, I abandon my car in a tow-away zone nearby.

Inside the terminal building you haul your backpack to a United counter. When I see the destination, my heart drops. Auckland.

It hadn't occurred to me you might be leaving the country. I assumed you'd be taking an internal flight, working your way eastwards towards the Big Apple like most other backpacking foreigners. Now I realise you could be going anywhere. Sweet Jesus, Auckland. I have a passport, obtained for my disastrous senior trip to Puerto Vallarta some years ago, but I don't even know if I need a visa to get to New Zealand.

I retreat to the other side of the departure hall, and pull out every item in my goddamned pack, swearing under my breath. I'm sure I put my passport in with my other personal papers, but I can't find it anywhere. It must still be in the room with my other stuff. I'm real pissed to come so close, and lose you because of a moment's lack of order.

My frustration draws the attention of one of the security staff, so I repack, and make myself inconspicuous behind the oversized baggage tunnel. I look again at the flight number on the sign over the counter. There's a stopover in Honolulu. I clench my jaw and pray. I even consider calling the pizza delivery guy to offer him a thousand bucks to break down the door of my room on North Point and bring me my passport.

When it's your turn at the counter, you pull a bundle of tickets from a money belt hidden under your T-shirt. The check-in lady smiles.

'Where are you travelling to today Ma'am?'

I hold my breath.

'Honolulu,' you say.

I sigh with relief. You'll still be in the US. If I have any chance of continuing this mission, I need to do some homework. I must learn your itinerary. I have to find out all the destinations on that bundle of tickets in your belt. Keeping you in my sights is essential.

I have the added challenge of figuring out how I'm going to get myself a new passport. A more pressing question is whether they still have seats left on the afternoon flight to Honolulu.

'JACOB SPENCER. MR Jacob Spencer is requested to approach a member of the crew at the gate.'

I wince when I hear my name announced like a siren over the public address system and leap out of my chair. I pull my cap down over my sunglasses, and circle the back of your seat. But I needn't have worried about you hearing. A yellow Sony Walkman lies in your lap, headphones clamped over your ears, and your head is buried in a book. I can almost reach out and touch your golden curls. Instead I pass by and continue towards the desk.

'Mr Spencer?' the stewardess asks.

I'm relieved her voice is quiet, that I no longer feel conspicuous with the intrusion of the echoing PA system. I nod, swallowing the frustration I've been feeling for the past hour.

My whole future depends on this moment.

'You'll be pleased to know a seat has been confirmed for you on this flight to Honolulu, Mr Spencer. Thank you for your patience while waiting for stand-by.'

Relief floods through me. I glance in your direction while you continue to read your book unawares.

'Here's your boarding pass, sir, and the receipt for your bag. We'll load it into the hold directly from here.'

I award the stewardess a rare smile; she doesn't know it, but she's changed my life forever.

SIX

'SANDY, IT'S SO good to see you!' said Roz when she met me at Honolulu Airport. 'I can't believe you're finally here. It's been like, eight years. Shit, time flies!'

She was my best friend in middle school. Her father worked at the world headquarters of the Nestlé Corporation in Vevey for a few years during our childhood, until he was reposted to Hawaii.

'I knew there was an important reason we became penfriends,' I jested. 'If I'd known how beautiful this place was, I'd have shipped myself with you in your suitcase back then.'

I loved Oahu the moment I walked down the gangway. Away from the airport and the pungent fumes of kerosene, the smells of the tropical vegetation were a world apart from our Swiss pine forests. A combination of the scents of frangipani and humid foliage drifted on balmy wafts of salty air, even in gridlocked downtown Honolulu. With the gentle cooing of the zebra doves, softer on the ear than their distant European cousins, the perfect sensory recipe was set for a holiday in paradise. After the stress of San Francisco's busy metropolis, I was looking forward to some lazy island time.

Roz had skipped a lecture at university to meet me at the airport. We boarded the shuttle to downtown, then took a bus to her small one-bedroomed home in the suburb of Moana.

'Saves on parking fees at the airport, and I can show you the route to the beach for when I'm at school.'

Sitting on her wooden front deck amidst a chorus of crickets and the clicking of geckos, we caught up on family news, sipping our guava cocktails.

'How's your dad?' she asked.

'It's sad, Roz, you wouldn't recognise him. Sometimes he doesn't even recognise me. My brother, Pierre, and his girlfriend, Marianne, are looking after him. A therapist comes by every now and then. I felt a little guilty leaving them in charge, but the farm is Pierre's business now. Everyone was dubious about me dropping the uni applications, but Pierre encouraged me to do some secretarial temping to save for this trip. They even helped a bit with my round-the-world plane ticket.'

'So how do you like the big old US of A?'

'It's great. Got to tick a few boxes. A dream trip so far. New England, Chicago, the Grand Canyon. When I reached the west coast, I bus-hopped north on Highway One along the Californian coastline to San Francisco. That was my favourite city. I'm looking forward to discovering Honolulu too.'

'I don't have class until Monday afternoon, so I can spend the weekend showing you around,' said Roz. 'After that, you know you're welcome to stay as long as you like. Think of it as pay back for all those awesome summers we had messing around on your farm. I seriously recommend going to one of the other islands, though. Honolulu's not a patch on what we've got on offer elsewhere.'

At the weekend, we drove around Oahu. We swam over the reefs at Hanauma Bay, and Roz surfaced, spluttering with laughter each time I squealed through my snorkel at the shoals of tropical fish swimming amongst the coloured corals. Afterwards, we ate fresh king crab from the Shrimp Shack, a yellow van parked on the side of the road north of Kaawa. Continuing round the island, on the North Shore we watched Roz's friends in a pre-season surfing competition on the Banzai Pipeline. The daring antics of the surfers took my breath away, reminiscent of black-run skiing in the Alps. Back in the south, Roz showed me her favourite spot on Waikiki Beach, where I spent most of the following days while she attended her courses at the university. Body surfing, watching endless games of beach volleyball and eating fifty-cent slush puppies were high on my agenda. But most of all, I relished relaxing into island mode.

Every dollar I could save on my travel budget was a bonus. I assured Roz if she ever came back to visit Switzerland, there would be a place to stay at the farm. But Roz had her own life to live without some long-lost friend monopolising her sofa. I took her advice and planned to visit another island before I overstayed my welcome.

'You gotta see the Big Island,' she said. 'It has so much to offer. I'm going back to live there when I finish college. Hawaiian Airlines is doing a special to Kona right now. Too good to pass up. I wish I could come with you, but I've just got too much on at college.'

So, by the end of the week it was decided I would head out to the Big Island on my own.

SEVEN

I COME CLOSE to busting my cover one morning when we're among only a dozen or so passengers heading to Waikiki on the bus. I'm worried you'll turn and see me. Recognition at this stage is my greatest fear. Although I long for the smile of acknowledgement, the unpredictability of an unplanned meeting is still terrifying. I keep thinking today will be the day I summon up the courage to introduce myself to you. Then I falter and remind myself of the advantages of learning all about you first. But baseball caps and dark glasses won't help if they've been clocked a couple of times. I don't want you to think I'm some kind of weirdo stalker.

Instead I rent a pick-up with a king-cab from a hire company downtown. There's a small parking lot outside the Lyon Arboretum along from where your friend with the spiky red hair lives. I hunker down at night in the back of the vehicle without disturbance from neighbours or the cops.

I listen in to conversations from a distance, filtering out everything else in the vicinity to focus on your voice, like one of those sensitive microphones used in spy movies. But it's not always enough. Spiky has already told you she only has one key for her place. It's hidden under the pot with the dead orchid beside the steps to the veranda. On Monday when I know you're down at Waikiki Beach and Spiky is at school, I let myself into her house, determined to uncover your whole round-the-world plan.

A backpack, a crumpled sleeping bag, and some clothes are stacked on the floor next to the foldout sofa in the living room. I pull a T-shirt from the pile of clothes and bury my face in it. It's the first time I experience your true essence. You are as I imagine. A strong forest scent, maybe pine or balsam, accompanies the musk of your body. Hooked onto my fingers under your T-shirt is a pair of peach-coloured panties. I push them into my back pocket and put your shirt back on the pile.

I want to lie down where I know you've been, inhale you, touch the places you've touched, but I know I can't linger. You or Spiky could come home at any moment.

I find your airline tickets tucked into your red passport underneath a map of New Zealand on the low table in front of the sofa. I flick the passport open. *Sandrine Bavaud.* I'm surprised you're Swiss but congratulate myself on recognising your French accent. I forgot they speak French there. I let your name roll around a few times on my tongue. *Sandrine, Sandrine, Sandrine.* I write down the details of your itinerary and the address from the back of your passport and hightail it out of there.

The fear of you getting on a plane without me being able to follow you is like a cancer in my gut. The day after I check out your flight tickets, I follow you to Waikiki. Once you're settled on your towel, I walk past Ala Moana to Downtown Honolulu, go straight to the passport office to declare that mine has been lost somewhere between San Francisco and here. When they explain it will take at least a week to issue a new one, my angst returns. The provisional date for your onward flight to New Zealand is exactly a week away.

No amount of tantrum-throwing or cash incentive can get those bozos to speed up my passport renewal. I've already paid for the express service due to the loss, and they say there's a backlog. There's a chance you might stay for longer. How could a girl like you come all the way to Hawaii and only visit Honolulu?

I plan on sneaking back into Spiky's place to steal your passport, but in the end, I don't need to. Later that afternoon, after the forms have been filled in, new photos taken, my social security verified, and all manner of checks done on my identity, I tail you from the beach to a travel agent on Kapiolani Boulevard. A guardian angel must be listening to me. You change your airline departure to two weeks later, and purchase a Hawaiian Airlines ticket to Hawaii, the Big Island.

EIGHT

I FLEW TO Kona after a week with Roz, and secured a cheap deal on a rental car with my flight package. Budget hotels and hostels were few and far between on the Big Island, so to compensate for the cost of the rental car, I camped in the small tent I'd bought when I was staying in the Rocky Mountains.

After a few days beach-hopping up the west coast, staying in state camp grounds for a couple of dollars a night, I drove over to the leeward side of the island. As I crossed the northern tip of Hawaii I passed the cusp between two constantly battling weather fronts. The view from Waimea was of two vastly different landscapes, one arid to the west and the other tropical to the east.

The east coast was lush, with significantly higher rainfall. Humid air, thick with the vegetative aromas of tropical plants, blew about my head through the open window. An azure ocean winked through the gaps in the trees.

After a visit to the main town of Hilo, I pulled into an empty campsite on a ridge overlooking the coast where I finally unpacked the tent.

The site was a flat grassy field surrounded on all sides by a thick forest. The place looked abandoned when I arrived in the afternoon. I pitched my tent in the middle of the field. Although this meant there was no shade, I avoided falling guavas and other sticky gifts dropped by the flocks of birds roosting in the trees.

As I was finishing a picnic of bread, cold meats and fruit purchased earlier at a store, a pick-up truck pulled into the campsite. It was towing an iconic cigar-shaped silver caravan. The driver reversed under the trees and leapt out. He patted a large black and brown mongrel tied to a rope in the open flatbed.

My anxiety spiked. A man on his own. With a big dog. I rummaged around in my pack to locate the pepper-spray the manager of a Chicago hostel had recommended I purchase from the local army surplus store. 'For your peace of mind,' he had said. I slipped it into my back pocket.

The man wound down the supporting jacks on his caravan and unhooked it from the truck. He stood up and waddled towards me, his flip-flops snapping on the grass.

'What's a *Haole* princess doing here in the middle of nowhere?' The heavy-set islander spoke with disarming Polynesian charm.

'I'm on a round-the-world trip,' I admitted hesitantly, pushing a tent peg into the soft ground.

'Where you from? East coast? That ain't no California accent.'

A red T-shirt stretched across his belly. He heaved up the pair of surf shorts clinging to his wide hips.

'I'm Swiss,' I said.

The big man whistled.

'From Swee-den,' he said, drawing out the vowels. 'They get snow there, right?'

I continued to peg the lines on my tent in silence. It wasn't the first time I'd met a local in dire need of a geography lesson, but I felt it was best not to contradict him.

'Well, looks like we got this place to ourselves for the weekend,' he said. 'It don't get busy until December round these parts. It's rare to see tourists in the campground at this time of year. Still rainy season, see, you'll probably get a good soaking later. Hope your tent's up to it.'

I tilted my head. In truth I didn't know. This was my tent's first big test. I looked past him to the dog leaping around in the back of his truck, tangling its rope around its legs, impatient to be free.

'You're lucky though. My cousin keeps the grass mown here. He swears if he left it for even a week, the forest would take over. He's the park ranger for this area.'

It was vaguely reassuring to know this man had a connection to the authority from whom I'd picked up my camping permit.

'Then I may have met your cousin this afternoon in Hilo. I've paid my two dollars. He told me this site isn't manned. I have my park receipt here,' I said with a smile.

He shook his head to indicate he didn't need to see my ticket.

'You sure are brave travellin' round on your own. Wouldn't let my sister be doin' that. Anyway, I'm goin' to the store. Gotta pick up some stuff. Might bring a few buddies back here tonight. Always an excuse to have a little party when there ain't no tourists around. I'd invite you to join us, but I don't think a purty thing like you'd have too much in common with my gang.'

He slapped his thigh and burst out laughing. I smiled to hide my alarm, unsure whether his suddenly sinister accent with the word 'purty' was a feeble attempt to make a joke about the Hawaiian equivalent of hillbillies. The muscles of his arms flexed as he pulled up his board shorts and sauntered back to the truck.

Taking a book, I lay on my sleeping mat in front of the tent and pretended to read in the late afternoon sun, watching the big man surreptitiously as he untied the dog. It jumped down from the flatbed, winding its way around his legs. The man propped open a panel on the side of the caravan. From inside he took a large bowl and filled it with water from the standpipe at the edge of the campsite. All the time the animal fussed around him. He tied it up, and left the bowl of water on the ground with some dry feed. Then he climbed back into his truck and drove away, gouging ruts in the grass with his heavy tyres. As the vehicle passed by, he shook a thumb and little finger 'hang loose' sign through the open window and gave me a wink.

As soon as the truck's engine noise faded in the distance, the dog settled down under the shelter of the caravan's rear panel and put its head on its paws to sleep. It looked friendly, but as it had quietened, I didn't disturb it.

Thinking it would be safe to go for a short walk, I tucked all my valuables into my money belt, and padlocked the zip on the tent – a mere visual deterrent. A path wound through the vine-strewn trees to the east of the campsite at the end of which was a clearing with a stunning outlook over the town of Hilo. The deep blue of the Pacific Ocean glittered in the distance.

The sky turned from orange to purple in the dusk. As I made my way back towards the campsite, the dog started to bark, making me jump. I thought it was reacting to me. Perhaps I'd surprised it with my movement through the trees. But when I came out into the open, I could see it straining at its rope, barking at something in the forest on the other side of the site.

The big man's truck was still absent. The dog continued its cacophony as I walked towards my tent.

'Hey! Stop that racket!' I yelled.

I felt foolish shouting at the dog, but hearing my own voice calmed my sense of unease.

The dog stopped briefly, looked at me, wagging its tail and flattening its ears with nervous familiarity. A thread of drool hung from its mouth. Then its ears and jowls swung back towards the forest as the whine wound up to barking again. There must have been an animal moving about in the trees. I hoped once it passed on, the dog would settle.

But it didn't stop.

Night fell swiftly, a phenomenon that took a lot of getting used to in the tropics. Within half an hour it was pitch dark. The campground facilities were limited. As the season had yet to officially start, there was no electricity in the ablution block. They'd warned me at the Parks Office in Hilo earlier. I found my torch and headed to the low building. The beam immediately attracted swarms of moths and other flying insects, so I postponed my cold shower until morning.

A swathe of stars in a moonless sky cast the tiniest amount of light when I turned off the torch. I allowed my eyes to adjust enough for me to see my tent. The silver caravan was a giant ghostly zeppelin against the dark forest, where the dog continued its commotion.

As I walked back to my tent, I switched on the torch and shone it towards the trees in an attempt to distract anything encroaching on the site. The only movement was the occasional flash of an insect wing caught in the beam of light.

The barking dog was beginning to give me a headache.

'For Christ's sake,' I shouted. 'Could you just shut the hell up?'

Getting angry with it wasn't working, so I turned and walked slowly towards the trailer, changing my tone. I saw the dog was male, but he didn't seem aggressive.

'It's okay, boy. Stop barking now. There's nothing out there. Calm down.'

I delivered my speech in a soothing voice. He stopped as I approached, flattened his ears and lowered his head. His tail wagged so forcefully, his backside swung from side to side as he strained at his rope. He cowered as I came within touching distance and licked my outstretched hand. I scratched behind his ears and stroked his head. He was a friendly beast.

'What's all the fuss, boy? Can you calm down a bit? This girl needs to get some sleep. Stop your commotion.'

He panted and turned, tangling himself in his rope. I extracted his legs, made him lie down, and went back to the tent to prepare my bedroll to sleep.

But as soon as I tucked myself into my sleeping bag, the dog began to whine again, and before long broke out into a renewed frenzy of barking. I now wished his owner would come back to the campsite. Even if he brought his unknown friends with him, at least he could stop the damned barking. It wasn't the first time I wished I'd persuaded Valérie to give up her job and come with me on this trip.

I attempted to read my book, tracing the words with the torch. But I couldn't concentrate.

I was about to unzip the tent flap and approach the dog again, when I heard a thump and a squeal, and the barking stopped abruptly. I made out a pattering of feet or paws, and what sounded like a yap from the other side of the campground. I hadn't heard the pick-up return. The ensuing silence was almost more disturbing than the barking. I wished I had the gift of x-ray vision as I strained to work out what was going on outside my tent. All I could hear was blood rushing in my ears to the rhythm of my thudding heart. I didn't know whether to unzip the flap and take a look, or stay where I was.

The minutes ticked by. I remained still, straining my ears, thinking I might miss something. The dog must have gone.

Sometime later a double light swept the canvas of the tent like a lighthouse beam. I heard the deep rumble of a motor turn into the field. A vehicle pulled up in the vicinity of the caravan, and a door slammed.

'What the hell?' the big man's familiar voice rasped, softened around the edges with alcohol.

I breathed out. I didn't think I would ever be quite so pleased to hear his voice.

'Brutus!' he yelled, and I snorted quietly at the name this big Hawaiian had given his soft-natured dog.

Curiosity got the better of me. I unzipped the flap of the tent. The pick-up's headlights shone on the spot where the dog had been tied. The rope hung empty from the hook. His owner stood scratching his head.

I clicked on my torch and walked towards him. He turned to me, pointing at the space where his dog had been.

'Goddamned dog,' he said. 'Chewed right through the darn rope.'

'He was barking for a while, and then it suddenly went quiet. I didn't hear anything after that,' I told him.

'Goddamn,' he said again. 'Don't know where he'll be now. Half way back to Hilo probably. Stupid mutt.'

I looked down at the rope end. It looked as though it had been cleanly sliced through rather than chewed. But the man must have been too drunk to notice. I stared towards the forest, my heart pounding.

'You going to look for him now?' I asked.

'Nah. Too damned wasted,' he said. 'He'll have found his way back to the shack. Just hope he don't steal one of the neighbour's hens. I'll get him in the morning. Gotta sleep now, man.'

''Night then,' I said as I made my way back to my tent, relieved he wasn't leaving.

NINE

IT'S PROBABLY THE heat and humidity that make you decide to leave that campsite in Hilo, despite me not knowing how long you originally planned to stay.

I initially thought to wait until Hawaiian Man took off with his Airstream. We'd have the place to ourselves, especially now the dog has been dealt with. But it's not as though I can appear to you like some movie hero and carry out a big seduction scene. The very thought still petrifies me.

This morning you stuff your belongings in the trunk of your rental car. I figure you're leaving before the big guy wakes up and engages you in some kind of morning talk. I realise he might blame you for the disappearance of his dog. Good girl for leaving. I don't want him monopolising your time any more than necessary. After I get over my error of judgement on the dog, I'm happy to see you on the move.

You drive towards Hilo. I run to my pick-up hidden in the trees where I slept, close to the campsite turn-off, and not far from the jungle gully where I dragged the dog last night. There was something immensely satisfying about silencing the animal that had been annoying you all evening. Whacking it on the head with a rock wedged into the branch of a tree and tied with my belt made absolutely sure it wouldn't bother you again. Then I slit its throat before rolling it into the steep ravine. The body will be far enough away from the campsite when the stench rises from its carcass later in this tropical heat.

My sleeping bag and Thermo-rest are still strewn across the flatbed. I watch them slide from one side to the other in my rear-view mirror, hoping they don't fly away as I hit the gas to follow you. From Hilo you head back inland past orchid farms and smallholdings towards Volcano Village in the National Park. I remain at a respectable distance on the long drive. You pull up in front of the unimaginatively named Volcano House on the edge of Kilauea Crater.

With my baseball cap pulled down over my eyes, I sit at a corner table in the crowded café while you order a cup of tea.

That voice of yours is so damned sexy. I'll never tire of it. The tone you use with the waitress implies you don't want to put her out. I think she might comment on your accent, but she acts like she's seen enough tourists for the season. She's probably wondering whether she should remind you to leave a gratuity.

The 'thank you so much' slipping from your tongue sets my heart beating. It's kind and sensual in a way I hadn't expected, nothing like Ma's soft mid-Western voice, but no less lovely. The closer I get to you, the more I experience a whole stack of emotions I'm finding difficult to identify.

You carefully count your coins, making it obvious you don't have the budget to stay in that restaurant for more than a drink. With the view from the wide window over the vast Kilauea crater, a wisp of sulphurous smoke drifting lazily in the distance, this is prime real estate, and refreshments don't come cheap. I wish I could take that tab and show you how much cash I have inside my billfold.

You clear out of there pretty quickly, perhaps embarrassed to have left so little change. As I calculate my own check I leave a few dollars by my empty Coke bottle, then pass by the table you've vacated and place an extra dollar bill on the nickels and dimes arranged in a neat little pile. I don't want some grouchy waitress sending you negative vibes for not coming up with a decent tip.

Outside, you examine a guidebook as you lean against the door of your car. Your feet crossed at the ankles emphasise your long legs. You're dressed in cut-off shorts and a denim shirt with the sleeves rolled up. You rub your arm with your free hand. I imagine your thighs sprouting goose bumps as a breeze ruffles the pages of your guide. I hang my arm casually in front of my fly to hide the swell in my jeans.

At this altitude, once the sun goes down, you'll need more than a shirt and shorts to keep you warm. I wonder whether you'll head for a campsite, or look for a bed under a roof tonight.

With time on my hands, I have every opportunity to study you in a way I know I'll not be able to do once we are together. It isn't something every guy gets to do on his first date – to scrutinise his partner before they meet. This way, I'm also getting to know your likes, dislikes, habits, and routines.

I figure I should do something about the acne on my chin before talking to you. This is my mission, and I have to get it right. It's time to start taking care of myself too. I've been a loner all my life. The counsellor at school once tried to find out why, but the only thing he taught me was that I'm good at keeping secrets.

Physical and character traits aside, by the time we meet, I will know you better than you know yourself.

TEN

A GROUP OF us were standing in front of the Current Activity bulletin board at the visitors' centre in Volcano Village. A gust of wind blew my hair across my face. I shivered as I reached up to pull it into a ponytail.

'A forty-degree low tonight. What's that in real money?' I asked nobody in particular. 'I hadn't expected such a chill breeze. This is supposed to be a tropical paradise.'

'We're at well over a thousand metres. There's a bite to the air. Brass monkeys and all that,' said a man with an Australian accent beside me.

He was shuffling through a handful of tourist leaflets. Several people milled around monitors displaying spectacular night scenes of exploding lava. I placed the plastic fob of my rental car key between my teeth, and pulled on a sweatshirt jacket. With such a gradual ascent on the way to the national park, I'd forgotten we were almost at the same altitude as our farm in the Alps.

A girl appeared at the side of the Australian.

'Do you have a car?' she asked with an American accent, staring blatantly at the key fob in my mouth.

I nodded.

'Where are you heading?'

I shrugged and finished zipping my jacket before putting the key in my pocket.

'I'm not sure. I'm looking for a campsite I guess. I haven't really decided.'

'Why don't you check out Kuwaki-aki, or something like that? It's about five miles down the road from here,' said the girl.

'What she's saying is, it would be great if we could get a ride with you,' said the Aussie. 'It's a free campsite, not many facilities. I don't know if that's what you're looking for,' he concluded, perhaps in an effort to forgive his partner's boldness.

'Did I hear you say you're driving to Kulanoakuaiki?' asked another tourist, the complicated name tripping easily off his tongue.

He and his partner turned to look at me expectantly. I stared at the four of them, would have laughed at their group cheekiness had I not realised they were all shoestring travellers like me, and it was a dog-eat-dog world out there. Everyone was on the hunt for a free ride.

'G'day, I'm Dave,' said the Australian, offering his hand. 'And this is my wife Suzy.'

I was surprised. They seemed so young to be married, about my age. Barely out of college. The other two were an older American couple in their early thirties called Drew and Krista.

I felt like a five-star taxi driver with my rental car full of backpackers. The boot was crammed with all our gear. What wouldn't fit was wedged between everyone's feet or on laps.

'This is my one luxury on my round-the-world trip,' I admitted as we drove along.

I hoped my newfound friends would make a petrol contribution, but I quietly accepted what might turn out to be my one act of altruism for the week.

AFTER I'D SET up my tent in the small campground, I rummaged in my backpack for an extra layer of warm clothes. The group of us gathered at a picnic table, having agreed to prepare a pot-luck dinner of various ingredients we'd brought with us. It was good to have company after the weirdness of the campsite above Hilo.

In the night, I thought I heard another vehicle. But this time, I didn't feel nervous. Once I'd warmed up in my sleeping bag, I slept soundly.

The following day, we all decided to head back up to Volcano and hike out to the crater. The Visitors' Centre had reported some recent activity linked to the main lava flow to the south of the island. We made our way across the ropey black surface of the crater. Steam and smoke belched out of the earth in the distance.

'Sorry, good people. I know you've hiked a long way, but I can't let you go any further.' We stood in front of the park ranger like children denied a visit to Santa's grotto. 'It's too dangerous today. Too much sulphur gas. She's getting itchy to have a bit of a blow,' he said.

My eyes widened.

'I don't mean like right now. She hasn't had a big grumble for a while, but she's building up to it for sure.'

He made the crater sound like a pet dragon due to wake from a very long sleep. He told us the crater hadn't erupted in its entirety for several hundred years.

Instead of instilling fear in us, in childlike defiance, we piled into my car and drove down to the southeast coast where the island was continually spewing its molten guts into the ocean. If the volcano was active up at the top, it should also be putting on a show down there.

At Kalapana, I parked the car beside a wooden post with a life-saving ring hanging on a hook. The post would have been at the ocean's edge five years before. It was now a hundred-metre walk to the water.

'This is one of the few places in the world we can witness an island growing rather than shrinking,' said Drew. 'Millions of tons of lava expanding it every day, defying the effects of the world's greatest steadily rising ocean.' He sounded like my school geography teacher.

The beach was steep, with coarse jet-black sand absorbing the heat of the sun. Most of us had kicked off our shoes at the top of the slope. We ran down to the water, screeching as the sand burned our feet. We immersed our stinging soles in the wild waves pounding against the beach. The ocean dragged at our legs, trying to sweep us away. There was the danger of a strong riptide, so we didn't swim.

Dave, the Australian, was wearing a pair of flip-flops. He retreated to a cool scrubby area at the top of the beach and shouted to us.

'It'll cost you a beer for the use of these,' he yelled, and threw them down so we could scramble back up the black sand one at a time.

I was the last to borrow them. As I passed the flip-flops back to him, his fingers lingered on the outside of my hand.

'*You* might have to forfeit more than a cold beer,' he whispered.

The laughter died on my lips. I flushed with alarm as I glanced towards Suzy who was tying the shoelaces of her sneakers next to the car. I was about to tell him that was totally uncalled-for, when he gently punched my shoulder and guffawed before walking over to his wife.

We drove further around the point until we reached a roadblock. Folds of black lava had spilled and cooled across the tarmac in the past year. The white line down the middle of the road disappeared under the solidified mass. The flow had brought with it old metal carts, hubcaps and items of furniture. We walked across the undulating lava towards the coast, taking photos along the way. There was no park ranger there to stop us, but I realised we were being reckless.

'Come on!' yelled Dave, and began jumping from one ropey mound to another across the barren landscape.

'Is this safe?' I asked.

'We'll wait right here,' said Drew, as Krista clicked away on her camera. 'Honey, don't wander too far out,' he told her.

Suzy pulled my arm to follow Dave.

'Aren't you worried these tubes might have thousand-degree rivers of lava flowing through them?' I asked her.

'Don't be a scaredy-cat,' shouted Dave before Suzy could reply.

I imagined hot magma underneath us spewing from the volcanic fissures within the bowels of the island. There were signs on the road where we'd parked warning us not to walk on the solid lava. If the ceilings of the tubes were weak, we could fall into them at any time. I stayed with Drew and Krista.

They didn't go any further than a hundred metres from the coast, where a wall of steam rose from the lava as it poured into the ocean. But we were all close enough to hear the roar of the seawater as it boiled against the hardening mass in the great swell. I would not be coerced into Dave's dare.

'Nature at its most impressive,' I murmured.

'As I said, a bit of a miracle. Unlike that boy,' said Drew, raising his chin in the direction of Dave. 'It'll be a miracle if he doesn't get into trouble. He's such a fool.'

I frowned as I heard Suzy calling for Dave to come back to the safety of the road. I thought of several words harsher and more appropriate than 'fool.'

IT WAS MY last day at Kulanoakuaiki before I headed back to the warmth at lower altitude. The adventurer's guidebook to the Big Island suggested I should hike up the trail towards the observation centre on Mauna Kea while the weather remained fine. It would be a long day's trek, but conditions were perfect. After preparing a picnic and filling my water bottles, I folded my map into my daypack.

Dave appeared at my side. He must have seen me preparing to leave.

'Can Suzy and I join you?' he asked.

Although the last person I wanted to hike with was creepy Dave, I didn't say no. It was safer not to wander alone in such a remote area.

As we set off in the car with the sun shining brightly on the surreal black landscape, I relaxed. Suzy cheerfully asked me about my travels on the mainland, and the places I'd visited in her home state of California.

'You guys are on your honeymoon? Where did an American meet an Aussie?' I asked in return.

'Thredbo, during the last ski season. I was travelling. Dave was working on the chairlifts. We're heading back to the US mainland. Figured we'd get married first, so we tied the knot in Sydney before we left. We're heading to Lake Tahoe. My family owns a lodge there.'

Her family had money, which led me to wonder about Dave's motives as a ski bum. The last thing he should be doing with a new wife was flirting with other tourists.

HAVING GROWN UP hiking in the Alps, I was well-prepared for the rough volcanic paths of Mauna Kea. Suzy didn't fare so well, in addition to which she suffered from the altitude. Her unsuitable footwear on the sharp glass-like scree of the rough path impeded our progress. We didn't make it to the top. A blanket of thick white cloud rolled in during the afternoon, so we made the decision to descend.

I picked up quite a pace on the way down, mainly to keep warm. Dave kept up with me. He should have stayed with Suzy, but I didn't say anything. The gullied slopes of the volcano meant that we lost sight of her in several places. I stopped from time to time to let her catch up. She didn't seem bothered that Dave was forging on. She waved her hand and said it was okay, she'd catch up eventually. She mentioned she wished she'd invested in a better pair of hiking boots.

When we reached the road, we had to wait for Suzy, so we sat in the car to shelter from the icy breeze.

'God, I wish she was a bit more like you, had a bit more gumption,' Dave said.

It irked me to hear him speak of his new wife so negatively to a virtual stranger. I shifted in my seat and looked out of the window towards the coast. It suddenly looked a long way down from here.

'I really like you, Sandy. In fact, I really fancy you.'

'Don't be an idiot, Dave. You're on your honeymoon,' I said, trying to keep my voice light.

'We all make mistakes. Perhaps she's not the right one for me after all. Holiday romances rarely last forever.'

'So, your attraction was driven by the fact that you could spend a couple of seasons powder-skiing in the US?' I raised my eyebrows.

He shrugged and looked out of the window.

'She's a lovely girl, Dave. You should make things work. Especially as you haven't even reached California yet. If you've married for a passport, I hope she knows it. But that's not the impression Suzy gives. What you've just told me, that's... weird.'

I wanted to be rid of him now. I felt uncomfortable, but I couldn't simply drive away leaving them on a cold pass. Pockets of snow lay in the ravines of the volcanic slope. Two people would quickly freeze up here. It seemed so surreal to have come from the tropical heat of the coast to a place that felt like the high peaks of home. I shuddered, but it wasn't from the cold. I began to feel nervous out here in the wilderness with someone who had read the wrong signs. I willed Suzy to hurry back.

'I'm not the only one who finds you irresistible,' he said.

'What do you mean, not the only one?'

I thought about all the travellers and backpackers I'd met over the past few days, how I was looking forward to some time alone again.

'There's one guy who can't take his eyes off you. And now I see why. We keep bumping into him on our outings. We even saw him on the slopes above Hilo just before we met you, and then at Volcano. Wondered if it was someone you knew.'

Dave touched my arm. I pulled it away. Anger heated my cheeks.

'What the hell are you thinking?' I hissed. 'You're just married! You've harmed the friendship we had. Suzy seems like such a nice girl. She doesn't deserve this. She doesn't deserve you, doing this to her.'

I opened the door and climbed out of the car. The cold wind buffeted my hair. I caught the flash of Suzy's red sweater as she gingerly walked down the trail. Watching her approach, I wondered who Dave was talking about. What guy? I didn't recall any single men travelling alone apart from the big man at the campsite. He'd been more concerned about his dog and his night out with his buddies. Apart from him, I was alone there.

As Suzy reached the trailhead on the other side of the road, I leaned down to speak quietly into the car.

'Look, Dave, I think you might have read a wrong message somewhere. I'm not about to start something or risk breaking up a marriage. If you're having problems, you need to sort them out with Suzy. This is not right. I think it's best we go our separate ways.'

Dave shrugged.

'Sorry to keep you waiting, guys!' said Suzy as she climbed in.

I started the engine, and we drove back to the campsite.

ELEVEN

THE AUSSIE DUDE follows you out over the lava field while you're taking a morning stroll.

Blood pounds at my temple with anger when I see him. I didn't follow you guys on the trip up Mauna Kea yesterday, but something happened on that hike. Whatever it was, I could tell you were really pissed. This dude needs watching closely. He'd better not lay his hands on you.

He's concentrating on your back, trying to catch up to you without making it look obvious. You're still a few hundred yards away. I'm far enough behind that you can't hear either of us. I only have this window of opportunity to protect you. His vibes are pretty bad. I want to tell this guy to leave you alone, that I know what his game is, that it's time to give it up.

I calculate we're about the same height. I even think we look kind of alike, except for my beard. But as I get closer I see he's a lot more muscular. His filthy lust washes off him in waves. The loathing rises like a red cloud in my head.

I lope the last few metres towards him and hold my arms out like a boxer. As I approach, I realise the dude is taller than me. I figure the conversation we're about to have would be better if I'm looking down on him rather than looking up at his face. I spread my hands and ram them into his back. He loses balance and goes down easier than a silent pin at the bowling alley. I learned a long time ago from my father how anger can spur a man's strength, but I'm still surprised.

I expect him to push himself up. I wait for retribution, a confrontation. I'm worried he'll yell and draw attention to us. I imagine he could put some weight behind a punch. But he doesn't move. When I stare down at the dude's head pressed against a jagged piece of volcanic rock, I swallow.

The black rock glistens where there was no shine before. I'm not sure whether it's fear or euphoria that expands in my chest. I crouch down and look towards you. The air is silent. Yellow grass stalks shiver in the light breeze. You're still walking away in the distance, scuffs of volcanic dust drifting sideways from your footfalls.

I doubt you're going to pass back this way through the sparse scrub but I should move Aussie Dude. His body is fucking heavy. I pull him by the ankles, and one of his boots slips off in my hand. It's impossible to pull him by both feet, as my fingers keep sliding free from his socked foot. I have to tie his Goddamn boot back on so I can grip both his legs. This is all taking too much time. Any moment now you could turn around and head back to the camp. I grab the waistband of his jeans and try to drag his body sideways, but I can only move it a few inches at a time.

A few feet further on I come across a collapsed lava tube. I roll the body into the shallow hole. I can't completely hide it. There's nothing to cover it with. I try to shove it further into the hollow. It's even harder to push than it was to pull. I'm too weak to do much with its bulk. We're a long way from the campsite, away from any marked trail. I figure no one will find it for a long time.

There's blood on my hand and arm. I know it's not mine. I grab handfuls of sand and some grass to try rubbing it off. It smears brown across my skin, and I gag.

I look up. You've come to a halt at the top of the slope, gazing east away from me. The sun has risen over the Pacific Ocean in the distance. There are a few clouds on the horizon. I know you'll turn around at any moment, so I decide to lie in the lava tube until you've walked back to camp.

I'm right next to him. I keep expecting the dude to wake up and move, grab me, plead with me to help him. We're both wedged in this natural coffin. The air smells like rust. The cotton of his shirt is warm against my arm, but makes me shudder. He doesn't move, as though we're experts in a game of hide-and-seek.

It's only after my heart has stopped thumping and the sweat has dried on my shirt that I realise I've just killed a man.

TWELVE

IT WAS TIME for me to leave my temporary travelling friends and head back to Kona, but not before taking a detour on the way. This time I was adamant I would go alone. No more free-riders.

An older Swedish couple at the campsite told me about a special place in the southwest of the island. They said if I only did one thing on the Big Island, I should visit Green Sand Beach. The couple had a jeep, and warned me that my Toyota wouldn't handle the rutted track from the parking area to the beach. I should be prepared to hike in.

Finally, alone and driving through a wind farm on South Point Road, I wound down the window to let the warmer air of the lowlands into the car. Rows of windmills hummed as I passed. The hypnotic spin of giant sails on the huge metal pylons towered above me, making me feel insignificant and isolated.

Once past the wind farm, I concentrated on the turquoise ocean beyond the tip of the island. When the hardtop road ran out, I drew up next to a red pick-up truck in the parking area at the trailhead to the beach. I had brought extra water and a picnic in my daypack. I exchanged my flip-flops for hiking boots before setting off down the trail next to the signpost for Papakolea Beach.

I was grateful for the advice of the Swedish couple. The road was bumpy. The ruts in some places were a foot deep along the three-mile hike. When I reached the beach, I was at first a little underwhelmed. From a distance, the green tinge on the shore looked more like an algae-covered bank of mud. But drawing closer, with the sun shining on the millions of olivine crystals packed together, the beach transformed into a trove of what looked like precious emeralds.

There were no concession stands, no cafés, no public conveniences, and no people. I wondered briefly where the occupants of the pick-up truck might be, and scanned the cliffs surrounding the bay. It felt good to be alone. I'd had enough of being everybody's taxi driver and babysitter. I relished the sound of the ocean and the sea birds.

The water looked inviting after the hot walk to the beach, but I stupidly hadn't brought my bikini with me. I saw no harm in a quick skinny dip, so pulled off my shorts and T-shirt, followed by my underwear, leaving them on the top of my backpack above the water line. The beach was steep. Rough waves pounded in all directions. I pulled my hair into a ponytail and waded into the water. The sea tumbled me around, so I stayed near the shore to avoid being swept away in the undertow. The frothing water against my nakedness was like a forbidden treat, and I laughed out loud.

Afterwards I sat on the beach next to my clothes, enjoying the feel of the warm wind on my bare skin. When I was dry, I brushed the tiny green gemstones from my backside and legs. As I pulled my T-shirt over my head, the glint of something on the cliff caught my eye. My heartbeat spiked. I looked towards the trail, thinking someone had arrived while I was sitting with my back to it, but I couldn't see anyone. I blushed with the memory of frolicking in the waves like a child. Pulling on my shorts and hiking boots, I made my way back.

When I reached the car park, the red pick-up truck had gone.

IT WAS LATE when I arrived in Kona. I drove straight to the Kona Hale Hostel on Ali'i Drive where I had pre-booked a room. I parked in front and made my way to the entrance. The lights were on inside. A breeze carried the heady scent of night-blooming jasmine. I'd been at the wheel of the car for more than seven hours. It had been a long day.

As I carried my pack up the steps to the wooden decking, I caught women's voices talking urgently through an open window. I opened the front door, triggering a bamboo wind chime, and entered the hostel. Before I had even swung my pack to the floor, Suzy rushed through a door into the hallway crowded with some expensive-looking bicycles leaning against the wall.

'Oh God. Sandy. Thank Christ you're here.'

I stepped backwards, confused. Of all the hostels and budget guesthouses in Kona, I hadn't expected to see Suzy there. The last person I wanted to set eyes on right then was her philandering husband Dave.

Suzy's face was red and puffy. It was obvious she'd been crying.

'Have you seen Dave?' she asked.

'No, I… I didn't think I would see you guys again.'

I was uneasy, wondering whether Suzy had sensed Dave's attraction to me.

'Lisa here told me you're booked in tonight. I've been looking for you all over town. I… Dave's gone missing. And I know you had the car… and I know you and he got along. I just thought maybe he'd hitched a ride with you or something. Or that you knew… He's been gone since this morning. Just disappeared. I don't know what to do.'

Suzy sobbed, her intake of phlegmy breath like a toddler on the tail end of a tantrum.

'I'm sorry, Suzy, I don't know. I've been on my own the whole day. I went down to South Point, to Green Sand Beach. I didn't see another soul. Honestly.'

She covered her face with her hands. Lisa, the hostel manager, put her arm around Suzy's shoulder.

'Honey, I'm sure your man will show up in the end. He probably just had one of those newlywed scaredy-cat moments, needed some time to himself.'

Lisa looked at me over Suzy's shoulder with a comical grimace. She wasn't sure what to say or do. Neither was I. Should I have felt guilty that he'd made a pass at me? It seemed a bit extreme to take off because he thought he'd made a mistake marrying this girl. She was better off without him anyway. But I wasn't going to tell her that.

'Why didn't you stay up at the campground? If he'd gone hiking, surely it would've been better to wait for him there,' I said. 'I thought you were both still asleep. I went for a short walk before breakfast, then left. The only people I saw were the Swedish couple who arrived yesterday.'

'I saw them too when I woke up,' said Suzy. 'They said they thought they saw Dave getting into a red pickup truck. They couldn't tell if he was on his own, but they thought he was driving. I can't think what he was doing. He wasn't in the tent when I woke up. I got dressed, tidied up, went to freshen up in the wash block. When I came back I realised he'd just... gone.' She began sobbing again. 'We're booked into the Sheraton for the next three nights. A present from my Dad. After I got a ride down here, I went to the hotel first, thinking he'd be there.'

'The Swedish couple could have been mistaken. I remember seeing a few other cars, but thought they belonged to people in the campsite. I'm so sorry, Suzy. I don't know.'

I bit my lip. Something she'd said about the red pick-up truck bothered me. I thought of the car I'd seen at South Point. But that had already been there when I arrived. Dave surely wouldn't have left his new wife on a whim, knowing he had the comfort of a luxury hotel bed for the next few nights? What a jerk. I wondered if there *was* a reason I should feel guilty. I was sure I hadn't given him any sign he would interpret as encouragement.

'I thought we were so happy,' Suzy continued. 'Why would he leave me now? We hadn't even gotten to the States. We have a big house in Tahoe, ready to move into. My parents…'

Lisa, seeing my exhaustion, and realising this wasn't getting us anywhere, rubbed Suzy's back, guiding her towards the door.

'Well honey, if your guy turns up here for any reason, we'll be sure to let you know,' said Lisa 'Dave, is it? Perhaps he forgot you had a five-star reservation tonight. Though I sure wouldn't miss it. The Sheraton's got one of the best pools on the island. You just go back to your room, and if he hasn't shown up by tomorrow, I reckon you should call the police. I'm sure he'll turn up though.'

Suzy looked at me, teeth gritted, on the edge of tears again.

After she left I thanked Lisa.

'There was some weird stuff going on between those two. I didn't want to get involved,' I said. 'The guy was a creep, to be honest.'

'Let me show you to your dorm. We're mighty busy this week. A bunch of triathletes have already showed up for the Ironman at the end of the month. You're lucky we had a cancellation when you called.'

I prepared a light dinner in the communal kitchen from food left over from the campsite, a can of soup and a packet of Mexican rice. The kitchen was full of triathletes cooking piles of chicken, mixing dubious powders and juices into food mixers, trying to satisfy their cavernous hungers. Their gluttony diminished my own appetite even more than Suzy had.

I sat on the deck facing the ocean with my dinner in a bowl on my lap. The hostel was set back from the beach in a residential area to the south of Kona's buzzing town centre. I couldn't face going in to town to explore the nightlife. I thought about Dave, hoping he wouldn't show up on the hostel's doorstep in the shadow of his poor wife, begging for my attention.

LISA CREPT INTO the dorm room before anyone was awake the next morning and quietly shook me out of my slumber.

'The cops are downstairs, Sandy,' she whispered. 'They want to talk to you about that guy Dave's disappearance.'

I shook the sleep from my head, pulled on some clothes, and paid a quick visit to the bathroom. As I walked down the stairs of the hostel, I reflected on the bad luck my doing everyone a favour had won me.

I felt sorry for Suzy, and angry with Dave, but knew a day in my rental car and an afternoon hiking in the national park didn't constitute an obligation to help either of these people in their dilemma. I wanted nothing more to do with the whole thing.

As I walked past a couple of cyclists getting ready for an early morning ride and went outside to talk to the police, I decided to book my flight back to Honolulu to make tracks south. Although I had enjoyed my stay in these beautiful islands, something was telling me it was time to move on.

THIRTEEN

THE PATROL CAR pulling into the hostel's parking lot in the morning wakes me from a dream about you. I'm in the back seat of the pick-up's cab, parked across the road in a side street. My vehicle is partially hidden by a row of giant fanned palms. I think I'm going to be busted for either illegally parking, or sleeping in my car, but they don't even look in my direction.

I hadn't expected the American girl to be such a bellyacher. When I saw you through the window of the Kona hostel last night being accosted by the stupid bitch, I thought maybe I should have put her next to her asshole partner in that lava tube.

The slamming of the cop car doors ruins the fantasy I'd been reliving of you on that green beach, your stolen panties in my hand. I'll never tire of the memory of your body rising out of the sea, water rushing off your breasts and belly, your pale skin where you haven't tanned. You so easily make me hard, make me want you. It brings us one step closer to our physical harmony.

AFTER TEN MINUTES, you come out of the hostel to meet the cops in your bare feet. I think for a moment they're going to haul you off to the station in their patrol car. You hand over your keys to one of the officers and wait on the driveway while they inspect your vehicle. They must be wondering if you had anything to do with Aussie Dude's disappearance. I run my fingers through my hair. Should I go over and give you an alibi? His stupid bitch must think you have a connection. I decide to wait.

The sun has already warmed the bitumen. You hop from one foot to the other. When you finally move to the shade of the hostel step, you have a frown on your face. I don't regret Aussie Dude is dead. You chew on a fingernail while you wait. I want to tell you not to do that. You shouldn't spoil those pretty hands.

The cops leave after half an hour. You seem more relaxed. I hope Snivelling Suzy leaves you alone too. Having listened to her whining, I'm shocked to find out they were newlyweds. You'd think she'd recognise the favour I did her, eliminating her cheating bridegroom. She must see he had 'adulterer' written all over him.

I breathe easier. I didn't realise I was holding so much tension. I'm glad I didn't have to choose that moment to declare myself your knight in shining armour.

It's still not quite time.

YOUR TRIP TO the Big Island wasn't on your original itinerary, and I'm not sure of your next move. Studying the flight schedules for United and Air New Zealand, I feel helpless that I don't have that control. Whatever you decide, I know you'll have to fly back to Honolulu from Kona to continue your international journey. When I calculate the flight times, I'm pretty sure you won't be hanging around the airport in Honolulu for eight hours until the next international flight connection. But if you do, I pray that the eight-hour transit will give me enough time to pick up my passport from downtown. Thankfully it's a weekday. But my plans would be a lot easier if you decide to stay an extra day or two with Spiky. I'm sure you'll be wanting to catch up with her, tell her your adventures, perhaps have a last shopping trip to Ala Moana Mall, or visit Waikiki Beach to satisfy your slush-puppy addiction.

Not that I'm religious, but I say a little prayer as we get off the plane in Honolulu, silently willing you not to turn towards the transfer corridor. When you stride towards the baggage reclaim area, I thank the twisted gods, who've never looked out for me before, for granting me some extra hours.

But you mustn't make it too long, sweetheart, as it's time for both of us to hightail it out of the US. There's an outside hope that the ancient lava tube in Volcano National Park will either collapse in on itself, or fill with hot lava during the next eruption. Any evidence would be conveniently incinerated.

It's more likely that a hiker will come across the body of a young Australian tourist. And someone might decide his bad fall on a hike through the lava fields wasn't an accident.

But by then we'll be half way around the world.

YOU CHECK YOUR watch as the bozos at Agricultural Control in Auckland Airport threaten to open your tent and give it a steam clean. Once you convince them you've only ever used it in a few sites on the continental US and Hawaii, they let you take the kit through. I wait for you outside immigration.

It's ironic I didn't get the same grilling, but in retrospect it's a great relief, as they missed the blood stain darkening the volcanic dust on the left toe of my boot. I only notice it when I look down as you're being questioned about your own footwear.

I wait to see where you head when you leave the airport. I'm horrified when you walk to the first major intersection, stand at the side of the road, and stick out your thumb. No, no, no, you shouldn't hitchhike! Why are you doing this now? Apart from the danger it presents, my plans are about to be thwarted. I haven't followed you across the remaining half of the Pacific Ocean only to have you disappear into some stranger's car. It's not the first time I wish I had some kind of tracking device.

My heart sinks further when I run back into the terminal and see the line of tourists at the car hire counters. I barge forward.

'Ma'am, it's a family emergency. My mother is terminally ill at the hospital in Auckland,' I say.

The businessmen waiting in line grumble and the tourists whisper half-hearted sympathy. I secure a rental contract, paying the highest insurance premiums to save time, and run to the parking lot. I'm thankful there are still cars available, and that Auckland Airport doesn't have an off-site rental car pool. I throw in my bags and take off without checking the vehicle, making an instant decision to pick you up if you're still at the intersection. The thought of you placing yourself in danger in some unknown person's car makes my stomach roll. For all I know, you could have car-hopped from east to west in the US, but somehow you don't strike me as a seasoned hitchhiker.

I pull into the line of traffic and crawl towards the intersection. As the road straightens out, I'm relieved to see you're still at the kerb. You're leaning against your backpack, thumb poised, holding your left arm up with your right, as though it's been weighing you down for hours.

My throat constricts with the anticipation of stopping for you. I hope my action of flipping the blinker triggers a look of relief on your face. I'm prepared to feign surprise to be heading in the same direction as you, wherever that might be. Our time together might be limited. My face burns with this sudden decision after so many weeks of procrastination. I haven't had time to consider what I'll say to you other than *Where are you heading?'* Christ knows how I'll get you to stay in the car.

The traffic moves at a snail's pace. The sound of the blinker echoes loudly. I glance at my reflection in the rear-view mirror and wish the heat on my cheeks would fade. Several hours cramped on the plane has done nothing for my looks. My beard looks tatty, my hair's a little greasy. I attempt to comb it with my fingers and notice a sour odour rising from my creased shirt.

The cars edge forward, and I bring my hands back to the wheel. My fingers catch the windshield wiper stick and the rubber blades screech across the glass, making me jump. My foot falls heavily on the brake, causing a short squeak of rubber on the road. You look briefly in my direction when you hear the screech, your thumb still held high. I'm about five vehicles back from the line of cars rolling towards the intersection.

An old jalopy pulls in to the curb and my mouth falls open. A man leans across the passenger seat to wind down the window. You nod, look briefly over the roof of the car chewing your lip, and open the rear door to throw in your backpack. Then you climb into the passenger seat. Before I can react, he sweeps you away into the traffic.

I lean uselessly on the horn, too late. The guy next to me in a BMW throws me an irritated look. I jut my chin, keep my eye on your car – a light brown Holden – and manage to weave my way through the traffic on the two-lane highway to slip in behind you on the road into the city. I focus on the back of your two heads, one close cropped, one with golden curls. Each of you moves occasionally with the conversation, and your shoulders relax.

I beg him not to touch you.

FOURTEEN

NEW ZEALAND FELT more like home, and I hadn't even hit the Southern Alps yet. The shoestring travel guide said it was safe to hitchhike everywhere.

After a few days in Auckland, I was excited to head south. I stopped in Rotorua, where I found a cheap youth hostel boasting its own giant hot tub with a constant supply of geothermally heated water. I met many more backpacking travellers than I had in the States. There was always someone willing to share their experiences or recommend an interesting activity.

'How've you been getting around?' asked the Irish girl, Morna, who I met while unravelling my sleeping bag onto my bunk in the dorm.

'Mostly hitching. I've been pretty lucky with my rides. Saving dollars. Everyone says it's safe here,' I said.

'I've been here a month now. Even way up north in the middle of nowhere you can get a ride. Jaysus, you'd be waiting days if you were hitching round Kerry,' said Morna. 'It's what the pubs were invented for. People who never manage to get a ride. No problem here though. Mind you, it's awkward to backtrack once you start getting into a dodgy-looking driver's car.'

'Oh, have you had one?'

'I got a ride here with a bit of a *stook*.'

I raised my eyebrows.

'An eejit. He was a nervous, spotty American. Said it was the first time he'd ever given anyone a ride. Said he was practising, for feck's sake. Practising his bad pick-up lines more like.'

Morna roared with laughter. I thought about how to avoid getting into the car of someone I might not completely trust. Not so easy when standing alone at the side of a road in the middle of nowhere. I wondered if I was safer now I was far south of the city.

'Do you ever hook up with others, for safety. Hitch together?' I asked.

'Sometimes. If you do that, it's important to know who you're travelling with. Make sure they're well presented. You don't necessarily avoid the tatty clothes, as long as they look clean, but they need to be non-smokers, and mustn't have too much gear to stuff into the back of a car. If ye meet an Irishman called Mick he's a sure bet. He's travelling with his accordion. Gets a ride every time. I teamed up with him in Cape Reinga and we got a ride all the way to Whangerei in a Maui camper. He played the fecking thing all the way down Ninety-Mile Beach.'

She pronounced 'thing' '*ting.*' I thought if I had a car I'd give her a lift to listen to her accent all day long. She would have been welcome company in Hawaii.

For the next few days we agreed to hitch together through the centre of the North Island. There would be some lonely stretches, especially along the Desert Road.

It meant I wouldn't have to get into a car on my own with a *stook*.

BEFORE HEADING FURTHER south, we spent some time in the tourist centre of Rotorua, visiting mud pools, geysers and a typical Maori village. A group of the hostellers convinced us to sign up for a 'mystery' day trip out of town, something that promised on the poster to be an unforgettable experience off the beaten tourist track.

We were picked up from the hostel in a rusty old Land Cruiser.

'You all got your hiking boots on?' the driver asked. We showed him our 'sturdy footwear' that had been recommended for scree-running.

I sat in the front passenger seat between Darren, our driver, and Morna. We drove past Lake Tarawera to the crater of the same name, a steep scar in the volcanic landscape with ridges running down each side of a giant crevasse. The Land Cruiser bounced to the top of the highest point of the ridge and we all piled out.

'Now's the chance to use your alpine skills.' Darren winked at me as we gazed down the steep slope to the base of the crater. 'I'll see you all at the bottom. Enjoy the run.'

We lined up along the ridge, and ran down. The scree avalanched under our feet as we took giant loping strides. Our feet were carried downwards on packed volcanic gravel. It felt like running on the moon or pedalling on cushions of air. Our whoops of delight echoed within the crater walls. When we reached the bottom, Darren was waiting in the Land Cruiser, watching our trails of dust drifting into the air like the evidence of a migrating herd.

'Can we do that again?' asked Morna. 'That was a helluva *craic*.'

'No time, sorry. Next stop, Lake Rotokakahi, Green Lake,' Darren said as we climbed into the Land Cruiser.

We bounced along a series of bone-shaking forest tracks around the south of Lake Tarawera, and I wondered if the Land Cruiser would arrive at our destination in one piece. We passed tree ferns taller than houses dotted amongst the tightly packed native forest, before arriving on the shores of a vivid green lake surrounded by trees sprouting red bottle-brush blooms.

'New Zealand's Christmas tree. The native pohutakawa,' said Darren as he turned off the engine.

In the ensuing silence a rich warble of birdsong reached us through the open windows. I tipped my head and closed my eyes.

'That's a tui. Another native to New Zealand. Fair amount of them out here. Nothing to disturb them.'

We clambered out of the vehicle like kids on a school trip.

'Are we going on a boat ride? It didn't say anything about this in the brochure,' said Morna, pointing to an old outboard motorboat floating in the shallows. I'd noticed a trailer parked amongst the trees as we drove in. Fresh tyre marks leading to the water indicated the boat had recently been launched in the lake.

'You scared of boats?' Darren asked. 'You can always wait on shore. We won't be long.'

'No, I mean that's really cool,' she said.

'This boat belongs to my second cuz. He's a full-blooded Maori. So his boat's permitted on this lake. He uses it to collect fresh-water mussels growing here. Strictly speaking, no white man is allowed on this lake. You might not believe it, but I'm part Maori.'

The tourists hung on to his every word. Maybe Darren did have some Maori ancestors, but it was hard to believe when he looked more like a Scotsman with his strawberry blond hair and freckled skin. And after doubting the permissibility of scree-running the crater, I wondered about the validity of the consent to put a boat on Lake Rotokakahi.

'Beautiful,' said one of the girls gazing across the calm emerald water.

'It's not always green,' said Darren. 'When there's an algae bloom the water turns pink and it's dangerous to swim in. Highly toxic.'

'Well I'm glad it's not pink today,' I said. 'I quite fancy a dip.'

From the back of the vehicle, we took out our daypacks while Darren pulled out an icebox.

'Here, give us a hand with the chilly bin,' he asked one of the Canadians.

We loaded the icebox containing our picnic onto the boat via a gangplank directly from the beach. After we'd all climbed aboard, Darren pushed it away from the shore with an oar. Once we'd drifted far enough, he tipped the motor down and started the engine. He piloted the boat towards the middle of the lake.

It was a calm day. The group settled into their seats, brandishing cameras or slathering on sun screen. I reached into my pack, pulled on a sun hat and enjoyed the peacefulness, watching the chevron of the boat's wake behind us as it forged its way across the bottle green surface.

I leaned back and gazed up at the sky, clouds scudding across its rich blueness. I was sitting in front of Darren, and pretended not to notice when he placed his arm casually along the gunwale behind me. I surreptitiously watched his fingers on the tiller and moved away from his other hand when it accidentally brushed my shoulder.

At the far end of the lake we approached a small island covered in what Darren told us were manuka bushes and the skeletons of a few old kauri trees. It was surrounded by a beach of bleached shells and pebbles.

'Can we stop there for a swim?' someone asked.

'Not allowed, mate,' Darren called back. 'It's *Tapu.*'

'Tarpoo?' The Canadian laughed. 'What the hell does that mean?'

'It means it's a sacred place. If we disturb the Maori gods, they become angry. Something bad will happen. I guess your North American Indians have the same kind of curses. The island is the resting place of Hinemoa, a great Maori princess. Some say those aren't actually discarded mussel shells on the beach, that they're really Hinemoa's crushed bones.'

'Ah that's such bullshit,' said the Canadian. 'Tell you what buddy, I'll give you a hundred bucks if you anchor at the island so we can take a dip in the lake there. How would your Mooree Gods react to a few loonies, eh?'

Darren looked a little uncertain. I could tell a hundred dollars was an attractive prospect. I thought the huge Canadian was crazy, giving away cash that would have lasted me a fortnight.

With only a moment's hesitation Darren leaned over and held out his hand.

'Deal,' he said.

They shook on it, before Darren turned the tiller to head for the island. He hauled up the motor at the stern as we approached the shallows. He took a rope as he jumped out to tie the boat to a tree above the water line. He unloaded the chilly bin and set out our picnic. Then he stood up and stared across the lake, biting his lip.

'I'll have to pay you later buddy,' said the Canadian. 'My cash is back at the hostel.'

'Mm. No worries,' Darren said, a little distracted. 'I think you guys should wait until we get back to the main beach for a swim. We can picnic here, but we shouldn't stay too long. I've done my bit for your bargain, mate, by mooring here, but I don't want anything to happen.'

'Like what?' the Canadian said. 'Sheesh, dude.'

He whispered the word 'chicken' under his breath.

The sharp shells meant a treacherous barefoot walk into the lake, so I was happy to wait to swim off the main beach anyway. When we'd finished our lunch, Darren hurriedly packed all the rubbish and cans into the icebox and carried it back to the boat.

'What's the hurry?' the Canadian asked. 'Scared of your Mooree Gods, eh?'

'Not really,' said Darren. 'But if my cuz knows we've visited the island, he probably won't lend me the boat again.'

When we arrived back to the shore, Darren tied up and carried the chilly bin to the Land Cruiser. Morna and I grabbed our packs and walked around the bay to the widest part of the beach. The others strung out along the shore. The Germans lay towels on the sand before stripping down to their underwear and diving into the lake. The Canadian rolled his eyes at the precision of the towel-placement, took off his T-shirt and waded in with his shorts. Morna and I both had our bikinis on under our clothes. The water was cool, but it felt good to finally wash the scree dust off our legs. Once Darren had loaded the car, he joined us on the beach and took a running jump into the water.

After the swim, I lay on the sand, letting the sun dry my body. I listened to the tuis in the forest canopy. Some of the group dozed. Morna skimmed stones with the Canadians on the smooth surface of the lake. I heard the Germans boasting to Darren about the distances covered and the passes scaled on their travel adventures.

An almighty boom suddenly split the air, and we all ducked involuntarily with the shock. My ears buzzed with the pressure of an explosive retort. A puff of rising blue smoke dissipated over the boat as the sound of objects dropping into the water accompanied the echo of the blast around the lake. We stared open-mouthed at the stern of the vessel. The explosion had blown away the gangplank and left a gaping hole where the outboard motor had been. Bubbles and steam rose from where it rested on its side, disabled in the shallows. With ears still ringing, I turned to stare at Darren.

'Holy fuck,' he said. 'The fuel can must have blown. My cousin's going to kill me.'

We could see in his eyes he was echoing our thoughts: *We were all on that boat ten minutes ago.*

'That's your tarpoo for you, Darren,' said the Canadian. 'Shit, man. I don't think my hundred bucks is going to cover that.'

'Well, seems like that party's over,' said his girlfriend.

I shivered as we climbed into the Land Cruiser.

'It was a freak accident,' Darren said. 'I'd better get you guys back. I can deal with this later.' He shook his head, clearly disturbed.

As we drove back to Rotorua, I thought about the powers *Tapu* might really have had over us. Darren was probably concocting his own Maori legend for his future clients in his mind as he drove us back to the hostel.

We found out later that evening that the entire Green Lake was under the spiritual prohibition of Maori Tapu.

We should never have been there at all.

FIFTEEN

YOU'RE SO FUCKING fit, and it's killing me. Since when did anyone consider this a vacation? Tramping, the Kiwis call it. Feels appropriate when every step is an angry stamp up the mountain.

Worse than the hostels and backpackers' lodges, are the Department of Conservation tramping huts dotted around the national parks. Some of them only have a handful of bunks for hikers, and it means I have to spend many nights under the damp southern hemisphere sky. Traipsing through what the trampers refer to as the 'bush' is frustrating enough. To think I could afford a five-star hotel room every night with all the modern comforts is driving me crazy.

I thought New Zealand would be another exotic destination in the South Pacific, like Hawaii in the tropics, but I wasn't prepared for how far south the country lies. I should have paid more attention to what you were carrying in your pack, and bought some warmer gear.

But I'll suffer the cold. I could be craving the hot summer nights of my childhood, without my father, of course. But I'm not. It's worth it for you.

I find out where you'll be on your tramping excursions mostly by studying the permit registers at the DOC offices. Initially I thought I'd stay put and wait for you to come back to the hostel. But each time I'm about to do this, I can't bear the thought of letting you go, and I end up following you.

I shun the attempts of other backpackers to engage in small talk. I sleep out in the open to avoid the huts. This isn't the Rockies; thankfully this country has no predators, except for the occasional weta – a gross-looking giant beetle – one of which I find in my boot one morning. But with the dew or drizzle eating into my bones in the middle of night, I'm half-awake most of the time anyway. There are moments when I dream about my mother, which is far preferable to dreaming about my father. Every time I see her, she convinces me I have to protect you, I have to let you continue on this journey of discovery and independence. She convinces me that you're mine.

After wiping the smile off that freckled fucker's face at the lake, I feel like I've gained an extra power. It was the same satisfaction I felt when I got rid of Hawaiian Man's dog. This time a cut fuel line and a smouldering rag was all it took. It was a mighty effective way of getting the bozo to keep his filthy hands off you at the end of the day.

I'M PLODDING UP to the Harris Saddle on the Routeburn Track near Queenstown. The trail is more like a staircase than a walking track. I know you're heading towards Lake MacKenzie from the entry in the DOC register. I calculate that you're an hour ahead of me. All I can think about is putting one foot in front of the other, so my heart about bursts out of my chest when I see you right in front of me as I crest the hill, sitting on a rock not far from the track.

'It's not safe,' you say.

I'm excited and confused at the same time. You've spoken to me! But… What's not safe? I can't speak because I'm totally out of breath and feel sick with the effort. You're with a small crowd of people on the saddle. I don't know whether your comment is encouraging conversation. I'm suddenly petrified. I touch the peak of my cap in acknowledgement and pull it down to hide my face. I give you a wide berth, but as I pass, you speak again.

'The ranger is advising everyone to wait until the sun's off the slope for at least an hour,' you say. 'They think it'll be okay to traverse at about five p.m.'

When you go back to chatting to another girl who was only a stranger to you this morning, I realise you've been here for a while. I clench my jaw when I see I haven't made an impression on you. I'm suddenly self-conscious of my tangled long hair, messy beard, and persistent acne. I mumble an 'Okay, thanks' once I've caught my breath, and go to sit on a hump of grass on the other side of the saddle. Perhaps your words have more meaning behind them than some information delivered to a friendly stranger. I watch as you chat easily to the others in the same way, and I'm confused. I go over each word you said, analysing the message.

The other hikers are milling around, sharing their trail mix and taking photos. I stay where I am, watching you on your rock, sitting there like a goddess. You're wearing your regular hiking boots with thick socks pushed down to your ankles. Your legs are still tanned from Hawaii and several days on the mountain tracks of the Southern Alps. You sit with one boot on the grass and the other tucked up on the rock in front of you. Your chin rests on your knee with an arm hugging your shin. Your cargo shorts slip up your thigh. I can see the paler skin where your Hawaiian tan has faded and the sun here has only coloured your leg to the bottom of your shorts. I push my hand inside the top of my pack where your panties are scrunched like a security blanket.

A guy with a rope comes over to you. You give him a warmer smile than the one you gave me. My lips tighten, and my heart beats hard as your eyes linger on him when he walks away.

The others convince you to play paper-scissors-stone. The wind ruffles your curly hair and you swipe it out of your eyes several times until you tie it back with a band. You take out a baseball cap and pull the pony tail through the half circle opening at the back. The brim protects your eyes from the sun, and they lose their squint in the shade, pools of golden-brown surveying the view. I place my sweatshirt on my lap.

You appear to become bored with the game. There's a lull in the conversation, the others move away, and you pull an apple from your pack. A voice in my head screams 'Now! Now!' and before I think about the consequences I shift off the tussock of grass and approach you. This is my big moment. I swallow as I walk up to you.

'I'm Jake.' Nervousness makes my voice break into an unaccustomed baritone. I've made you jump. As you look up you appear to cover your shock, then you smile, and everything in the world feels good.

'Nice to meet you Jake, my name's Sandy.'

I hold out my palm. You're cutting the apple with a Swiss army knife, placing the slices in your mouth directly from the blade. You raise your two occupied hands and shrug to indicate you can't shake my hand. Disappointment burns.

'I guess the expert knows best,' I say, nodding towards the guy with the rope, sitting near the snowy slope.

'Greg's looking after us,' you say. I bristle at the use of his first name. 'He's a ranger. Knows what to do.'

I hope the smile you give is for me, and not for the ranger. Your eyes crinkle, and you nod. It feels good knowing we're in this thing together. You look down at your apple and cut it with exaggerated care. I'm suddenly uncertain about standing there, so I go back to my hump of grass on the saddle. I feel like I'm on top of the world.

There are several of us all together, waiting for the snow to harden. As the sun dips lower and the trail falls into shadow, the ranger begins uncoiling the rope slung over his shoulder.

'I'll go first. You,' he says, pointing to a tall, broad-shouldered man. 'Take the other end. You can act as the anchor on this side. We'll cross one at a time. But I need to get to the other side of the slope first.'

The big guy holds the rope while the ranger crosses the traverse. The old snow has sunk in rivulets where it must have melted underneath. The incline widens to a steep funnel below us, so steep we can't see the bottom. It might be a twenty-foot drop, and it might be a thousand. I swallow.

Once the ranger reaches the other side, he tells you to cross next. I hope it's because you're one of the lightest of the group, and not that he wants to save you first. It's not a contest, but I feel ashamed that I'm chosen shortly after you, my slim build mistaken for puniness. The heaviest in the group will take the final traverse. They'll be making the deepest foot-holes in the snow.

I make it past Ranger Jerk on the far side of the traverse. As I'm about to step onto solid ground, one of my boots breaks through the crusty snow, and I slip. You gasp, and lean forward to grab my hand. Our fingertips touch. You hold my hand! You can't imagine the joy that courses through me. I wish you could feel it through our grip. I know a shift has come in our relationship. If it wasn't for the sequence of our crossing, we might never have touched.

You turn back to help the others. We've made physical contact. Skin to skin. It's now a tenable thing. I am in seventh heaven.

SIXTEEN

THE GROUP ARRIVED at the MacKenzie hut together in a jovial mood, as though we had been through some life-changing event. As there was only one wood-burning stove, we shared our food, clubbing together to create a concoction in the two available saucepans. After dinner, a group of us played a game of Spoof with pebbles near the warmth of the stove. The prize was a gulp of beer from the single can of Lion Brown one of the trampers had carried with him from Queenstown.

I volunteered to do the dishes, and heated some water gathered from the rain butt outside the hut. As I washed the pans with a headlamp strapped to my forehead, Greg came out to help. I remembered the static tick that had connected our hands as we introduced ourselves to each other earlier on the saddle. He'd described the transformation of crystals to those who'd never seen snow, his striking green eyes and engaging smile putting everyone at ease. My heart quickened as he began stacking the mismatched plates and utensils.

'You look like an experienced tramper. Have you been in New Zealand long?' he asked.

'Not long, but I'm used to hiking in the mountains. I come from Switzerland.'

Greg raised his eyebrows.

'The northern Alps. Granddaddies of this lot.' He swept his hand towards the shadows of the mountains around us, bright stars twinkling above them. 'I was probably being over-cautious today on the Harris Saddle, but snow like that is unpredictable. Didn't want to lose anyone.'

He smiled, and I hoped he meant me in particular.

'Better to be safe than sorry,' I said.

'I wouldn't normally have been here. I was fixing a trig beacon above the Dart Valley when the office radioed through about the traverse. I'm glad I came.' He spoke as though this chance meeting was a surprise for both of us.

'People who don't live at altitude don't know about the dangers of snow. In the Alps we were taught from a really young age to respect the mountains at all costs. My brother used to take loads of risks when he was younger, *hors piste* skiing in spring. Until he lost a school friend one season. Putrid snow is the worst kind.'

We chatted about the Alps, our common love of skiing and mountaineering in the wilderness. I explained how I'd always wanted to see the Southern Alps and how they felt more familiar to me than the volcanic parks of the North Island. A small seed of melancholy planted in my mind that my time with Greg would be all too brief. We were heading in different directions in the morning. My provisions had almost run out anyway. I needed to get back to Queenstown.

For the sake of decorum in the cramped hut, the women slept on the upper bunks and the men down below. We were like an extended happy family on an annual outing. Any feeling of homesickness I might have felt was eradicated as I experienced a travelling comradeship I'd not yet felt on my journey, even with Morna. Against my better judgement, I couldn't stop thinking about Greg sleeping in one of the bunks below me. I was determined to summon the courage to ask him for his contact details before he left in the morning.

SEVENTEEN

AS EVERYONE SETTLES on the bunks and the quiet chatter fades, I imagine this atmosphere is what a frat party must feel like after everyone has drunk themselves into a stupor. I was never invited to any of those gatherings back in Kansas, but walked past the comatose bodies spread throughout the dorms the morning after such occasions.

The girls are all on the top bunks, and you've cleverly scored the one nearest the fire. When it was decided the guys would take the lower bunks, I hastily chose the one diagonal to yours, to have a good view of your mattress.

This is the first time I've been in the same room as you. I desperately hope it won't be the last. The hut smells of the remnants of the meal and smoke from the dying fire. I think of my pathetic contribution to the dinner – a can of beans and a bag of peanuts – I'm glad you didn't notice they came from me.

There's no point sleeping outside tonight. You've already seen me, and it might cause alarm if the ranger notices I'm missing. He counted us like sheep before we all traipsed down the mountain.

I sit on my bunk after eating so I can watch you from the shadows. I've been trying to catch your conversation all evening, to work out your travel plans over the next few days. I don't join in that stupid drinking game.

I try not to think about the way you looked at Ranger Jerk this afternoon. He's sitting on the lower bunk close to the door and I want to poke his eye with a burning stick from the stove to stop him looking at you.

I initially thought this would be my big chance. Circumstances beyond my control have thrown us together, but I can't seem to pluck up the courage to talk to you again. A trampers' hut is hardly the place for a big seduction scene. The ranger decides he's going to help you wash the dishes outside. I kick myself for not thinking of it first. What can you be doing out there for so long? I'm on the verge of making an excuse to go out for a piss, when you come back in, eyes sparkling and a flush on your cheeks.

I hate him.

When everyone turns in, his breathing deepens even before you've finished changing clothes inside your sleeping bag. He can't see you from his bunk. I'm the one who watches you turn and settle until you find a comfortable sleeping position. When you're motionless, I study the slope of your shoulder. A puff of your hair splays on a pillow of sweaters and fleeces. I could reach out and cut a lock of it for a keepsake. But I don't get out of bed.

It's dark and muggy in the hut; the air has been sucked up the chimney from the stove. As my eyes droop, I think I hear Pa whispering in my ear beside me on the mattress. The acrid smell of cooling ashes in the stove reminds me of the diesel oil on his hands. But I don't let him in. I'm not scared of him anymore. I'm not frightened of his ghost. And when he says, 'Do that thing I showed you,' I cancel out any thought that he has ruined my capacity for passion by fantasising about your body on our beach in Hawaii.

Until the big American in the next bunk suddenly says: 'You've got to be kidding me,' and I turn onto my stomach to stop the rhythmic hiss of my hand moving under the nylon of my sleeping bag.

EIGHTEEN

MY ENTHUSIASM AS I woke in the morning for another day on the trail and a chance to chat up Greg was dashed when I saw his bunk was empty. His pack had gone. After the disappointment, I told myself it was crazy to have invested so much in a moment of instant attraction.

A few of us had pre-booked the trampers' minibus the next day to take us back to Queenstown. The meeting point was at a place on the map called The Divide on the road from Milford. Our rendezvous there was scheduled for late in the afternoon. There were several people already on the bus when it stopped. As I shuffled into the seat behind the driver, I narrowed my eyes at the familiarity of the passenger sitting up front. When he turned to look over his shoulder, Greg's smiling eyes made my heart miss a beat. I wondered if he'd planned this.

'It's you,' I said. 'I didn't think I'd see you again. Job done?'

'In the nick of time, it seems.' He grinned at me. 'I still had something to fix above the Hollyford track. I left MacKenzie before dawn and didn't want to disturb you. Worked like buggery so I could meet your bus at Marion Corner this morning before it stopped at The Divide.'

'You must have hiked like the wind.' I said, hoping he'd done this so he could meet me.

'The Hollyford Valley this morning was spectacular. I should have asked you to come with me, but didn't know how much bushwhacking I'd have to do off the trails. Turns out it wasn't so bad.'

'I hope you weren't disturbing any flora and fauna by drifting off the marked paths,' I said in mock admonishment, quoting the DOC signs posted at every trailhead.

'I took great care, I'll have you know, your Alpine Majesty.'

I reached forward to punch his shoulder playfully, and he grabbed my fist. Heat flushed my face.

As we approached Queenstown, Greg said he'd be at Eichardt's Pub later for a drink. He mentioned it casually as though he wasn't sure anyone else would be interested. Then he asked the driver to drop him off on the outskirts of town.

'See you later then,' I said hopefully as he hopped out of the van and slid the door closed.

I was desperate to shower four days' tramping sweat off my body, shave my legs and shampoo my hair. I was looking forward to going out for the evening. I felt like a schoolgirl preparing for her first youth club disco, and suddenly wished Valérie could be here to help me get ready. I owed her a letter or a postcard. She was probably getting tired of my endless descriptions of foreign vistas, national parks and the intricate details of youth hostel travel. I smiled at my reflection in the shower room mirror as I combed my newly washed hair. I hoped to provide more excitement for her in my next correspondence.

Although I'd already convinced myself I wasn't looking for the complications of romance, a girl was still allowed to have a little fun, surely?

THE PUB WAS rowdy when I entered, with a group in the corner singing along badly to *"Don't Dream It's Over"* by the new down-under sensation Crowded House twanging out of the speakers. Jugs of Speights beer passed constantly back from customers gathered three-deep at the bar. The locals were letting their hair down as much as those of us who'd been socially deprived in the bush after several days on the tramping trail.

Greg and I shouted our brief life histories to each other over the noise of the crowd. As the barman called last orders, we escaped the muggy interior at the end of the evening, not quite ready to say goodbye.

We walked towards the promenade on the lakeshore. He bought a punnet of kumara chips at a take-away stall on the corner.

We'd both had a fair amount to drink. We were exhausted after the long day, with our respective hikes out of the national park taking their toll. Several nights in the rudimentary facilities of the DOC huts and shelters meant we were both sleep-deprived. But attraction crackled between us.

Leaning against the railing at the lake, I placed the empty chip punnet on top of a concrete pillar and swayed in for the inevitable kiss. Greg's hand touched my cheek, he threaded his fingers through my hair, and our mouths met. He tasted of salt and ketchup. When I closed my eyes, my world tilted. I stumbled against the pillar. The chip container clattered to the ground, breaking the moment.

We pulled apart breathlessly, both knowing we were far too drunk to make sense of this passion. I laughed and bent to pick up the carton. Greg held my arm to stop me from falling over. When I'd tossed the carton into the bin, he grabbed my hand.

'I'll walk you back to the hostel,' he said.

I felt light-headed and pouted in the dark, not entirely sure I wanted him to walk me anywhere, but allowed him to lead me along the lakeside. As we reached the steps up to the deck of the hostel, Greg turned to hold me in an embrace.

'I'm not good for much tonight, Sandy,' he whispered in my ear. 'What are you doing for breakfast?'

I almost asked whether he would prefer to call me or nudge me, until I remembered I was sharing a hostel dorm with five other girls. I wanted to invite myself back to his place, but figured he'd have asked if he wanted me to go home with him.

'I'm having breakfast with you,' I said instead.

'I'll take the morning off work, and meet you here at nine, right here on this deck,' he said. With his arms around my waist and his mouth against my lips he whispered: 'Sweet dreams, Sandrine.'

My head was starting to throb as the result of too much strong micro-brewed beer, but I knew there was the thrill of something we hadn't quite finished. Although I hadn't even considered the logistics of *starting* something, I felt a long-forgotten squeeze in the pit of my stomach, and climbed slowly to my dorm, looking forward to seeing Greg the next day.

NINETEEN

I WATCH RANGER Jerk saunter down the street. I'm in two minds what to do. When you touch your mouth after he pulls away and you turn to go into the hostel, I want to run after you, pull you round, put my mouth on yours. I want to wipe his scummy saliva off your lips.

I'm so over this guy getting your hopes up, dashing them, and getting them up again. I saw you look at his empty bunk this morning, and wish you'd looked at my empty mattress like that.

While you were in the long-drop hut doing your morning business, I packed and snuck out. Waiting for you amongst the trees on the westward trail, I never saw if you gave my bunk a glance.

I didn't think we'd see Ranger Jerk again. As you passed on the trail I heard you talking about your plans with another tramper. You told her you thought you'd hitch south to Te Anau once you'd checked out of the hostel in Queenstown.

But when we got on the bus, there he was, sitting up front next to the driver, smug as a sewer rat.

As I watched you walking down the street after we left the pub, your faces together, now I think this guy has made you change your plans. That didn't look much like a farewell kiss to me.

INSTEAD OF FOLLOWING you into the hostel, I turn around and tail him. He's humming a tune like some love-struck schmuck. How can he leave you like that? I'm sure he's made plans to see you again. I clench my fists as I pursue him down the road.

We're on the edge of town. In the distance, the street lights are still on. Two cars drive past and a handful of drunken people are wandering away from the pub which has just gone dark.

As I get closer to him, I need something to make me feel safer. Flowerbeds and trees are planted between the Esplanade and the sidewalk. I remember Aussie Dude's accidental encounter with the ground in the lava field. I bend down to grab one of the fist-sized rocks scattered amongst the bushes. I weigh it in my hand and close my fingers around its comfort. Standing, I continue after the guy. He's not walking straight. I catch up to him and tap him on the shoulder. He turns, surprised.

'Leave her alone, asshole. You gotta leave Sandy alone,' I say, trying a forceful voice.

'Mate? Are you all there? What's your problem?' he asks, and then narrows his eyes. 'Hey, weren't you on the saddle yesterday? Jilt you, did she? Well, you can fuck off, bro.'

His last words make me lash out. The rock is in my left hand, but I automatically clench my right fist and swing my arm towards his face. He grabs my hand before it makes contact. He might have been drunk before, but he sobers up pretty quickly. I feel a tick of alarm as he pulls himself up to his full height. His steady hold on my wrist makes me realise he's a lot stronger than me. He stares me down.

'Ah, come on, mate. Leave it out,' he says, relaxing a little. 'I don't want to fight. If it makes you happy, I have to leave in two days on a temporary transfer. I doubt she'll come up my way, she's already done the tourist bit there. She's all yours. But mate, are you sure she'll have you?'

My ears ring when he says this. At first, I think it's just an insult. But then I ask myself if it's pity, and clench my jaw. I want to wipe the sneer from his face. Is he trying to be generous? I swing out with my other arm and he ducks, but not before the rock in my hand scrapes across the top of his head.

'Argh!' he yells, and releases my wrist, crouching to put both his hands up for protection.

The momentum causes me to pirouette. I accidentally let go of the rock. It skitters away on the sidewalk. He pulls a hand away from his head and I see the dark shine of blood on his fingers. I look around. It's about three in the morning. There's no one about now. The ghostly shape of a tourist steamboat is moored in the distance, a sliver of moon glinting on its funnel. I scramble along the sidewalk to retrieve my rock. Ranger Jerk rises for the attack, drunken anger mingled with confusion on his face. Blood trickles down his brow.

I stay in a crouch but shift my feet to gain purchase. As he stumbles towards me, I rise up to meet him, the rock in my right hand. Winding my arm as though preparing for a baseball throw on the Frank Myers field, I swing it with all my strength, and aim for the little dip between his ear and his forehead. He makes an 'oof' that deadens the noise of contact, but I feel a soft crunch along the tendons of my wrist. For a moment I wonder if I've broken my hand. But when he silently falls and sprawls on the ground, I look at the rock in my palm and can't believe it was that easy. The only movement is one of his heels rolling to stillness, and then nothing.

I stare at his body and remember Aussie Dude, how hard it was to drag him across the lava field. It's surprisingly easy to move this guy on the hard blacktop of the sidewalk. I drag him over to a copse of bushes while I decide what to do. I've no doubt he's dead. I've seen that emptiness before. Now I have to work out how to get rid of the body.

A car drives along the Esplanade. I keep still and turn my face away so I won't be seen in the dark. We're hidden from the road by the bushes and the headlights diffuse amongst the branches. The car keeps going.

At first, I think I'll go get my car, which is parked down the street from your hostel. I change my mind, knowing I'd leave traces of his blood and DNA in the trunk. Even if I'm not caught straight away, there would be a trail to me later from the rental records.

The easiest solution is the lake, but I don't know whether the body will sink or float. I can't recall what happens in crime movies.

I'll be exposed once the sun begins to rise, so I know I have to hurry. The sky is already turning blue along the tops of the mountains to the east. I drag him down the slope to the beach and am surprised I don't leave a trail of blood as his head bumps over the paving stones down the steps.

Ranger Jerk is wearing a pair of jeans and a hoodie. I begin filling his pockets with rocks and pebbles from the beach. I pull off his sweat shirt, tie the neck closed with the string from the hood, and try to fill it with more stones. I soon run out of space. I look at his T-shirt, but don't see how I can tie it closed, so I leave it. I've no desire to set eyes on his bare torso. He's probably sporting an impressive six-pack.

I take off his shoes, an expensive pair of alpine Scarpas. I turn them over in my hands. Smart, but too big for me. I remove the laces and tie the bottom of the sweatshirt closed, using a double hitch Pa once showed me, to stop the cloth slipping open. Shifting the body closer to the edge of the lake, I tie the heavy cushion of the sweatshirt firmly around his waist with the sleeves.

A duck quacks on the water close by, making me jump. Its repetitive tone fades as though it's been woken from sleep and is gradually settling. The only sound is my heavy breathing and my heartbeat in my ear.

I look down at the body. Will it really sink? Only one way to find out. I pull it into the water, careful not to disturb the knots tying the sweatshirt to the body. It's now heavier, and my shoulders protest. The water is cold around my ankles, seeping into my shoes and weighing down the lower part of my jeans. But as I move further into the lake, it takes a little pressure off my load.

I'm still not convinced the body will sink. Before I wade too deep, I check the head is under water, then stand fully on his chest, first one foot, then the other.

A string of bubbles fizzes out of his mouth and nostrils before my foot slips on the cotton of his T-shirt. I fall backwards. The splash sounds as loud as Niagara to my ears. I calm my breathing, look up and down the shore. The town is still quiet. I have to get the air out of his lungs. But with that thought comes the memory of a cow I once came across on our Kansas farm. It had been dead for a few days, by which time the gases in its stomach and guts had swelled until the animal looked like a parody of a kid's helium balloon at the county fair. Or a life raft. In any case, it would have floated if we'd had a body of water big enough. In short, it's not only his lungs I should worry about.

I leave him half submerged and head to my car. Opening the trunk, I tear away the flap of carpet covering the spare wheel. In the hub of the rim is a canvas bundle I'm hoping will contain what I'm looking for. I unroll it, search through the metal tools:

a tyre jack, a spark plug cover and, at the bottom, an interchangeable screwdriver. I unscrew the Philips head and attach the flat one, testing the sharpness of the edge with my thumb.

Shivering, I run back to the shore as best I can in my water-logged clothes, cursing that I didn't undress before entering the lake. Ranger Jerk's body is mostly submerged and I have to search for him when I get back. I locate him when I spot his denim-covered knees, side-by-side, bobbing in the shallows.

I push the cushion of rocks to the side and stand above the body. With the screwdriver in both hands, I close my eyes tight and bring it down as hard as I can onto Ranger Jerk's stomach. The first hit lands on his sternum. The tool judders in my hand. But as I stab him over and over, the screwdriver pierces his flesh. My rhythm is broken only because it's harder to pull the screwdriver back out than it is to jab it in. The T-shirt sucks up each time I pull away the tool, and tiny puffs of dark blood swirl away in the lake. But he doesn't bleed heavily. I imagine each of his six-pack muscles bursting with the impact.

I move down to the more vulnerable area of his abdomen and keep punching at his body, piercing the flesh until I think he must have more holes than a colander.

I pull him into the deeper water and shuffle in until the lake reaches my armpits. I shove him with my foot as far as I can along the sloping lake floor. The ball of his stone-filled sweatshirt drags him away. I watch the shadow of his body roll into the depths, and wade back to the shore.

I'm proud that I have saved you from the creep.

This has been my first immersion in water for several weeks. I know you're tucked up in your hostel bed in angelic slumber, but I wish I could tell you this has been a baptism for both of us.

TWENTY

WE'RE ON THE red-eye from Auckland to Sydney. You discreetly survey the cabin like a seasoned traveller. You've come a long way from the nervous darting looks of a rookie backpacker a couple of months back when I first saw you on the bridge.

I'm seated about twelve rows back. You swing your backpack onto the armrest, shrug off your jacket and tuck a stray lock of hair behind your ear.

You reach up to push your pack between a carry-on case and a handbag, tidying the straps into the belly of the overhead compartment. One of your shirttails frees itself from the waistband of your jeans. The smooth tanned skin of your midriff shows briefly, revealing that tiny mole on your left side. Lowering your arms, you bend to retrieve your jacket from the seat.

You scan the cabin one more time before sitting. As you turn to the front, all I see is the back of your head. There's a fraction of a second's hesitation, a moment of complete stillness, and I know you've registered recognition. I've mistakenly relaxed my cover. You sit down and, for a moment, don't move. I imagine the cogs of your brain frantically cranking and clicking, eyes perhaps half closed, calculating where you've seen my face before. Then your elbow moves into the aisle and I hear the distant click of your seatbelt as you secure yourself into place.

I wonder how many coincidences I can afford. I feel stronger and more confident after eliminating the ranger, but with that power has come the certainty that you're not ready for me yet. I want you to look at me like you looked at him. Before I approach you again I have to do something about my appearance. I have to change the way I dress, maybe cut my hair. I've been considering shaving my beard, but after a flare up of acne, my skin has been too sensitive for the razor.

I hope the identikit calculations in your brain aren't enough to make any other connections, and that this doesn't turn out to be an error.

During the flight, I sleep with my face turned towards the window, my static-charged blanket pulled over my head, safe in the knowledge that there's nowhere for you to go.

AFTER WE'VE MADE our way through immigration and agricultural control there's a guy waiting for you in the arrivals' hall. He wraps you in a bear hug. I narrow my eyes, observing him carefully. There are plenty of smiles, but his lips only touch your cheek. He doesn't kiss you on the mouth – he's not a lover.

I assumed you'd either hitchhike again or take a bus into town, and hadn't counted on someone meeting you. The customer lines at the car rental counter go around the corner past the foreign exchange office. I don't think my sick-mother-in-hospital trick will work twice in a row. The rental car parking lot here is probably miles away as it's a much larger airport.

Instead I follow you and the guy out of the terminal. He doesn't offer to carry your backpack. Or maybe he has offered, but you insisted on carrying it yourself. It confirms there's no romantic connection. That's the first thing I would do for you.

I follow the two of you towards the parking lot, bending low between the rows of parked cars. You're animatedly describing your travels to him. I strain to listen. I only catch the occasional phrase now and then, but at one point I do hear him ask:

'How's Uncle Daniel?'

The roots of my hair tingle as you reply:

'Papa's not doing so well. Pierre and Marianne have…'

A car drives past and I don't hear any more, but I smile. A relative then, a cousin. I wonder who Pierre and Marianne are. Siblings? The two of you stop beside a box-shaped white Volvo. Cousin unlocks the trunk, and you throw in your backpack. When you climb into the passenger seat he starts the engine. I quickly write down the license plate on the back of my boarding pass, along with the name of the Volvo car dealership advertised on the bumper sticker.

HOW MANY VOLVOS can there possibly be in metropolitan Sydney? I don't recall the brand in Kansas, but back there everyone's hung up on the American dream of monster motors that make more noise than power-to-speed. I try not to let anxiety affect me. I will solve this conundrum.

I change some money and buy a coffee to get some coins. There's a payphone near the terminal exit. I begin by calling information, hoping your cousin has the same name as you. But the woman tells me there are no Bavauds in greater Sydney. I don't even know your cousin's first name.

I call the police, claiming to have left my wallet in the car of someone who's given me a lift. I tell them I noted down the license plate, but they insist I go into the nearest police station to register the loss and get a duty sergeant to make 'further enquiries.' They're not willing to simply give me Cousin's number. I certainly don't want to get the cops involved, so I thank them and hang up.

It means I have to visit the Volvo dealership.

It's late afternoon. The dealership is in Mosman, north of the city. I decide to keep the same story I'd fed the cops. It would be a bit dumb to swan up there in a rental car, so I flag down a cab.

The driver says he's not keen to go there in commuter traffic, that he'd rather take a local fare as he's going off duty soon. A fifty-dollar bonus soon changes his mind.

'If you can get me there before the place closes, there's another fifty in it for you.'

'Mate, you're on,' he says, hitting the gas and speeding to the on-ramp of the freeway.

It pisses me off that down here I'm everyone's mate.

I need to use the bathroom, but try not to think about it.

As I walk into the dealership, a salesman is showing a young couple around the cars. Shakin' Stevens has been dragged out for a second year to wish everyone a merry Christmas over the speakers. There's a girl up a stepladder hanging tinsel across the area above the reception desk. She steps down unsteadily in her wedge platform shoes and asks if she can help.

The salesman glances at me from across the room. He clocks my clothes, my beard, and the backpack. It's the same look the taxi driver gave me. He turns back to his customers. He's wearing a pair of shiny grey pants I guess are the bottom half of a cheap suit, and a thin black leather tie against a white shirt. He looks like a dweeb, but I feel my face redden all the same under his scrutiny. I figure I hardly look like car-purchasing material. If only these bozos knew.

I turn to the girl.

'I got a ride in a Volvo yesterday from up north to the city. I left my wallet in the car, and I have to find it. It's got my ID and a load of important stuff in it. I was wondering if you had a record of cars sold over the past year. It looked pretty new. I'm hoping the same guy still owns it.'

She bites her lip.

'You'll have to wait for Ethan. I can't help you with that. He shouldn't be long, unless they want to test-drive something,' she says, pointing her chin at the couple.

'Eeth,' the girl calls. 'Have you got a sec?'

Snake-Tie turns with a frown, and reluctantly approaches. It's obvious I'm not there to boost his commission. I repeat my story to him.

'I can't give out customer information. Sorry.'

'Ah, come on! It's my wallet. I've got all my ID stuff in there. And credit cards. I'm pretty much screwed if I can't get it.'

'Nah, sorry mate.'

'Ethan, give the guy a break,' says the girl as she passes by with an armful of tinsel. 'Perhaps you can call the owner for him.'

That's not particularly great news, and my heart pounds.

'Well…' Snake Tie sighs, and beckons me into his office.

I can tell he's not long had a computer on his desk. He sits behind it with a proprietary air. I can hardly see him. The great bulk of the casing on the back gives off the smell of new plastic and an unpleasant odour of burning electronics. As I give him the details, he types in the colour: white, and model: 740. The computer tick-tick-ticks and groans as it searches the data.

'That's not our most popular model,' he says. 'Although… Wow. Five white ones sold in the last year. Must be because of the excellent crash test results, won the Traffic Safety Award in Europe.'

I slump in my seat. The salesman frowns and turns back to his computer. I'm itching to be on the same side of the desk as him.

'Did you notice any unusual design features on the car?'

I narrow my eyes, remembering the boxy Volvo pulling out of the airport parking lot, the back of your curly blonde hair disappearing out of my life.

'The wheels, for example?'

'I don't know… They had a funky rim design. Like inverted pizza slices.'

'Double-spoke diamond alloy. Good choice. He has taste,' he says, as my eyes drop to his ridiculous tie.

Tapping the keyboard some more, he pulls at his shirt cuff and his bony knuckle sticks out. A few dark hairs sprout from the sleeve. For some reason, it reminds me of Pa, and I am vaguely repelled. I tap my foot in synchronised impatience. He looks past the computer monitor at me with a frown. I lift my hand in apology.

Then his eyes focus above my head, and he flashes a smile.

'Excuse me,' says the guy who was looking at the cars, 'My wife and I would like to know if it's possible to test drive the 780 this afternoon.'

Snake-Tie's eyes widen briefly before he flips his wrist and looks at his watch. It's the end of the day. I can see he's torn. I'm the last person he wants occupying his selling space right now.

'Go ahead,' I say, although he's already out of his seat.

'My assistant will be right with you,' he tells me as he guides the man out into the showroom.

The girl is back up the stepladder, hanging more Christmas decorations. As Snake-Tie approaches her and they both have their backs turned, I push myself out of my seat and hurry round his desk to focus on the computer screen. On a spreadsheet are five invoice numbers, and next to them the owners' names. I pull a pen from the holder on the desk and take out my boarding card from my pocket. I scribble to make the pen work, filling up precious white space on the ticket. I click on the invoice he's highlighted. My eyes ache with the speed with which I have to scan the purchase extras. And then I see it. *Double-spoke diamond wheel rims.* Bingo.

The assistant's ass stretches the material of her skirt to bursting point as she climbs down the ladder. I'm back on the other side of the desk before she even starts walking towards the office. I tear open the zippers on my backpack, dig out my wallet. I hold it out in front of me in one hand and place my other hand on my forehead. The assistant raises her eyebrows as she enters the room.

'This is so dumb! I found it while looking for my notebook to write down the address. What an idiot!'

'But…'

'Thank you so much for the offer of help. Sorry to hassle you so late in the day.'

I get up to leave, and I feel the assistant's eyes burning at my back. Snake-Tie is fiddling with the mechanism to open the garage door of the showroom and doesn't see me as I walk out of the side door. I head to the nearest intersection to flag down another taxi.

WE'RE APPROACHING THE longest day of the year, and it's still light when the taxi stops at Avalon Parade. I walk around the corner to Surfside where the houses in a quiet cul-de-sac near the beach speak of money. I experience a twinge of doubt. Cousin surely doesn't live here. If these are your relatives, why the hell didn't you fly directly here to spend your year in luxury? I feel conspicuous with the clothes I still haven't changed from the flight, my scuffed backpack hanging off one shoulder.

I look down at the address again to be sure, and approach. A woman is moving around what looks like the kitchen, but it's not you. I stand uncertainly at the end of the driveway. An older man appears from the side of the house carrying a garden hose. He looks up and sees me standing on the sidewalk.

'G'day,' he said. 'You lost? Backpackers' is on the Parade. Just past Bellevue.'

I gauge the guy. He looks nothing like your cousin, so I can't be sure. But I hope he's your uncle. I ask him if he has a white Volvo 740.

'My son-in-law drives a Volvo,' he says warily.

I decide to give him a different story to the one I gave the police.

'I was parked next to him in the lot this morning, and clipped his wing mirror as I drove in. I wanted to leave him a note with insurance details but had no pen and paper. I went back to the airport terminal to get something to write with, and when I got back he was pulling away. I took his license number, and traced it to here. I feel real bad about it.'

'Well, that's amazing you've gone to the trouble,' he says.

As he's being so friendly, I think of adding some fuel.

'I also think I might know the passenger. We travelled together in the States. Sandrine Bavaud?'

The guy slaps his head, and a smile spreads on his face.

'Sandrine! Sandy Bavaud. That's Steve Barrow's cousin.' He pauses. 'They changed their name to Barrow,' he says conspiratorially before continuing. 'She arrived this morning. Steve was picking her up at the airport. They'll all be with us for Christmas. Let me get the phone, I'll give Steve a call.'

'No!'

My abruptness halts the guy in his tracks. I force a gentler tone.

'No, it's okay. I'm not staying in town. If you can give me the address, I'll drop the insurance details off, or put it in the mail to him.'

'You can always leave the information with me, son.'

'Sir... Mister... it's okay. I want to get it to him as soon as possible. I'll be moving on next week, and I feel like he should get them before I hand in the car.'

The old guy looks past me to the empty road.

'I'm around the corner, wasn't sure what number you were,' I say hastily.

The guy pauses for a split second. He's checking out my appearance. If it had been you, people would be falling all over you to give you information.

'I'm really not comfortable doing that, son. The best I can do is offer to give Steve your papers. I know you know Sandy and all, I'm just not sure...'

This guy is pissing me off. I can't believe he's so mistrusting. This isn't the States. Anger rises.

'You know what?' I say, 'I'm just trying to do the dude a favour. He can deal with the damage himself. I don't need this shit.'

His eyebrows rise almost to his hairline and he stares at me as I turn to walk down the driveway. As I glance back, he's going down the side of the house, leaving his garden hose sprawled like a snake across the dry lawn. I'm pretty sure after he's pointed me out to his wife, he's going to call his son-in-law.

Before I turn onto the road, I stop beside a tree with blooms like tiny red toilet brushes, and with relief I urinate against the trunk. Fucking asshole.

AFTER I'VE CHECKED the directory at the payphone outside the gas station down the street, I hail another cab. Climbing in the back I pull the page I tore out of the phone book from my pocket. Barrow, the only S in the book.

'Manley, please,' I say as I sink into the seat.

The traffic going towards town is quieter. My new driver stays on the coast road, giving me a chance to study the beachfront. Watching the waves as we speed along makes me feel dizzy. I haven't eaten since the plastic meal on the plane. My stomach grumbles. The driver ID on the taxi dash says Ravi. A garland of plastic flowers hangs from his rear-view mirror. His car smells vaguely of curry and onions, but as the journey progresses, it's eclipsed by my own underarm odour. I hope you'll be staying here for a few days, as I'm seriously in need of a shower. I wonder whether the father-in-law will call Cousin.

Manley is closer than I thought to downtown. Ravi takes a wrong turn. We end up on the peninsula overlooking the Harbour Bridge and the Opera House. It looks like a postcard, but there's no time to linger.

'Take picture,' he says.

'I don't have a camera,' I reply.

'Crazy tourist. No camera,' he mutters.

I shrug as he swings the taxi round and we find the address of your cousin. There's only street parking here. The white Volvo is nowhere in sight. I tell Ravi to take me to the Novotel we passed on the way in, down near the beach. I pay his fare, and he drives off.

It's late when I check into the hotel, but still warm. It's hard to believe it'll be below freezing back in Kansas. I take a room overlooking the ocean. I wonder if you're down there somewhere along the beachfront, enjoying the balmy evening.

By the time I've walked up Raglan Street, it's completely dark. The Volvo is parked outside the old Victorian house. There are a couple of lights on in the upstairs apartment, so I hang about on the street.

And then I see you. You're carrying a load of clothes, probably laundry, past a window. I hope you'll be here at least until after Christmas. I guess that's what normal people do, spend Christmas with their families, even on the other side of the world.

I look forward to staying in a real hotel, knowing you're safely tucked up for the night. I can afford the luxury of not having my bag ready to chase you for a few days.

I've got my own laundry to deal with.

Back at the hotel I tip everything out of my pack to give it a good airing. I sort my clothes to send to the hotel's laundry service. As I shake the pack to get every pair of underpants and the last stray sock out, there's a thud on the floor. I look down at my old passport. It must have been wedged in a fold in the lining. I stare at it, laugh out loud, remembering the anxiety I went through to get a new one. I tuck it into the top pocket of the pack.

It feels so good to sleep in a real bed, with real sheets, a real TV and 24-hour room service. I take advantage of the latter until I can't eat another slice of pizza or slug another bottle of beer.

I wake at dawn the following morning. You're still within my sights after crossing half the world. It must be a sign. It must be *right*. I'll hang back for a few days, make sure you don't think I'm tailing you. After our encounter in New Zealand, it would seem weird if I did the same thing again. I flick through the tourist leaflets in the room, imagining you and me discussing our plans for the day.

The traffic is permanently gridlocked, so it's pointless to hire a car. I call down to reception and ask where the nearest bike rental is. You'll most likely take the ferry to the city. I have a better chance of following you on two wheels. If I miss you, I know where you're staying.

The concierge recommends a rental shop on the Esplanade, not far from the intersection outside the hotel. I head down there first thing.

As I walk towards the beach, I smile. I always have plan B if none of this works out. The emergency address in the back of your passport is imprinted on my brain. And although I don't want to spend any time without you, both those pieces of information have been my insurance since going through your bags in Spiky's house back in Honolulu.

I will never lose you.

TWENTY-ONE

'I THINK I know him,' I hissed.

Clutching Steve's arm, I dragged him into the shadowed porch of a sport store.

'Who?' My cousin raised his brow.

'A guy – American I think – I saw on a tramp near Queenstown. He was one of a group of us who got stuck on a pass because of avalanche danger.' I reached for my throat, a tingling sensation working its way up from my chest. 'Jake... that was his name. I remember now.'

Steve followed my gaze, and we watched Jake cross Market Street in the distance, pushing a bicycle. He was still a long way from us, but if it was the same guy, he'd trimmed his hair and beard. He looked less like a vagabond, but it gave the impression of youth rather than maturity. He still wore a baseball cap but had swapped his square-framed sunglasses for round ones, John Lennon style. They suited him even less.

He reached the other side of the road. Centrepoint Tower pierced the bleached Sydney sky in the background.

'Amazing coincidence,' said Steve. 'Why are you hiding? You should say g'day to the guy.'

Steve took a step out of the shadow of the shop porch as if to call out to Jake, but I grabbed his arm and pulled him back.

'Wait!' I paused. 'I guess it's not that much of a coincidence. I know I've seen travellers several times on the circuit round New Zealand, and this is downtown Sydney. Loads of tourists pass through. But… no, we'll let him be. He was a little creepy.'

Steve pouted comically.

'Seriously, forget it.'

'Linda's dad told me about an American with a baseball cap looking for my Volvo. Said he'd clipped my wing mirror in the parking lot. I couldn't find any mark on the car. Do you think it might be the same guy?'

I bit my lip. As Jake paused on the pavement, he glanced in our direction. I drew my head back into the shadows. I felt awkward not showing myself. I hoped Jake hadn't seen me jump back. My face prickled with heat.

'There's always the chance he's looking for you, Sandy,' Steve joked.

I didn't laugh. A chill ran down my spine.

A memory pushed its way forward. *Coincidences.*

I was pretty sure I'd caught sight of him on my flight to Sydney.

I'D WANTED TO be in Australia by Christmas. After Queenstown I continued my journey through the southern Fjordland on the South Island, but was beginning to look forward to the comfort of family.

Greg hadn't shown up for our breakfast date. I stayed on the hostel's front deck an hour beyond the acceptable waiting time, beyond the moment a girl knows she's been stood up. I imagined him waking with a hangover, thinking he shouldn't be leading some tourist on when she was only going to be around for a day or two. Or worse, after the excitement of our adventure on the traverse, that he'd made a terrible mistake. It was only a few passionate kisses. I didn't even have his phone number, or a last name, and had no idea where he worked, only that he was a DOC ranger.

Something was telling me it was time to move on.

Two cousins, sons of my uncle on Papa's side, lived in Sydney. We hadn't seen each other since childhood. When I was little we lived together on the farm, which had enough rooms to accommodate the two families. We occupied a different floor of the chalet, a Swiss tradition dating back centuries where several generations worked on the same farm. When Uncle Jean decided to seek his fortune in the southern hemisphere, he bequeathed the business to Papa, who in turn passed it on to Pierre. When Uncle Jean sold the sheep station, he moved to Sydney, changed his name to John Barrow, and started working in real estate.

A few years my senior, cousins Stéphane and Guillaume now called themselves Steve and Will, although their anglicised names didn't seem to fit them. They said it was to avoid the confusion of the spelling of their names on official papers. I thought it was sad they'd given up part of their identity. They barely spoke French anymore and had no intention of returning to Europe. Steve had married a young nurse, and Will was head chef at a gastro pub in Double Bay.

Steve's wife Linda's parents emigrated from England after the second-world war and put down roots in New South Wales. They'd settled well into an affluent Aussie life in this area north of Sydney, but they still insisted Christmas lunch should be the traditional *fayre* of the old country. The Barrow Family were all invited, although Will was working. The festivities were of neither truly English nor Swiss tradition, and I felt a little disconnected.

Everyone helped set up the Christmas banquet next to the pool. Linda's father tried in vain to angle a giant sailcloth to shade every area of the table. We brought out platters of steaming vegetables, roast potatoes and a massive stuffed turkey with all the trimmings ready for carving.

The weather was hotter than usual for December. We'd seen Santas in Bermuda shorts rolling in on surfboards at Manley Beach on Christmas Eve. I couldn't conjure one single comparison to our traditional *Noël* in the Alps. We would have been gathered round a roaring log fire sipping *vin chaud* with snow falling outside.

When all the food had appeared from the kitchen, Steve stared at the festive table.

'Strewth, I can't bloody face that meal in this heat,' he said to Linda.

She looked at her mother, who was wiping her hands on her apron before swiping at a strand of hair plastered to her forehead with the back of her hand. She nodded to her husband.

'It's true, pet,' she said to him. 'It's too humid out here. Crank up the air conditioning in there and we'll bring everything back inside before everyone loses the will to eat.'

Each of us took dishes, table settings, plates and cutlery inside to re-lay the table with slightly less finesse than before. As I carried the linen napkins inside I stopped by the pool, wishing I could have a dip. Sweat trickled down the channel next to my spine, and I entered the dining room where glacial air was now cooling the feast.

Linda's father began carving the turkey and we all helped to dish out the vegetables. Linda ran out to fetch the cruet set, the last thing left on the patio table.

'Mum, didn't you tell me the neighbours were down in Melbourne for Christmas?' Linda asked as she slid the door closed with her foot behind her. 'I thought I heard someone next door.'

'They're not back until after new year. Could be possums. They've been a real nuisance lately.'

'Oh, I've never seen a possum!' I jumped up from my seat and went towards the window.

The purple jacaranda blooms in the neighbour's tree quivered, and I concentrated on the branches.

'They're a bloody nuisance,' Steve said. 'Don't open the door Sandy, you'll let in the heat. Come and eat lunch before it gets cold. You'll have plenty of time to see the possums. They'll be hanging out on the porch roof later. Pests.'

I closed the window and sat back at the table with a sigh. They wanted to start the meal, but my hunger had dissipated. This show of English tradition was a farce, and although I couldn't imagine not being with some kind of family on Christmas Day, I knew I wouldn't be here for long. I felt sorry for Uncle Jean and my cousins who had abandoned their heritage to try and blend in here but with Linda's family holding them back with an event like this. Steve and his family should be barbecuing on the beach with the rest of the population.

I thought of Papa, hoped he would still be there next year for a Swiss family Christmas with Pierre, maybe Marianne, and me. If I couldn't have that now, I'd rather be back on the road exploring the outback.

I wanted to see them all: Koalas, kangaroos, wombats and possums. They weren't pests to me.

And I still had a whole new continent to discover. I'd soon be on my way to Asia.

TWENTY-TWO

I'M ACHING TO ring the bell of the house in Avalon. This whole festive occasion looks more like Thanksgiving than Christmas, although that's something I've only seen on TV. Neither celebration warranted more than an extra bottle of hard liquor back in Kansas.

The whole party moves back inside the house. The discussion about the weather around the table at the pool that led the group to decamp was ridiculous. It's so hot, not even a puff of steam rose from the feast as it was set out under the giant sun shade. When you carry the last of the table trimmings back in through the glass doors, I see beads of sweat gathering on your upper lip. Then the door closes and I'm alone in the heat pounding up from the paving of the neighbour's terrace.

This house is shuttered up. They must be away for the holiday. Their tree is the perfect place from which to spy. As the family sits down, you come to the window and look in my direction. I almost drop the binoculars, and pray you don't see me. I don't move a muscle. Jesus. You're staring right at me. I lick my cracked lips.

After what feels like an eternity, you return to the table and sit where I can only see half of you. I'm thirsty. I didn't bring any water with me, and my head is spinning. The woman called

Linda is facing me, and I know if I move, she'll see me. So I'll wait until she gets up from the table. My sweat drips onto the foliage below.

There are a bunch of adults and a couple of brats. The guy I met a week ago stands at the head of the table and sharpens a carving knife. The woman, who is presumably his wife, dishes out vegetables. Voices rise to a crescendo through the closed window before falling silent as everyone concentrates on eating. My stomach rumbles and the heat puts me in a soporific daze.

Suddenly the window slides open, and you race outside onto the terrace with your napkin in your hand.

'I'm not coming back in until someone kills that thing!' you yell.

I hear male laughter, then the old woman shushes them.

'Don't jest, boys! If it was a huntsman, sure. But a redback is no laughing matter.'

'Bloody hell, it must have been hiding in the tree,' says Linda.

'Linda! Language! Kids!' says the woman who must be the mother of the children, possibly Linda's sister.

Voices are raised, and there's a rapid triple thump.

'I'm not coming back in until I see that thing dead!' you repeat, standing on the other side of the pool.

Cousin comes out holding what looks like a Christmas card in the palm of his hand. You approach him, tuck your hair behind your ears and lean in to inspect what's on the card.

'Okay,' you say simply, and walk back into the house.

Cousin throws the crushed body of the spider into the flower bed and goes back inside.

I shift on my branch, my ass having now lost all feeling. The old lady comes out and surveys the garden, hands on hips. She looks up, and her gaze falls on the gently swaying blooms of the tree I'm sitting in. She narrows her eyes, then with a puff of her cheeks turns away to enter the house, leaving the sliding door a few inches open.

Nobody rises to close the window. I'm so dizzy from the heat, and should get down, but am compelled to stay a little longer now I can hear the conversation again. You speak to the Uncle in French. Your voice is so goddamn sexy. As dessert bowls are scraped clean and coffees are served with port and brandy, you switch back to English with the others and I learn that you love the tropical heat, roast potatoes, and New Zealand sauvignon blanc. I learn that you want to Scuba dive, hang-glide, and of course you're scared of spiders. I know that after your trip around Australia, you'll be visiting Bali, Malaysia and Thailand, amongst other countries I don't get to hear because the kids are screeching.

But my vision is starting to go. If I don't get down from here, I'll pass out. When Linda leaves her place to carry out some dishes, I climb down the tree.

The cycle back to the hotel seems to take ten times longer than it did on the way out. I almost crash twice. When I get to my room I push the air-con to maximum, gulp a gallon of iced water, and collapse onto the bed as the room spins. I probably have heat stroke. But I'd go through worse for you.

My final thrill is taking a cold shower on Christmas night. Then I lie on top of the bed, missing you like crazy. Like a junkie needing his next fix.

TWENTY-THREE

I WAITED OUTSIDE the Chang Mai guesthouse for almost an hour, my hair an uncontrollable frizz in the sultry atmosphere. I'd lost count of the times I'd already listened to the mix-tape Valérie had made for me that I collected poste restante in Bangkok. The sweat-soaked earphones of my Sony Walkman kept slipping from my ears.

I wondered whether anyone would actually show up and kicked myself for taking the cheap option. I'd handed over my precious Baht the day before to a suspicious-looking agent off Thapaie Road. There were two of us waiting outside the guesthouse.

When I approached the man sitting near me on the step, I discovered he'd booked the same tour several days before me. We compared tickets and decided they were genuine. The flimsy receipts written in Thai script wilted in our hands from the humidity.

Our arrangement was for a group tour on a five-day trek through the tribal communities of the Karen people. The agent had told both of us a bus would collect us at sunrise, and that there was some distance to travel to the jungle. If it hadn't been for the other man, I'd have probably given up waiting by then.

As the Jeep pulled up, I puffed with relief. It skidded to a stop in front of us. In the southeast-Asian-style I had become accustomed to, two boys leapt off the roof and swept up our backpacks. They didn't even ask to see our receipts. As we were the only Westerners sitting on the step, they must have assumed we were their passengers.

'Jungle tour?' I asked, to make sure.

They smiled and nodded. Dust settled from their arrival. The boys tied down our packs to the luggage already precariously balanced on the roof.

This was not the comfortable mini bus I had expected. One of the boys indicated the other man should sit up front with him and the driver. He opened the door at the back for me and I gazed into the overfilled vehicle.

'Move over!' he yelled to a woman with braided hair. She smiled resignedly and unstuck her bare thighs from the torn plastic seat to reposition herself closer to her neighbour.

'Hi, I'm Mary,' she said as I squeezed in. 'And this is my husband Ron.'

She nodded towards the man sitting beside her, who looked like he was in a bad mood. Mary sounded jolly, as though she was over-compensating for Ron's anger. I wondered what they'd been promised on their jungle tour. I was determined to enjoy the experience, however far from the small-print in the agent's brochure we were being led.

The humidity pressed upon me. I sucked in the heavy air in the cramped space.

'Can we get going?' Ron asked, his voice rising.

His face was red, sweat beaded on his nose, and I sensed the panic of overheating flashing in his eyes. The Jeep set off, our heads jerking backwards with the unexpected acceleration. As we pulled away from the guesthouse, I stared across the road at a person sitting in the shadow of a tree.

A memory flashed through my mind. I glanced away and blinked in confusion. I strained to look back again to the figure to confirm my suspicion, but he had gone. I had to wonder whether I saw him there at all. I shook my head.

'What's up? Are you okay?' Mary asked.

'I'm fine. I thought I saw someone I knew. Someone who's supposed to be in another country.'

'That happens to us all the time, doesn't it, Ronny?'

Ron stared with clenched jaws out of the other window towards the sun rising in a blood-red haze over the Ping River.

'We're constantly bumping into people on the Southeast Asia trail. Everybody's doing the same route. Travelling south to north in an attempt to avoid the worst of the monsoon. It's kinda cool. It makes you think we're all one happy family on the move. Where you heading next, Cambodia? Laos?'

'I wanted to go to Vietnam, but they've only recently opened up to tourists and the visa application was too complicated. After this I'm heading to one of the Thai islands for some beach time, then probably Nepal. Maybe India. Then it'll be time to make tracks home. My father's not well. I can't stay away too long.'

I bit my lip. I felt a wave of remorse and tried to remember the last time I'd called home.

As soon as we picked up speed, air filled the car, although it was as warm as a hair dryer. Nothing could eliminate the prickling feeling now creeping up my neck.

'Sorry, air-con not work!' the driver said.

I closed my eyes and the image of the figure under the tree flickered in my mind.

'That's not what we were told at the agency,' grumbled Ron. 'Said we would be transported in an air-conditioned minibus!'

Was it that guy, Jake? Was this a traveller's inevitability, as Mary had suggested?

'My God,' I murmured.

'You okay? Not feeling good?' Mary shifted away from me.

It was a cheeky way to get a little extra space in the back of the Jeep. I was tempted to say I felt travelsick.

'I'm fine. I'm fine,' I said instead.

I turned to look at the passing barren paddy fields, waiting for the rains for planting. Buses, tuk-tuks and scooters all vied for a place in the middle of the dusty road ahead.

The last place I'd seen him was Sydney. Before that? Queenstown, or Te Anau maybe.

'Ya, sorry, group not big enough. Two cancel. Open windows wider. Open, open. Air con. Same, same,' yelled the driver.

My face flushed hotter from the humidity. Or was it from the memory that I had deliberately ignored the guy all those weeks ago crossing a crowded road in Sydney. If it was the same guy, what was he doing on a street corner in Chiang Mai?

And if it was him, had he seen me?

TWENTY-FOUR

THERE'S A SPLIT-SECOND of eye contact as the Jeep drives away. I leave the shade of the tree opposite the guesthouse. I had intended to wait until your return from your tour. The last thing I want to do in this wretched heat is get into more fucking hiking. But there's a guy with you, and I panic. Where the hell did he come from? I can't tell if it's someone you know or if he's a random tourist.

When you step towards the curb and look up and down the street at the increasing traffic I see his eyes travel up and down your body. I want to wipe the smirk from his mouth. The compulsion to be near you, to protect you, takes over again.

I flag down a tuk-tuk and give the driver the address of the agency near Thapaie Road where I know you organised your tour. I cling on to the seat in the back as he weaves in and out of the traffic. Did you recognise me outside the guesthouse? I'm unsure. It was such a brief moment. In any case, I don't know how to interpret the expression on your face. It looked more like you were being abducted than setting out on a tour. I tell the tuk-tuk driver to step on it.

I should have booked myself on your trip. A five-day trek in the wilderness would have been the perfect opportunity for you to get to know me. I certainly don't want that other guy getting to know you.

I push open the door of the grubby travel office. There's a man with greased hair wearing a fake Lacoste polo shirt and a pair of fake Ray-Bans sitting behind a desk full of papers. I can't believe you handed over your money to this sleaze ball.

'I need a guide for a jungle tour,' I say.

'Next tour, Friday,' Sleazeball says.

'I need one today.'

'Today tour gone.'

'I *know*,' I say, trying to quash my patronising tone. 'I need a private guide with a fast car to follow *today's* tour.'

The salesman leans back in his chair and takes off his glasses, blinking as he can probably see better in the darkened office without them. I pull a fistful of hundred-dollar bills from my pocket and place them on top of the papers between us. He raises his eyebrows, and his mouth forms a tight little 'o' like a cat's anus. I've bought him.

'Oh, sir,' – I am suddenly 'sir,' flashing those greenbacks – 'my cousin, he available. We find you place. Private tour? No problem.'

It's amazing how quickly things happen when you have money. After a couple of phone calls, it's not long before an old Mercedes pulls up in front of the office and a similar-looking guy with the same fake aviator Ray-Bans is shaking my hand. Panit is my guide for five days. Once it's established we are 'like brothers,' he drives me in relative air-conditioned comfort to the northern Thai town of Fang. The comfort is only relative because the car has to avoid potholes, ruts, domestic animals and oncoming traffic that can't stick to the correct side of the road. On the way, I explain to Panit that I want to participate in the same tour as the one that left that morning.

'You follow girlfriend?' he asks.

My face reveals he's right, before I realise he was joking. I want to punch him for guessing my motives. He sniggers at his discovery.

'They trek near border of Burma, in Doi Pha Hom Pok. Not so safe. Freedom fighters.'

Not so safe. What does that mean exactly? I can guard you from the occasional horny tourist, but I'm not so sure of my ability to protect you from terrorists.

He starts talking about the trek. I've already resigned myself to the fact we will have to journey on foot if I want to stay close to you, but it is with reluctance that we start hiking out from the end of the rough track where the Merc can no longer navigate.

Panit tells me the trekking companies are numerous. He says the tribes all take a cut of the tours. I'm sure he's exaggerating the 'danger' crap to make this whole thing seem more authentic and intrepid. The authorities wouldn't risk putting anyone in danger for fear of losing tourism revenues.

I hate it. The fake danger. The fake tribes.

'Lucky not rainy season, then you never keep dry,' Panit says, pointing under his armpit like some ape.

The jungle isn't quite what I expected, more like a tall dry forest with dusty tracks everywhere. Patches of trees are joined to bare areas where the vegetation has been cleared. I wonder how far into the wilderness we will have to go before we're having an 'authentic jungle experience.'

We trek up dry gullies to villages of thatched huts with children running around barefoot wearing grubby fake Calvin Klein T-shirts.

Your group is spending the day riding through part of the jungle on the backs of elephants. There's no way I'm getting on one of those things. Panit seems relieved.

'We travel faster on foot. They stop to bathe elephants in river. We go on to next village, different way. Be there before them tonight.'

We arrive in a small community of the Black Lahu tribe. Panit negotiates a place for me to stay with a family on the outskirts of the village. He makes it clear my presence is not to be made known to your group. Panit explains that this happens all the time. When two groups accidentally find themselves staying in the same village, the locals keep them apart so they feel like they're still having a 'unique jungle experience.' I wonder how many thousands of tourists are wandering around north-western Thailand unaware of each other's existence.

I eat dinner with my 'family.' It's a surprisingly delicious meal of rice, chicken and vegetables. The host shoos away curious kids from the other huts.

I needn't worry about drawing attention to myself. The rest of the village surrounds your group. After dinner I sit on the high veranda of the hut and watch your interaction with the tribe down in the communal clearing. I'm relieved to see you're not really engaging with the other guy you were waiting with outside your guesthouse this morning. He appears to be hitting on one of the other women in the group.

As I watch you playing with the children, a strange emotion comes over me. Whether for my own lost childhood or some inherent paternal feeling, I know you will make a fine mother one day. The way you play with those kids, make them sit on your lap and let them touch your sun-bleached curls is endearing. My own memories of 'family' are so horrific. I can't imagine what a happy childhood would have been like.

WHEN I'VE DONE my business in the long-drop and climbed back up to the hut, Panit is nowhere to be seen. I suspect he's staying in a brick and mortar house with access to a TV and hot and cold running water.

After we've eaten, the host beckons me over to the fire. He offers to share the pipe he's smoking.

'Kratom,' he says, smiling. 'Kratom.'

I have no idea what he means.

'Kratom. No opium.'

He looks at me with eyebrows raised as he offers the pipe again. I shrug. Now you've gone to bed, I'm bored. I clasp the pipe and draw a toke, hoping he's serious about the 'no opium'. It tastes surprisingly sweet. I take another drag and begin to feel a pleasant calmness. By the time I'm ready to lie down, my body is relaxed enough not to notice any discomfort. I fall into a deep sleep with the occasional dream that you are there beside me and our children are scattered about the hut on their sleeping mats.

In the light of morning I feel rested and at peace, but before I've even sipped the coffee offered by the host's wife, Panit shouts from the bottom of the ladder.

'Get dressed. Girlfriend gone!'

'What do you mean?'

Our voices wake the children, and the chief's wife frowns at me. Her husband delivers a retort and she chews her lip.

'Group leave. Okay, no panic. But we go. Not sure how far down river they float.'

'Float? They're on a boat? How will we follow them?'

I pull on my shirt and stuff my belongings into the pack.

'They walk to bamboo forest first. Then they make rafts. We go overland. You ready for walk? Big hill to cut off bend in river. Hot day.'

Why can't you have a normal vacation? The girls I remember from college would have headed to the beach weeks ago.

IT ALMOST KILLS me, but it almost kills Panit too. He stops often, mostly to light up a Marlboro. I envision the precarious livelihood of the Karen Tribes being wiped out in one huge forest fire.

'We go over Kiewlom Ridge, to get there before girlfriend's group.'

I no longer correct Panit on the girlfriend comments. After a while it sounds perfectly natural.

The path out of the valley is steep and rutted. The humidity blocks my throat like cotton wool and if I try to move too quickly my head pounds. The plastic bottle I filled with water at the last village is almost empty. Panit seems to be surviving on very little to drink, but his face is shiny. Each time he stops for a smoke, I have to stand several yards away from him. It's as though he's sucking all our air in through his cigarette.

He carries a machete to cut away the occasional vine or branch blocking our path. The weapon seems alien in his hands. His shades stick out of the breast pocket of his shirt and his shiny Reeboks scuff the trail.

'This path only used in rainy season. Jungle keeps growing, even in dry season.'

He brandishes the machete. I take a step back, eyebrows raised. He smiles, thinking he's frightened me. Moron.

The higher up the path we climb, the more birdsong and animal noises we hear in the forest canopy. The sky is a white backdrop through the gaps in the trees above us. I can't work out whether it's cloudy or hazy. The smoke from Panit's

Marlboros can't cover the occasional waft of another kind of smoke, different from the smell of the villages' cooking fires.

'Something burning?' I ask Panit.

He looks at his cigarette stub on the path, a thin wire of smoke still rising from the paper. He grinds it out with his shoe, before understanding my question. His chin points west.

'Slash and burn. Not here in Fang or the national park. It's no longer allowed. Across the border they clear forest each dry season for cultivation. For growing pineapple and palm oil.'

'Don't the fires spread here from Burma?' I ask.

He shrugs. I guess he has no loyalty to the national park. He probably doesn't even come from Chiang Mai. Just in it for the 'tourist dollar.'

'How high does this damned path go?' I ask.

'Over two thousand meters.'

'Two thousand? You'd think we'd be heading into cooler weather by now.'

I lift my armpit and take a whiff. I stink. Panit smiles.

'This the path the guides take to bring supplies. You'll see. There's a camp by the river on the other side where your girlfriend will pass. If we follow in canoe, she see us. And point is you not want her know you follow her, right? Guides use this ridge path for supplies when river flooding. You no used to our climate,' Panit concludes, sneering at my damp shirt, although his own is also patched with perspiration.

Every time I stop to take a breath or wipe the sweat from my face, I close my eyes and imagine your face to reinforce why I am here in this Godforsaken place. It's hard to imagine your group is actually having fun. I wish we were back in New Zealand, in the Southern Alps. The moment we touched seems so long ago.

I haul one of my dirty T-shirts out of my pack. Your panties come with them. I hurriedly stuff them back before Panit sees. I wipe the sweat from my face with the shirt.

'When was the last time it rained?'

'Now is end of dry season. We wait for rains. When monsoon comes, these paths turn slick. Be glad for dust. Mud is worse. And flash floods.'

Panit fans himself with a broad leaf cut from the jungle and plods slowly on up the trail. I follow him, eyes fixed on the bright orange rubber soles of his fake Reeboks, listening to the occasional slice of his machete through a vine.

PANIT'S TIMING IS correct. Coming down the other side of the ridge is even more challenging than going up, but he knows his stuff. We sit on the ground hidden by the trees to watch your group on the bank of the river. The tour guides are stringing huge bamboo poles together to make large rafts. The tourists don't really help much. It's too hot to do anything. You all sit in the shallows of the slow-flowing river, splashing each other half-heartedly.

Your T-shirt, smudged with the soaked dust of the jungle, is getting wetter and wetter in the river. I can see the outline of your torso. As the water soaks upwards along the stretchy cotton fabric, I make out the swell of your breasts. Fire rushes through me to see you're not wearing a bra. I know everyone else can see it too. I want to shout out, make you cover yourself. The tour guides stop briefly to watch you frolicking in the river. You're unaware that you appear to all the world to be half naked.

'Why you not just go to her? What crazy is this?' Panit asks when he sees my agitation. 'You know she finish jungle trek in two days. She go back to guest house in Chiang Mai. She go to market, buy cheap fakes with tourist dollar. She do what all the other rich white girls do when they travel through Southeast Asia. You think waiting weeks for her is going to change the way she open her legs for you?'

He doesn't get it. He doesn't understand. I have to make sure everything is perfect.

BACK IN CHIANG MAI a few days after the tour has finished, I hire another taxi to follow your long-distance bus back to Bangkok. When we arrive in the city, I feel bold enough to check into the same guesthouse as you. I wait until you and the girl you've travelled with on the bus have been shown your room. I approach the old crone who appears to be receptionist, cleaner, and washer-woman all rolled into one. I luck out and score the room next to yours.

The room is grubby. A faint smell of urine wafts from the hole-in-the-floor toilet down the hall. There's a strip of narrow Perspex at the top of the connecting wall. But I'm happy because the shadow of your squeaky ceiling fan is a constant reminder of your presence next door.

One evening as you're getting ready to go out, you talk about your family with your roommate, and you mention your mother. I learn she died of cancer, just like mine. Fate means us to be together.

I'm lying naked on my bed in the evening warmth, holding your panties like a set of prayer beads in my hand. As your conversation moves on to describe your time with those tribal children up north, I close my eyes. The sounds of tuk-tuks, Asian music, a Super Mario game nearby on Kao San Road, and someone hawking in the alleyway are a distant backdrop to the sweet harmony of your voice. I stand up from the bed and put my ear to the wall to hear you better. My palms lie flat against the barrier between us. I press the length of my body against the yellowing paint, slick with tropical humidity and the congealed dust of a thousand travellers. As my hardness presses against the wall, I imagine this is your skin, smooth and cool, an oasis in the oppressive heat. I long for the day I can be inside you. I move against the wall, the connection to your space conjuring the essence of you.

In my moment of release, a gasp catches in my throat. The conversation on the other side of the wall ceases.

'What was that?' your roommate asks.

'Probably rats. This guesthouse isn't the best I've stayed in,' you say.

'Do you think there's anyone next door?' the girl whispers. Heat rises to my face as though I've been caught out.

'Don't think so. I didn't hear anyone on the stairs and it's been quiet for ages. I'm starving. Come on, Nisha, we can grab some street food on the way to pick up our tickets.'

A sense of shame dulls the passion, but my mood improves when I hear you're heading to the travel agent to pick up your ticket for Surat Thani. We are finally heading down to the islands in the South China Sea.

But I am beginning to wonder when my patience will run out.

TWENTY-FIVE

THE BUS RIDE took all night. Nisha and I wished we'd invested in a cushion or an inflatable neck support. In our cramped seats, the only entertainment was *Saturday Night Fever* playing on an endless loop on a small TV screen at the front of the bus. Not even full volume in my Walkman headphones could block out the film. The air-conditioning was turned up full. Shivering most of the way, I thought longingly of all the clothes in my backpack in the luggage compartment under the bus.

When we reached Surat Thani, I said goodbye to Nisha who was continuing to Penang in Malaysia, and stepped into the tropical sunshine. Free from the smog of Bangkok, I inhaled the salty aroma of decaying fish and rotting seaweed. It was strangely pleasant, a preferable alternative to the charcoal stoves, diesel fumes, and occasional whiffs of effluent on Kao San Road.

The ferry to Koh Samui was a small wooden boat with bevelled windows and a highly polished wooden deck. I was one of the first on board and grabbed a seat on the bow to get the best of the sea breeze. Numerous long-tail boats buzzed back and forth beside us like teenagers on mopeds chasing a school bus. It was busier than I had imagined.

Once on Koh Samui, I shared a tuk-tuk with three other backpackers to the north of the island. I stayed a night at Bo

Phut Beach before negotiating a fare with one of the long-tail boatmen for the crossing to Koh Pha Ngan.

I was grateful for the previous advice from fellow travellers to make the extra effort to get there. Before I'd even stepped from the boat into the tepid water lapping the white sand of Sunset Beach, I was calculating the maximum number of days I could stay without jeopardising the rest of my trip.

The beach was busy with travellers lying on the sand or floating in the turquoise water. I lifted my pack out of the boat and walked up to the tree line. A man was sweeping fallen palm fronds from between two bungalows. I asked him whether he had any free rooms. He shook his head.

'Busy now. High season. Sunset Beach full. Try over on Haad Rin Nok – Sunrise Beach.'

I continued through groups of bungalows and restaurants scattered amongst coconut palms. Within minutes I came to the eastern side of the peninsula. I asked at three sets of bungalows, feeling more dejected as the last lady shook her head.

'You try Haad Khontee or Haad Yuan!' she yelled as I walked away. 'Ten minutes through trees. There!'

She pointed to a dense swathe of jungle at the end of the bay. I hauled on my pack and made my way to the end of the beach where I discovered a partially overgrown trail. Two minutes into the walk up a barely defined path, perspiration had soaked my clothes. Ten minutes turned into fifteen. I began to think I'd been sent on a wild goose chase. I could see hints of sea through the trees to my right. I felt vulnerable, far from civilisation.

The trees thinned and the path widened. As it descended, I was afforded a view of a secluded white-sand beach. Turquoise waters spilled gently onto the shore with a coral reef spread like a colourful map on the sea floor at one end of the bay. I stopped and took in the beauty of it. I'd finally reached my paradise beach.

I walked down past the bungalows to a palm-thatched shelter with a cooking area at one end and a handful of tables with plastic table cloths and mismatched chairs. I shifted my pack to the floor and a short Thai woman approached me.

'You look for bungalow?'

'Yes, I hope you have one available.'

She smiled in assent, exposing a gap between her two front teeth. I wanted to hug her.

'One remain. Hundred baht a day.'

'Can I see it first? I mean, I'm sure it's fine. I want to be sure.'

The woman puffed, reached for a key on a hook in the kitchen and lifted her sarong. She walked across the shelter without a word.

I reached for my pack.

'You'd better take the bungalow,' said a man with a north American accent, making me jump. I peered into the shadowed corner where the voice had come from.

'Although it's far from five-star,' he continued, and I felt awkward for the woman who would surely take this as an insult. 'You'll take it because Mimu's cooking is the best on the island.' I heard the smile in his voice.

'Mister Kai…' said the old woman, and giggled.

She waved for me to continue following her and shuffled barefoot along the path between the bungalows. She led me to the hut near the trailhead where I had moments ago come out of the forest.

I said yes before my eyes had even adjusted to the darkness of the simple palm-covered wooden bungalow, identical to the others clustered above the beach. Inside, there was barely enough room for the pallet bed and a space to cram my pack.

Crude wooden shutters covered the glassless windows. But the hut was dry, had a mosquito net, and was protected from the afternoon sun by the jungle behind.

Once I'd handed Mimu money for my first week's lodgings, I pressed my palms together.

'*Kob khun kah!*' I said.

She gave me her gap-toothed grin in return. I followed her back down to what I now realised was the resort restaurant.

'Welcome to Bovy Bungalows,' said the man in the corner.

As he came out of the shadows, he leaned a guitar against a table and held out his hand.

'Kai,' he said simply.

I clasped his strong dry hand. I could hardly get the 'Sandy' out of my mouth.

Kai, a tall, tanned Canadian, was bare-chested with a sarong tied around his waist. I wasn't sure where to look, at his striking blue eyes or the well-defined deltoids and rippling muscles of his upper body.

I sat at the table next to his guitar. He explained he had been living at the bungalows for several weeks. He was working with a group setting up a Tai Chi retreat on Sunrise Beach.

'Why are you staying all the way out here?' I asked. 'Surely there are bungalows closer to the retreat.'

'It's too busy over there. This place is peaceful. I love coming back here at the end of the day. When you've walked that forest trail a few times, you'll get used to it and it won't seem so far. And I like Mimu's food. Did I mention that?'

'Sold it for me,' I said, realising I was now starving.

Mimu heard her name and looked up. She was wrapping fresh fish and flavoured rice into banana leaves to put into the bamboo steamer. I placed an order, and watched Kai as he ran down to the beach to 'take a dip' before eating. His shoulder-length hair, spun tightly into dreadlocks, was bleached blond by the sun and the sea. His manner was friendly and easy-going. He threw a friendly greeting to a couple of other tourists as he passed their bungalow.

'All girls like him. He not easy to catch. Good fish.'

Mimu wagged a finger. I smiled. I had the feeling I was going to enjoy my days doing nothing on a Thai beach.

I SPENT LAZY days in the water swimming and snorkelling. Kai often joined me on the beach in the late afternoon after his Tai Chi. He sometimes serenaded me on his guitar, or we would sit in the warm shallows talking about our dreams. He taught me to fish off the boulders at the end of the beach. We threw back most of what we caught, the ones that were too small to eat. But every now and then we took a decent catch back to Mimu. She would prepare a romantic meal at our favourite table nearest the beach. Mimu's watchful eye was always on us, as though vicariously enjoying our growing attraction for each other, but mostly wanting positive appraisal for her cooking.

I loved it most when we lit a fire on the beach, lay on a mat watching the flames, occasionally brushing sand and salt from each other's bodies. I wanted to put my hands on his strong shoulders and run my fingers down his chest to the bone fish hook he always wore, carved for him by a Maori artisan in New Zealand.

One evening he described what he planned to do when he returned to Canada. He and a group of friends wanted to cycle across the continent from east to west. He asked me if I would like to join them. They would raise money for human rights. I wasn't sure how I would be able to pay for such a trip, but I told him I would love to go.

I was doing exactly what I promised myself I wouldn't. It didn't take long in that island paradise to fall in love.

TWENTY-SIX

I'VE OVERSLEPT THIS morning, and awake with the cold fear that I've missed you. For a moment I don't know where I am, then recognise the bungalow I managed to score on Sunrise Beach close to the trail to Haad Khontee. That was after sleeping two nights in the open. Some guy called Lee who runs the beach bar on Haad Khontee said the last bungalow had just been taken. That must have been you. He said the others all had long-term occupants.

I usually get up at dawn to get to my stakeout in the trees above your beach before anyone uses the trail. But as I'm later than usual, I hope I haven't missed you going on an excursion. Especially when I don't see you on the beach or in the restaurant.

Then I have the sickening feeling you might have spent the night with *him*. Feeling more bitter by the hour, I decide to sit in my regular spot and wait for your return. Thoughts of Hippy Boy eat at me.

You met him on your first day. He often sits on his own in the restaurant talking a few words of Thai with the gap-toothed old woman in the kitchen. He sometimes practises a weird martial art on the rocks at the end of the beach, standing for hours on one leg, arcing out his arms in some strange spastic pose. His stupid Canadian accent makes him sound like a pretentious prick, infecting everybody with purity and freedom as though he's part of some greater universal peace plan.

I hate him. I hate him for making you notice him. I can see it in your eyes when he plays his guitar on the beach. I hate that he makes you want him.

I can't see the front of your hut from where I sit, as it faces the beach, but during the morning the girls in the bungalow next door approach and disappear up your steps out of my view. One of them comes straight back out and runs down the path to fetch Hippy Boy from his bungalow. He comes towards your hut with a frown on his face. I'm relieved you're not with him. I don't know if he's had you that way yet.

Hippy Boy shouts down to the old woman in the kitchen. I've never heard him raise his voice other than his stupid singing. I realise something is wrong. The old woman brings a bag and a bottle of water back up to your bungalow. I want to know what the hell is going on, but daren't go down there. I sit and chew my fingernails.

An hour or so later, Hippy Boy collects some things from his own hut and hurries along the trail towards Sunrise Beach, passing within a few yards of me. He's so close I can see the crease on his brow. I want to take advantage of this perfect opportunity. I prepare to jump onto the trail to knock him towards the rocky outcrop below. It would be so easy to blame it on an accidental slip of the feet. But I hear two girls who share the bungalow next to you coming towards me on the path, and I let them all pass. He throws one of his self-righteous Zen greetings to them, and they converse in anxious tones for a few seconds before he jogs on. I press my lips together and hope I don't regret that missed chance later.

When he disappears, and the girls have passed by, I stand up amongst the undergrowth and slide down to the trail. As I walk down to the restaurant above the beach, I look back towards your bungalow. Your door is closed.

The old woman is sweeping the packed earth floor of the kitchen area.

'Is Sandy okay?' I ask.

'Who are you?' the old woman asks, immediately suspicious.

'Sandy's a friend of mine. I'm staying over at Sunrise Beach.'

'She sick. Dengue fever.'

'Dengy? Jesus what's that? Is it serious? Can I help? What does she need?'

The old woman rolls her eyes.

'Like malaria, but not malaria. Dengue from mosquitoes. But not here. Can't catch dengue here.'

'It must be from the jungle. Up north. Chiang Mai. We... we were in the jungle together.'

The old woman's face relaxes. She believes we know each other.

'Then you can help your friend. She need lot of rest. You letting her sleep,' she says and turns away.

She changes her mind and turns back to me.

'You take her water. She must drink. Important with fever. Not to dry out.'

'Is it bad?' And then a thought. 'Is it catching, this dengy sickness?'

'Here, you take this.'

She hands me a large bottle of water, still chilled from a cooler box full of ice next to the gas cooker. I take it and she holds out her wrinkled brown hand. I look at her, confused.

'Ten Baht.'

'Ten? What a rip-off!'

The old woman narrows her eyes and pulls the bottle out of my grasp.

'You really friend of Sandy?'

I flash her a reluctant smile and give her a ten Baht coin. I know water only costs a couple of Baht at most, depending on the proximity to the jetty and the friendliness of the bungalow owners. It's not like she can see money dripping off me or anything. But some people can smell it. Like those pirates in Chiang Mai. Any excuse to exploit a Westerner.

She walks with me to your hut. I wonder how you'll react when you see me. Inside your bungalow, which is really more like a shack, the shutters are closed and it's dark. The old woman pulls back the mosquito net around your bed. My anxiety about your potential reaction spikes. But you're completely out of it. Your breathing is rapid and shallow. I touch your arm.

'Holy crap. She's burning up!' I say. 'Is there a doctor around? Can someone at least take her temperature?'

The old woman places her hand on your forehead.

'She okay. Not die, silly. Give her water, maybe cool her head. She need few days' rest.'

She waddles back to the kitchen, her sarong flapping around her legs. I sit on the edge of your bed, watching your fever-ravaged face. I take off my T-shirt and soak a section of it with water. Squeezing some onto your lips, you automatically swallow as the drops hit your tongue. But you don't open your eyes. After a few sips, I wipe your forehead and neck with the damp shirt.

'It's okay, angel,' I whisper. 'I'm here to look after you now. I'll make you better. Please get well.'

All those weeks holding back, wanting to touch you, wanting to twist your hair in my fingers, wanting to moisten your lips with my tongue, and here I am, sitting right beside you. I trail my finger down your arm. You don't move. I cup your breast, loose under your damp T-shirt. You draw one knee upwards and groan. I snatch my hand away, afraid you'll wake up, but you sleep on. Under the sheet, you're wearing a flimsy pair of batik shorts. I place my hand on the top of your thigh where your bent knee has fallen to the side. Your skin is hot. I want to climb on top of you, possess you, be in you.

There's a thump on the step up to your veranda. I pull away my hand and cover you quickly with the sheet. I squeeze more water into your mouth.

A girl in a bikini steps into the tiny space of your hut.

'Oh, cool. I was just going to make sure Sandy had enough water. Is she okay?'

I nod, wanting her to go away.

'Just making sure she doesn't choke,' I say, turning back to gaze at your face, waiting for your swallow reflex to kick in.

'I'll come back later then.' Bikini Girl relaxes when she sees I'm there to help.

I've seen her before with her friend on Sunrise Beach. She appears to recognise me, so my presence doesn't provoke any questions. Her flip-flops slap back down the steps and her footfalls fade. I reach up to comb your hair away from your forehead with my fingers.

I think of all the missed opportunities, of the times I should have just walked right up to you and given it my best shot. I lean down and kiss your hot, dry lips.

I don't want to lose you now.

The Thai woman charges me eight Bhat for a second bottle of water and I leave it next to your bed. I touch your breast again through your cotton top, and push at my shorts. Voices drift up from the beach. I stand up to tuck the mosquito net around your mattress. It's time to go back to my bungalow before the old woman and the girls start to get suspicious.

When I leave, Hippy Boy passes me as I head towards the trail. He must be back from his ridiculous slow-motion calisthenics on Sunrise Beach.

'Hi. You new? What were you doing?' he asks, glancing towards your bungalow.

He is immediately mistrustful, looking me up and down. I want to take a slug at him, but figure I won't be doing myself any favours out in the open.

'I'm a friend of Sandy's. We travelled together for a while in New Zealand and Australia. I heard she was sick. I came to see if I could help.'

'Wow. News travels fast,' he says. 'How's she doing?'

I shrug.

'Breathing better. Her face is less flushed.'

'I brought her some oranges,' says Hippy Boy. 'I'll tie them round the beam so the rats can't reach them. She needs...'

'I know what she needs,' I say forcefully. *She doesn't need you.*

Hippy Boy's brow furrows.

'Relax, man. Don't stress.'

I roll my shoulders and turn to leave.

He waves a hand dismissively, and heads towards your bungalow. I sneer at his sissy-boy back.

TWENTY-SEVEN

'MY MOTHER USED to say the idle invite trouble,' I told Kai as we sat side by side on the beach. 'I still can't believe I was out of it for three whole days. I didn't even need to pee all that time.'

I blushed as I said this. When I'd moved my legs over the edge of the bed to stand up on day four, I could barely support myself. I just about made it to the door, and Kai was right there, rushing up from the restaurant to check on me. He had to help me down the steps on that first morning, but I was too weak to make it to the toilet block, so he held me under my arms as I peed at the side of the bungalow. It was probably the most selfless thing anyone had ever done for me, however much humiliation I was feeling.

'If it hadn't been for the girls next door, you might have been in a bad way. They brought you water straight away.'

'I remember Mimu at some stage saying "Dengue, dengue" in her high voice. And I remember gentle hands lifting my head. Drinking water from the bottle. Was that you?'

'Maybe,' Kai said, smiling.

I leaned in to his shoulder, breathing his strangely erotic smell of fresh garlic and cumin.

In the middle of my delirium, I recalled someone combing my hair with their fingers and drops of cool water across my dry lips. Someone had talked about my mother. I'd seen her, floating like a shining angel, felt the feathering of her cool dry fingers across my cheek.

Moments missing from those days weren't without their nightmares. Another time, in the middle of a night where a three-quarter moon cast shadows and a ghostly light through the cracks in my shutters, I saw a net bag containing what I later saw were oranges tied to the beam under the roof of the hut. The bag swung back and forth as though we were at sea. Two sets of beady eyes glistened at me from the top of the beam. I tried to shout out, to chase the monsters of fever away. My mouth was dry, my throat rasped. My shout came out as a croak. As I sank back into oblivion, the scratching noises and shuffles in the jungle forest outside my hut faded to a rustling of palm trees in the tropical breeze that sounded like rain in the night.

'Did you bring me the oranges?'

Kai smiled again.

'You're so kind. Where did you get them?'

'They had them at the market over on Sunset Beach. My gift to you. You need them to build your strength and get well. I had to compete with a friend of yours on the first day for water duty though.'

'One of the girls next door?'

'I don't know his name. Haven't seen him again. But he said you'd travelled together.'

His name? I sat up abruptly, looked up and down the beach. The sudden movement made my head pound. I was still a long way from complete recovery. The bells of alarm weren't improving things.

'Hey, take it easy. What's up? You're a bit jumpy. Relax. When you feel well enough, I'll take you to lunch somewhere exotic, and show you a new swimming area with the most amazing corals I found on Haad Yuan.'

My gaze scanned the line of bungalows against the forest and the restaurant where Mimu was preparing dinner, then down the steps to the beach bar where Lee was opening the bamboo panels ready for his afternoon customers. I couldn't see anyone who looked like *him*. I didn't have the energy to explain to Kai. Was it Jake? Who else could the 'friend' have been? I shivered, but not because I was cold. I no longer thought it was the common occurrence Mary and Ron had mentioned up north. Could it be possible he was following me?

'I think you were delirious.' Kai's comment drew me back from my thoughts. 'You asked for *"Maman"* a couple of times. The soldier's cliché.'

'I can't remember,' I said with a frown. 'But there was something about my mother. She died two years ago of cancer. God, I must have been really sick to have done that. Thank you for bringing me water.'

'We all help each other round here,' Kai said, holding me in a way that sent a thrill running through me.

EACH DAY AT Haad Khontee I felt stronger. Mimu plied me with bowls of fish soup and herbal tea. I soon felt strong enough to walk to the end of the beach and back. One morning I sat in the hut near Mimu's kitchen, popping slivers of pineapple into my mouth.

'Thank you for everything Mimu, for looking after me.'

'Not me girl. I have kitchen to run. You have men to help you. Lot of attention. You lucky girl.'

Lucky to be alive, I thought. I couldn't believe I'd been so ill. There were still three days missing from my life. I gazed down to the beach where Kai was helping Mimu's husband Vish change a cracked propeller on his long-tail boat.

'Yes, he's my saviour,' I said, then more quietly, 'rather a lovely saviour.'

'You have more than one savvy,' Mimu said, waving a cloth.

I swallowed.

'Who, Mimu?'

'Boy come. He think your sickness catching. He bring you water then I chase him off. He not come back.'

I needed to be sure.

'Mimu, can you tell me what this boy looked like?'

'Hair dark, long, not nice, not clean. Not boy I see you being with. But he care for you. Like a father or brother.'

With a racing heart, I carried on studying Kai, looking like Adonis in a pair of cut-off jeans soaked up to his thighs in seawater. I wanted nothing to ruin the romance we were building. If Jake was here in my paradise, I hoped my relationship with Kai would ward him off.

'COME, DANCE WITH us. Come on Sandy. Don't let those flames hypnotise you,' Kai teased. 'Let's have some fun. I know you want to dance.'

It was the night of the Full Moon Party. The tepee of wood on the beach bonfire collapsed, sending a shower of sparks up into the star-strewn sky. Smiling faces glowed in the firelight. Bare feet kicked up the soft white sand. Someone turned up the volume on the little speaker attached to a Walkman and the song distorted.

'You're very persuasive,' I said as I took his hand.

I let him pull me to my feet, the heat on my face a combination of too much Mekong whisky and our proximity to the fire. Kai swung me around, his hand on my waist. My lips lightly brushed his cheek before he guided my arm under his in a classic rock and roll move.

When the song finished, Kai turned off the music and picked up his guitar. He sat on a log to play. I went to the other side of the bonfire so I could see his face. I loved to watch him strum and sing. Warmth spread in my belly at the prospect of spending the night with him. He looked at me occasionally across the shimmering heat. Someone passed a bottle of Mekong and I took another swig. Kai frowned slightly before launching into the next chorus of *Hotel California*. I wondered whether that was lust on his face or concern about the amount of alcohol I'd consumed. I was determined to seduce Kai that night, and the whisky had given me the courage to do it.

As the full moon rose in the sky, everyone stood up to dance again. More Mekong was consumed. I lost my balance in the sand. After one boisterous pirouette, my head didn't stop spinning. I needed a break from alcohol.

'I'll be right back. I need to get some water.'

'Good idea.' Kai kissed the top of my head. 'I'll be here.'

Candle lanterns were dotted about the beach shelter, otherwise lit by the orange glow from the bonfire down on the beach.

A few couples sat together at tables in the restaurant, but the bar area was empty. I ordered a bottle of water from Lee and pushed a few Baht across the counter. The water was warm but I drank most of it, then recklessly ordered an expensive drink of fresh pineapple to help sober me up.

Lee prepared my juice and I smiled gratefully. After downing the water, I needed to pee. I hopped down from the bar stool and told Lee I would be right back.

When I returned five minutes later, the music on the beach had ramped up again. I heard raucous laughter. I caught a glimpse of Kai's face reflecting the flames of the fire. It was time to make my move. I swigged down my fruit juice to wash away the warm, metallic taste of water. Over the sweetness of the pineapple I tasted something bitter on my tongue, and narrowed my eyes at Lee, certain he had spiked the drink with a shot or two of Mekong. I winked, wagged my finger at him, and skipped down the beach to join the others.

The music continued. People were singing. I looked for Kai amongst the crowd. I peered towards the surf tipping onto the beach, the foam flashing white in the darkness. Figures were milling by the water but I couldn't see him. My vision blurred. I tried shaking my head to clear my eyes. But that made my temples pound. I worried about dehydration after my illness, and returned to the bar to retrieve the water bottle I'd abandoned earlier. It was almost empty. I finished it.

I didn't feel so great, wanted to lie down and sleep. I felt so stupid, having drunk too much whisky too quickly, especially so soon after my illness. I might have ruined my chances of spending the night with Kai. I figured if I closed my eyes for half-an-hour I would feel better and go back to the party, so I headed back to my bungalow.

As I lay down on the mattress, my nausea died down. I clung to the notion that I was going to feel better in a few minutes. My eyes burned and my head was pounding, but as long as I didn't move, I felt a sort of comfortable numbness. I just needed half an hour...

TWENTY-EIGHT

I IDENTIFY HIPPY BOY by the silhouette of his dreadlocks as he walks along the trail back to his hut. His guitar is slung over his shoulder, the neck pointing downwards. The fire has died down on the beach in the distance. The moon casts its ghostly light on the scene. A few figures still meander by the water line. The party is coming to an end. For all I care, those empty-headed travellers with their leather sandals and their nose rings can wrap themselves in their tie-dye sarongs and sway until they collapse in the sand.

As Hippy Boy approaches I stand in the clearing that has become my daytime home above the trail leading to the bungalows. Dead leaves and trampled undergrowth have formed a comfortable niche in the jungle. I'm hidden by the foliage from the path, but high enough to see the rear corner of your bungalow, part of the steps leading down, and most of the beach where you've been hanging out for the past few weeks.

The pile of empty plastic water bottles to one side of the clearing grows daily, along with the pungent smell of urine and rotting food scraps. Rats have been here during the night when I'm not around. The cicadas are still deafening, even though the pounding heat of the day is over. They've been kept awake by the brightness of the moon. The night is otherwise still.

Hippy Boy approaches. I creep towards him. As he passes under the shade of the palms, moonlight and the shadow of palm fronds streak across his face. He's concentrating on the path, humming an annoying tune, so the element of surprise is on my side when I meet him. His muscular arm is wrapped around the body of his guitar. In his other hand, he's clutching the necks of two empty bottles he has scooped up from the edge of the trail. Doing his bit to save the environment. Jerk.

With his hands full, concentrating on his stupid song, my appearance is unexpected. When I move onto the trail in front of him, the hum fades in his throat and his mouth opens. Recognition flashes in his eyes.

'Man, you scared the shit out of me. What the –?'

I move swiftly behind him and raise a simply fashioned weapon over his head. Two sticks of bamboo with a section of heavy-duty fishing line I scavenged from Sunrise Beach. I pull it tight around his neck. He hasn't let the bottles go. His guitar is too precious to allow to fall. If anything, his grip tightens as the muscles in his arms and neck bulge. This is to my advantage. In those two seconds, I am able to drag him uphill off the trail. He takes first one, then two steps backwards with me, our combined momentum driving him up the slope towards my clearing. Then the moment of surprise passes and he releases the bottles. They roll back down to the trail, the glass tinkling against occasional tree roots and pebbles. He lets go of the guitar. The weight of it pings the strap from the base and it crashes to the ground, rolling over with a discordant thrum.

I hope no one chooses this moment to pass by, but it is late at night; they're either in their beds or sleeping on the beach. Hippy Boy reaches up with his hands and grapples at his neck. But the fishing line is now tight and he can't get his fingers under the wire. The sounds coming from his throat are drowned out by the buzzing of the cicadas. We are still moving together towards the clearing when he loses his balance. We fall backwards. I'm surprised at his weight on top of me. By now I've twisted the two pieces of bamboo around each other, and even if I let go, the wire won't loosen. His body briefly knocks the wind out of me, but I realise I am in an optimum position, underneath him. He begins to kick. His heel meets my shin, but I move my legs out of the way.

I'm more worried about his arms. He's making a different kind of humming noise now. Once he realises he can't get to the wire at his neck, he tries to reach me with his hands. But I'm directly under him, lying flat in the undergrowth, my elbows still bent either side of my head with my hands on those two pieces of bamboo. He tries to raise his head. My fingers burn when I tighten the wire. I don't know how much longer I can hold him. He tries to twist, to reach his arms around him in a bizarre semblance of a hug, but I'm safely pinned underneath his sweat-slicked body. The putrid smell of his skin stings in my nostrils. He finally begins to weaken, and I know the end is near. Although my fingers and hands are aching, I hold on for several more minutes after he's stopped moving.

When I push him off me, his limp body rolls onto the dead leaves. Breathing hard, I struggle to stand up. I scramble down to the trail and retrieve the bottles to hide them.

I turn and look down at my work, the moon seeping into the clearing. The only mark on him is the angry dark line around his neck, a track of blood where the wire has broken his skin. Other than that, a fleck of frothy saliva glistens on his lower lip. I imagined I would see terror in his bulging eyes and his square Canadian jaw in the rictus of a silent scream, but his eyes are closed. He looks sickeningly beautiful in his permanent slumber. Jealousy sends adrenalin pumping hard through my veins. I find the strength to pull his body further uphill a good thirty yards from the trail. I retrieve his guitar and take it back to the body, wishing he could see me smash the thing around the trunk of a tree. The splintering wood and popping strings echo in the jungle. Once I've finished, I strain to listen to any movement from below. All I hear are the cicadas continuing their tinnitus hissing.

I leave the shattered pieces of the instrument lying on his body. I come back to the clearing to tidy the space, smiling all the while because I know Hippy Boy will not be trying to seduce you again.

I have you to myself once more.

TWENTY-NINE

WHEN I AWOKE, the sun was shining through the shutter of the bungalow, casting its stripes across my eyelids. I blinked hard and looked down at my body. I was still wearing the blouse I had put on for the beach party the previous night, but I was naked from the waist down. I scratched at a pair of mosquito bites on my elbow and cursed myself for not tucking in the net.

And then I knew. A crustiness on my inner thigh and a dull ache around my pelvis. When I acknowledged the vague burning between my legs, I was certain I'd had sex. The realisation made me blush. I looked around for signs of Kai's presence, experiencing a tweak of alarm when I didn't find any, not even a used condom. I blinked hard, trying to recall the evening. I wanted to remember every moment with Kai.

After I'd drunk some warm water from the bottle by my bed and visited the bathroom, I still couldn't recall what had happened the night before. The last thing I remember was talking to Lee at the bar. I rubbed my eyes and smoothed the sheets on the mattress. I sat on the edge of the bed and combed my hair with my fingers. Could I have had a relapse of the dengue fever? No, this was different. Nothing like this had ever happened to me before. I couldn't believe a few glasses of Mekong could do that.

When I had tidied both myself and the bungalow, I headed to the kitchen shelter where Mimu was preparing a late breakfast for a few people. The bonfire on the beach still smouldered. Vish was raking the sand around the bar. Lee was nowhere to be seen.

I recognised a few people sitting on the beach from last night's party. It looked as though some of them had slept on the sand. Sleeping bags and sarongs were scattered in piles around them. I couldn't see Kai.

To try and clear my head, I went back to the bungalow to change into my bikini. I waded into the bath-warm water of the bay and floated on my back between the gentle lines of surf. A wave lapped over my head. When I resurfaced, the soaking only served to make my temples ache and my eyes sting. Still no recall from the night before.

As I lay in the water, I studied the shoreline and the beach. I could see Kai's bungalow, but it didn't look like he was home. A sarong flapped in the breeze on the line strung under the overhang of his roof. I willed him to come out and see me. But it was late. He was probably already at the Tai Chi retreat giving a class.

I imagined him walking back along the trail, appearing above the beach next to my bungalow. I tried to think of the signs he might display to indicate he had slept with me last night. I licked the salt off my lips, and remembered I wasn't wearing any sunscreen. If I stayed in the water any longer, I would burn, even though I already had a deep tan.

Should I go and find him now? Try and gauge his mood? I was in a dilemma. I couldn't ask him outright. What would he think of me? He might have had a beautiful memory of us together in this tropical paradise, and yet I couldn't remember what had happened, although I desperately wanted to.

Then I imagined his face when I asked if he could tell me exactly what went on the previous night. He might hold my hand, describe every tantalising moment. He might be sad that I couldn't recall our magical night together. But my greatest fear was that he might be disgusted I had drunk so much that I'd lost my memory.

Until I could piece together the events of the night before, I couldn't ask.

OF ALL THE places I'd visited, Koh Pha Ngan was the hardest to leave. It wasn't only because I'd been cheated out of a week of my travels by the dengue fever. It could have been worse. I'd heard of some travellers picking up malaria in the rainy season in the Golden Triangle in Northern Thailand. They repeatedly suffered relapses later in their travels. At least dengue was a one-off deal.

The passion I thought was mutual seemed to have died. The decision to leave wasn't taken easily. After the full moon party, Kai disappeared. I knew he had begun to teach full-time Tai Chi courses at the retreat over on Sunrise Beach. He'd already talked enthusiastically about the tasks ahead. It was as though the party had been his last wild night before some serious work. I thought he must now be staying over there. The same sarong hung from the line on his balcony, but when I asked Mimu if he'd moved his things, she shook her head.

I still had little recollection about the night we spent together. I tried to drag up images from a fuzzy memory. His hands and mouth on my body. But the longer I left the space between the blank of our night together and asking him about it, the more my confidence faded. He must have been avoiding me. A part of me wondered if he felt bad that he'd taken advantage of me in a drunken state. It was all a confusing mess. I didn't have the courage to go and find him at the retreat. I wanted to apologise. For what, I wasn't sure. But the more I thought about it, the less I wanted him to think I was a promiscuous drunken tramp.

On the second day after the party when I asked Mimu if she'd seen Kai, she seemed worried. With a mixture of sign-language and agitated pidgin English she said she'd been to his bungalow. It looked like he hadn't come home. I'd heard a story on the night of the party about an inebriated backpacker who had drowned while trying to swim round the peninsula from Haad Rin Nok the year before. Mimu sent Vish out in the boat to search the water off Haad Khontee Beach. But I was sure Kai had been behaving too sensibly at the party to do such a thing.

My time on the island was running out. I couldn't forfeit my plans. I still wanted to visit Nepal. Kai had a full-time job. There was nothing I could do on this remote island to increase or even maintain my travel funds. Any jobs were already taken by locals. Despite our playful romance, I was getting a little bored with the beach.

Maybe this was Kai's message. Perhaps he was making things easy for me. I calculated my options, figured out the futility of my crush, and decided it was time to move on. I was determined not to miss out on the things I had planned for the remainder of my trip. As I sat at a table in the restaurant and told Mimu I was leaving, she seemed genuinely sad.

'You have to find Kai first. He be sad you leave.'

I shook my head.

'He must be staying at the Tai Chi Retreat, Mimu. He'll be back soon. He's making it easy for me. He knows this relationship is impossible.'

'No, no!' She was agitated. I put my hand on her arm. She shook her head, muttering to herself in Thai.

THE FOLLOWING MORNING, I paid Mimu what I owed her. With my Baht clutched in her hand, she put her arms around me and hugged me hard. My eyes stung with tears. I'd only ever seen her touch Kai, her favourite.

'Have you seen him?' I asked for the final time. 'I thought in the end I should say goodbye.'

'No, three days now. Hard working man. Rich tourist pay big dollar for his magic.'

Her words made me want to cry again. I walked back along the jungle trail for the last time with my backpack. The day before, I had negotiated with one of the fishermen to take a longboat to Koh Samui from Sunrise Beach. From there I would get a ferry back to the mainland.

I was about to settle in the middle of the longboat, gazing at the cluster of wooden buildings at the end of the beach where the retreat was based, when I stood up.

'Wait! Can you stay here for ten minutes?' I asked the boatman.

When I pulled a handful of Baht out of my money belt, he agreed. I left my pack in the boat, I knew I could trust him as he was Vish's cousin, though at this point I didn't really care if everything I owned apart from my money belt went missing.

'There's another bonus when I get back,' I said, jumping into the water, soaking the bottom of my cotton trousers.

I ran barefoot up the beach to the retreat and hurried into the open atrium at the front of the building. A woman walked from behind a bamboo screen with a pile of towels.

'Excuse me, have you seen Kai? Do you know where I can find him?'

Her expression clouded.

'We also like to know about Mr Kai. He not come to the retreat today or yesterday. People wait for him. Pay good Baht. And he not come.'

I looked at her, bewildered. I contemplated going back to his hut. But Mimu already told me he wasn't there.

I wondered if he'd left the island all together. Or was purposely hiding. Perhaps he felt he'd made a huge mistake. But there was no message, no note. I couldn't help thinking of Greg in New Zealand. That I'd been royally stood up again.

I'd already made the first step of my onward journey by walking the jungle trail back to Sunrise Beach. I couldn't keep dithering about my emotions. With sad determination, I went back to the waiting longboat.

I climbed in, told the fisherman I was ready. He gunned the engine towards Koh Samui. A rooster tail of sea water arced behind us, the wind bled tears from my eyes. I swallowed the lump in my throat, turning to stare at the turquoise water off the bow without looking back.

THIRTY

YOU AND I are amongst a dozen or so Westerners on the Thai Airways flight to Kathmandu. Everyone else seems to be a Nepalese national, each wearing at least five layers of clothing. Their short bodies are padded out to Pillsbury Doughboy proportions. I know we're heading to the world's highest mountains, but it can't be that cold in the capital.

At check-in, you stand a head above the others in the queue. It's easy to spot the Westerners amongst the passengers. I decide to stand tall, not hunch in the line. But I still feel self-conscious. Despite over a month in the tropics, my skin is paler than the Nepalese faces. As we gather in the cramped gate area waiting to board, I sit in the corner and pretend to read the magazine I've found on one of the seats. At one point your eyes sweep over me. As usual my baseball cap is pulled down, but there is no denying you've recognised me this time. Your expression hardly changes, but your gaze rests on me a split second longer than the other passengers.

I wonder what you're thinking in that moment. I have the feeling you're on the point of approaching me, but then boarding for the flight is announced. I let you take your place in line to get on the aircraft before me. I allow myself to be carried along in the padded flow of passengers behind you. It's unlikely I'll see you on the plane, as the only way I could get on the same flight was to book a business class ticket. But it doesn't stop my heart pounding with anticipation.

I don't know your seat number. As I turn left into the front section of the plane, I wonder how close you are in the economy section behind me. Knowing I've been seen, I wonder if you're expecting me to pass you in the aisle. Perhaps you're preparing to say something to me. I experience a little thrill. Since Koh Pha Ngan, I've kept my distance between us to allow the memory of Hippy Boy to dissipate, but you'll be over the confusion of his disappearance by now and looking forward to our next adventure.

There are no padded passengers in this section of the plane. I would have found their fashion choice amusing, if the air conditioning wasn't cranked down to just above freezing. I ask a hostess for a blanket, and inquire about the over-dressed passengers in chicken class.

'Same, same. Every flight,' she says, handing me two blankets. 'They're avoiding import duty on cheap clothes from Thailand they will sell on the markets in Durbar Square and Ason Chowk.'

I arrange myself in the ample space of the business class seat. It's a late afternoon flight. When we've been served a meal, the lights are dimmed so we can get some sleep. I tuck my blankets up under my chin, recline my seat and close my eyes.

I'm dozing off, when I feel rather than hear heavy footfalls down the aisle. I instantly know it's you. I smile, and feel like a child in a game of hide-and-seek. I pull my blanket over my head, creating crackling static sparks in the darkness, and pretend to be asleep.

The footsteps stop and I sense your presence beside me. Grinning like a kid, I peer out over the blanket, my baseball hat creating a mailbox slot of vision. Your hand grabs a fold in the cloth. I think you're about to snatch it away. How fun, this is a game! And then I see a moment of hesitation in your eyes. I'm not wearing my sunglasses. I realise you're suddenly doubting it's me. Your hand hovers over the blanket. I'm about to throw it off and say 'boo!' when I see the hostess hurrying towards you along the aisle.

To avoid any blame for causing a commotion, I pull the blanket back up to cover my face again, but the movement makes the guy next to me who's been watching the in-flight movie jump. He spills the coffee he was about to sip. It goes over both of us. Another hostess follows the first, rushing towards the scene.

'Ma'am, you must go back to your seat,' the first one says to you. 'You're not allowed in business class.'

The second hostess offers paper towels to me and the man next to me so we can wipe the coffee from our laps. I notice the delicate but firm hand of the first hostess holding you by the elbow to guide you towards the back of the plane.

'The game's up, Jake!' you stage whisper, resisting the hand of the hostess. 'Whatever your plan is, it...'

I don't hear the rest of your sentence as the hostess pushes you back up the aisle. Some of the other business class passengers are starting to grumble as they're disturbed from their slumber. I have an overwhelming urge to hit something.

I couldn't hear what you said because of the complainers around me and the hostess who's dragging you away. Were you teasing me? This is intriguing. A riddle! It was our special moment, and they've ruined it. You were willing to play along; I recognised your tone, it was conspiratorial. Yes, a game! You said it yourself. You were about to say something really important. We were about to have a big connection. I'll have to wait until later to find out.

People around me are now unsettled. I don't want to draw attention to myself by following you to the back of the plane, so I decide to stay where I am until the end of the flight. I'll savour the moment. Now I know you want me to come out of the shadows, I feel confident we've started something. Your words mean you don't want me to hide any more.

When we land in Kathmandu, the business class passengers are first to deplane. As I turn to walk down the steps, you're standing in the aisle in economy class. Our eyes meet over the heads of the other people, and I smile. I have to look away before I see you smile back, as the passengers begin to move towards the door, and I don't want to hold them up.

For such a basic airport, I'm surprised to see the business class bags are given priority as my pack tips onto the squeaky conveyor belt. After I've picked it up, I organise a taxi for us. Once I've given the driver a few dollars and promised him a load more if he'll wait for us, I make my way back to the luggage hall. Hundreds of bulging red and blue striped canvas bags are interspersed with the occasional high-tech backpack on the conveyer belt. It's obvious which luggage belongs to which passenger group. The traders and the trekkers.

You're engaged in deep conversation with a western couple, and I frown. I want to get you on your own, ride in the taxi without the annoyance of others present, so I hang back, hoping you'll shake these two. They continue to chat with you while you're waiting for your pack. I'm not close enough to hear the conversation or their accents. They seem to be monopolising your time. It looks like I'm going to have to follow you from a distance into Kathmandu after all.

THIRTY-ONE

A FEW TOURISTS were waiting for taxis when we came out of the terminal building. I stuck close to Alex and Anne as we approached the queue. I had to look like I knew what I was doing, if only to shake Jake. I hadn't let on to my new companions that I was being followed. They may have thought my engagement with them was a bit intense, but in truth I was probably no worse than any newbie trekker fresh on her travels.

We'd already agreed to split the cost of a taxi. As I looked at the line of Maruti Suzukis at the stand, I was glad I had sold my sleeping mat to another traveller on Haad Rin to reduce the size of my pack. With a last glance back to the reflective windows of the airport building, we squeezed ourselves into the next little white car in line.

The pink fur across the dashboard and a string of plastic orchid flowers hanging from the rear-view mirror helped the three of us bond, crammed in that confined space. There was much eye-rolling and suppressed giggles.

Alex and Anne had travelled together from Edinburgh to trek in the Himalaya. They weren't married, but I could tell by their body language this wasn't a Dave and Suzy scenario. They had an idea of where they would look for a guesthouse. I asked if I could tag along. I had nothing planned, and only had a few pages of recommendations torn out of a shoestring travel guide to rely on. It was dark, and we had no idea where we were heading.

I hadn't seen Jake at the taxi stand, thank God. I thought of how he might be trying to follow me into the town. I wanted to turn around, check whether we were being followed. But I was wedged tightly in my seat and couldn't look over my shoulder. Darkness had fallen, and the streets were pitch black. I breathed deeply, trying to feel relieved that I was in the company of the couple in the taxi.

'How come there are no street lights?' I asked the driver.

'Power cuts. Fuel shortage,' he explained. 'Big problems with India. Government cut supplies. We may not have fuel for taxis soon. Bad for tourists. Bad for Kathmandu. Bad for Nepal.'

We arrived in an area of the city frequented by backpackers and the taxi dropped us off. As we hauled our packs onto our shoulders, it began to drizzle. The occasional waft of an open sewer mixed with the pungent smell of rain on hot cooking coals. We picked the closest guesthouse on my list.

'How much you pay? All in one room?' asked the boy at reception.

I shook my head.

'Two rooms. We're looking for something around the ten-dollar mark,' said Alex.

'Hah, no husband?' The boy jutted his chin at me. 'You need husband? Can find husband for you.'

'No husband,' I said.

As we filled in our details on the hotel register and handed over our rupees, I didn't want to break the connection I had with Alex and Anne.

'What are your plans while you're here?' I asked.

I wanted to keep the company of others in this more remote environment.

'We're applying for our trekking permits tomorrow. We want to do Everest Base Camp and the Annapurna Circuit. In no particular order. How about you?'

'I only have time for one trek. The Annapurna Trail is the one I'd really like to do. Three weeks from Besi Sahar to Pokhara. A teacher gave a talk in my high school about Poon Hill, and it's been an ambition of mine since.'

'We could get a bus to Dumre with you. Then negotiate a truck. It's better to travel in numbers.'

I wholeheartedly agreed.

The following morning, we went together to the trekking office to secure our permits for the Annapurna region. Later we arranged to take a bus to Dumre where we learned we could find a space on one of the old Russian army transport vehicles heading out to Besi Sahar.

We had two days until our bus left, so spent the time visiting the sights of Kathmandu, temples, monasteries, markets, and the renowned Durbar Square.

I was nervous, kept scanning the crowds. I'd recognised Jake at the airport, but I didn't really know what he looked like. I'd always seen him with his face hidden behind a scraggy beard, shaded with a baseball cap. The human brain is supposed to be capable of mapping and recognising even the most common of facial features, but I couldn't muster a clear image of him in my mind.

There were hundreds of backpacking tourists milling around the streets of Kathmandu, and I saw him everywhere I looked, though I don't think it was ever him. He, on the other hand, would have no problem spotting my blonde curls, especially if he had truly been following me throughout my travels.

The thought made me queasy. I figured it must be psychosomatic, but it turned to reality later that day as we were scaling the Swayambhunath temple. I suddenly felt a little faint, and had to sit down on the narrow brick steps of the edifice.

I couldn't stay there for long. Wild monkeys climbed all over me, grabbing at my clothes and my hair. Anne warned not to let them touch my face in case they were carrying disease. The coloured prayer flags waving in my periphery at the top of the temple enhanced the feeling of seasickness.

'This sounds like a bit of a joke, a thousand miles from the ocean. But I could swear I've just climbed off a boat,' I told Alex, when he asked if I was okay.

'The smell of the sewers probably doesn't help,' laughed Anne.

I made it to the top of the pyramid temple. The view of the city was worth the effort. I had to sit down again after the descent, and watched the local women doing their laundry in the waters of the Bhachaa River flowing past the foundation stones. The mesmerising rise and slap of white sheets against smooth rocks calmed my head and made me feel better. I took a sip of water from my bottle and followed the couple back to the main road to hail a rickshaw to take us back to the guesthouse.

'HOW MUCH FOR three passengers to Besi Sahar?' Alex asked the driver of the first Russian army truck lined up on the edge of the road out of Dumre.

We had taken a bus from Kathmandu and were now inspecting a few sorry-looking vehicles for the next stage of our journey.

'Thirty dollar!' said the Nepali.

Alex circled the old truck dubiously.

'Look at the slits in the tyres! How can they possibly stay inflated? We'll give you twelve for the three of us,' he haggled.

The driver shook his head.

'You want leave first, you pay twenty dollar. Truck almost full. We leave soon.'

'I don't want to hang around here,' I told Alex. 'It's okay with me. We should take this one.'

I felt more comfortable once we'd put a few hundred kilometres between us and Kathmandu, but I still didn't want to stay in Dumre a moment longer than necessary. Trekkers, Sherpas and locals milled about in the dusty road. Despite needing time to get to the high passes for our bodies to acclimatise, I wanted to make it as hard as possible for Jake to follow. Alex shrugged his assent and we handed over US dollars rather than rupees, the preferred currency in this economy. Alex thought he could have haggled the guy down even more, but I was impatient to leave.

It had been a bumpy bus ride from Kathmandu, but it was nothing compared to what was to come. Packed like sardines into the back of the truck, we set off along the track to the foot of the Himalaya, more potholes than road. Half the passengers were trekkers and the other half Nepalese citizens travelling back to their mountain homes. We'd only been driving a few minutes when the truck stopped near a river. The driver leapt out with a bucket to fill what turned out to be a leaking radiator. He stopped at every subsequent water source to repeat the process and I began to regret our impatience to be on the first departing truck.

Clouds gathered on the horizon and rain began to fall. As we made slow progress, the Nepalese passengers complained to the driver. He stopped so the tarpaulin could be untied from the bars over the cab, then rolled out over the cold, damp passengers and our soaked luggage.

We arrived in a town called Bhote Odar and the driver pulled up to an abandoned garage. There were no other vehicles on the treacherous road. A heated discussion ensued. A man brought out a jack and undid the nuts of the wheel with the worst of the tyres. He mounted a different wheel as we all stood around waiting. When the jack was let down, there wasn't enough air in the replacement. Without a compressor and pump to fill the tyre, the only solution was to change it back to the old one again which at least held a little air.

Many of the Westerners abandoned the truck and checked into the only guesthouse for the night. But Alex was adamant we had paid for our trip to Besi Sahar. He said we might have to fork out the same again in the morning on a new truck that could be just as bad, so we waited with the other Nepalese passengers. I was happy to keep on the move.

In the middle of the night we set off again. We had a little more room with fewer people on board. Our shoulders knocked against the roll bars as the truck navigated the ruts. Our heads lolled in unison with fatigue. When the rain stopped, the tarp was rolled back off the frame. A bright moon in its last quarter appeared as the clouds cleared.

As we crested a hill and descended into a valley, fireflies accompanied us like magical fairies the rest of the way to Besi Sahar. I began to relax, thinking I had finally put enough distance between myself and my stalker.

THIRTY-TWO

WITH KATHMANDU ON your itinerary, I know we're in for more footwork. But a three-week permit! The Annapurnas! That's like Everest, right? Madness!

It was an inconvenience when that couple hooked up with you at the airport. I need to get you on your own. I saw you searching for me when you were in line for a taxi. You kept glancing back to the airport entrance. It gave me a tweak of satisfaction knowing you were looking for me rather than the other way around. I should have leapt out of the car, called you over. But you were being generous with your time; that couple was obviously in need of your travel advice. You seem overwhelmed by them. We won't let people like that distract us when we are together.

To kill time until you left on the bus, I did a little shopping. On the Sukra Path to the east of Durbar Square is a row of glittering jewellery stores. At night, the narrow street is lit up like Christmas, full of the type of tourists who aren't carrying backpacks or living off rice and dahl for weeks at a time.

I chose something I know you'll love, a delicate Bhaktapurian twenty-four karat gold ring. The filigree setting houses over two dozen diamonds. It's the only shop in southeast Asia that has accepted my American Express card.

I keep it in the box it came in. It's become my talisman, and lives in the pocket of my trekking pants. I touch it often, my fingertips humming against the nap of velvet on the lid. The action calms the anxiety of knowing that soon we'll be travelling in the high mountains again. I'm planning that magical moment when I give it you.

FOR THE FIRST time since my inheritance and winning that jackpot in Vegas, I have little choice about where I can spend money. There are no five-star resorts up here in the Himalaya. When a trekker buys his bed for the night, it comes with only one choice on the menu. By the time we've left the treeline behind, I'm sick of dahl and tea. I look forward to getting somewhere I can tuck into a big juicy steak with fries.

But there are some small 'luxuries' I have been able to arrange. I hired a Sherpa in Kathmandu who has organised a private Land Rover to take me to Besi Sahar. His name is Tenzing. The irony of this is not lost on me. I am hoping to avoid going up any steep peaks, but once I discover you're heading to Dumre on the bus, Tenzing immediately knows you are intending to trek the Annapurna circuit all the way to Pokhara. This is further confirmed when he checks the records while securing my trekking permit from the Ministry of Home Affairs.

'Why you follow girl? She break your heart?'

'No, on the contrary, I care for her very much and...'

Tenzing shakes his head. He seems distinctly less understanding than Panit.

But he also knows his stuff, and he knows where to get the best gear. He takes me to an alpine-outfitters in Kathmandu. He gets me all the modern state-of-the-art equipment and clothes, a new pair of comfortable hiking boots which he makes me wear wherever we are walking in town, and a supply of high protein food and energy bars for our journey. He calculates how long it will take the bus to get to Dumre and instructs our driver to only leave Kathmandu to coincide with the arrival of the bus.

'You could save her a lot of hassle by offering her a ride,' he says later while we are watching the buffoons of mechanics trying to change the tyre on the Soviet truck. Tenzing tells me they would have purchased the tyre third-hand from some Pakistani trader.

I don't elaborate on the reasons why I need to follow you. A few extra dollars soon shuts him up.

THIRTY-THREE

IT WAS A relief to tie the bootlaces the following morning. After a breakfast of Tibetan bread, eggs and muesli, we set off up the the Marsyandi Valley. The *'Namaste'* greetings slipped from our tongues like hurried versions of 'Have a nice day.' For a population living in one of the poorest economies on earth, everyone was generous with their smiles. Each time we passed through a village, children ran after us happily demanding pens, sweets or rupees.

We fell into a daily hiking rhythm. The Himalayan peaks pierced the blue horizon ahead. We crossed stomach-dropping swing bridges, skirted magnificent forests of rhododendrons in full bloom, and pressed ourselves against sheer rock walls to allow donkey trains to pass on the narrowest of paths.

When we reached the high altitude of the Manang Valley, the natural supply of wood for cooking and heating became sparse. Deforestation was widespread. The smell of kitchen fires in the villages changed from pine to juniper and finally charcoal, sacks of which were carried in on the backs of donkeys and sherpas.

AS WE APPROACHED Manang, the number of trekkers increased. There was only one destination on our minds from there: Thorung La Pass, the highest point on our trek. As we climbed, the air thinned. The journey between villages took four times longer, as it was impossible to maintain the same tempo we had kept at lower altitude.

Alex complained from time to time of a headache. The sherpas we met urged him to drink more water or tea. We'd already agreed if any of us were to suffer the more severe symptoms of altitude sickness, we would either stay at the same altitude until we felt well enough to go on, or head back to Dumre. But we'd come this far. The fastest way to get to Pokhara, our final destination, was over the pass. It was the goal of our trek around the Annapurnas, and none of us wanted to be the one to let the team down.

So when I began to wake up feeling a little queasy, I kept quiet. We did most of our trekking in the morning, by midday finding a guesthouse to provide us with a warm meal and plenty of tea, after which I usually felt better.

But Alex apparently felt progressively worse, disappearing after lunch every day to sleep off his weariness. In his absence, Anne and I spent time with the families providing accommodation in these remote areas. We often walked with them to the fields where they tended their yaks or met supplies on the mule trains coming up from the valley.

After a few days above four thousand metres, I knew Alex and I would only say something if things got frighteningly out of control. Stoicism might be our downfall. Anne seemed unaffected. The effect of altitude sickness was a lottery; we'd met some alpinists who were suffering, even though they'd spent three weeks more than us acclimatising.

I often saw Alex holding his head, rubbing his temples. He had no appetite and his face was grey. I was truly concerned for him, but also worried about my own niggling symptoms. The smell of a charcoal fire with dahl bubbling gently over the flames was occasionally nauseating, but I nevertheless seemed to be acclimatising as we spent more time at altitude.

We were about to be faced with our biggest challenge.

'I HEARD YOU throwing up last night, Sandy,' Alex said as we sipped our tea at the table in the kitchen next to the yak stable.

'How did you know it was me?' I asked. 'Everyone else in the dorm was coughing and hacking all night.'

The guesthouse at Phedi was crowded with trekkers, providing a concert of snores, groans and laboured heavy breathing throughout the building.

'Oh, come on, you've been feeling like crap too, haven't you? We've just got to get over this ruddy pass. I saw you get up in the night. The next minute I heard retching outside. I figured it was you,' he said.

It was the morning of our last ascent. Many of the others in the bunkrooms had also slept badly.

We'd woken at four a.m. The wife of the yak herder cooked us unleavened bread and porridge. I wasn't hungry but forced the food down, knowing it was a long trek to the pass.

'I feel a little better this morning,' I said to Alex. 'You make the pass sound like a dreary chore rather than an achievement.'

'To be honest, I think I'll be happy when we've done it. I need to get back to lower altitude, but not the way we came. I think we've been playing a dangerous game with Mother Nature in more ways than one.'

I wondered exactly how bad Alex was feeling. Anne and I exchanged a glance.

We started up the pass at 4:30 a.m. There were other dangers. If we left it too late, the sun would rise and destabilise the snow on the shaded ascent to the pass, making our crossing dangerous. Much like the Harris Saddle in New Zealand, but on a mammoth scale.

About twenty of us left in small groups within several minutes of each other. Each footstep took an immense amount of energy. The temperature was well below freezing. I wore almost every article of clothing in my pack, reminding me of the passengers on my flight from Bangkok to Kathmandu. Having chosen not to bring extra clothing for this one high-altitude pass, I wrapped a sweater around my head and wore socks on my hands. The only way I could keep warm was to keep moving, although progress was slow.

We no longer talked about our pounding heads, the fluid in our brains expanding to dangerous proportions – the possibility of a cerebral oedema we'd heard alpinists talking about along the way. At every step I silently repeated the mantra *Almost there, almost there.*

Alex took up the lead, with Anne behind him, and me to the rear. We were within a couple of hundred metres of the pass when I saw Alex stumble. He put his hand out to the steep, snowy slope at his side to brace himself. He was falling, and there was nothing I could do to stop him. I thought he might slither down the slope, but his backpack wedged into the snow, anchoring him to the side of the path.

Anne yelled out. With help from two other trekkers who caught up with us we managed to get him back to his feet, the effort exhausting us all.

'Should we go back down?' I asked.

Alex was mumbling. 'Leave me here. I'll just sleep for a bit. I'm so tired. I can't go on.'

'Mate, if you go to sleep here, you'll never wake up,' said one of the men who'd stopped to help. His New Zealand accent reminded me of Greg and our adventure in the Southern Alps. It seemed like a long time ago now.

I felt weak myself, and wasn't sure I could support Alex, but the two young men who'd stopped to help pushed him the rest of the way.

The achievement I should have felt reaching Thorung La Pass was marred by the pressing urgency to get Alex to lower altitude before any swelling on his brain made him lose consciousness.

But the concern for Alex had nothing on the shock I experienced upon seeing someone else I knew at the top of the pass.

I DIDN'T KNOW it was Jake at first, not until he spoke my name. He was dressed in a Gore-Tex mountain jacket with the hood pulled over a traditional yak-wool hat. The first reaction I had was jealousy at his sophisticated alpine clothing in those freezing conditions, but that was quashed by a simmering anger. I hadn't seen him since the flight to Kathmandu and had cast him from my mind.

He took off his mittens and thrust a bar of Cadbury's milk chocolate towards me. I stared at the farcical luxury, as we were hundreds of miles from any shop selling such confectionery. There, on a remote pass in the Himalaya, it was the one thing every trekker craved, instant replenishment for spent energy. The trail snacks we had brought with us from Phedi paled in comparison.

I glared at him. He was taunting me.

'Go on, take it,' he said, his voice muffled behind the cagoule stretched across his face.

He slid his thumb down the outer wrapper. The inner foil glinted enticingly, along with something else in his other hand. Before I registered the other object, I couldn't stop myself reaching for the chocolate. My body was acting of its own accord, sending a message of need to my brain without waiting for rationality.

I took the chocolate, and was ready to break off a square, when I noticed what was in his other hand. He was holding a gold ring out to me.

'What the hell is that? Are you mad?' My voice shook as it raised an octave.

I swiped at both his hands. The piece of jewellery and the chocolate bar flew up in the air. The ring landed on the rocky ground behind him and the chocolate bar bounced a few feet further on. The purple wrapper blew away in the wind. I chased it along the ground, not wanting to litter the pass. I caught it and turned. This was absurd.

Jake approached me. I held up my hand as though stopping traffic at a junction, and backed away from him. I saw the chocolate bar near my feet, placed the heel of my hiking boot on top of it, and ground it into the snow.

'Hey, wait! I bought that in Kathmandu! I've carried it all the way up here for you!' He laughed as if he was mad. 'You mustn't worry about a little chocolate ruining your figure, you've had plenty of exercise these past couple of weeks.'

I stared at him, speechless. This was a nightmare. He must have matched our journey from Kathmandu.

I looked at Anne. She had her hand on Alex's shoulder where he sat, drained and empty, beside the cairn marking the highest point on the pass. I moved my foot. The chocolate was half-crushed into the Himalayan shale. I slid my pack off my shoulders, and bent down to retrieve the remaining squares from the ground. As I gathered the broken pieces to take them to Alex, I felt the palm of a hand between my shoulder blades. At first I thought it was Anne, but then I knew. Jake's hand seared my back. Before he could speak, I stood up. He was still holding that tacky gold ring towards me. I lashed out again, hitting his arm harder, hoping this time the ring would be lost forever in the snow.

I turned towards the cairn, tears of anger freezing on my face. I reached my hand towards Alex, the morsels of chocolate in my palm.

'But… Sandrine…'

Jake was close behind me. How did he know my full name? I turned abruptly.

'Leave me alone!' I yelled, mustering the last of my energy. 'Stop following me. You are such a creep!'

The trekkers who were gathered round the giant cairn stopped their jubilatory chatter and stared at us.

For a moment, all anyone heard were the prayer flags tied to the top of the rocks flapping angrily in the wind.

Anne had been taking care of Alex and didn't fully understand what was happening. She looked at me in the ensuing silence with worry on her face.

'We have to get both you and Alex down to lower altitude as quickly as possible,' she said, glancing at Jake who had backed away.

She took hold of my elbow, looked intently into my eyes. I realised she thought my outburst was an effect of the altitude.

Alex was still slumped on the ground.

'Just let me sleep for a bit. I'll be okay. I'll catch you up later,' he said.

'You are not going to sleep,' said Anne. 'We have to get you to lower altitude. I've found a couple of people to help.'

Anne turned to me.

'Are you okay?' she asked.

She narrowed her eyes. I felt ice on my cheeks from my tears. She looked towards Jake, who was watching us from a distance. She shook her head.

Anne took Alex's backpack, and we carried it between us. As I turned to take one last look at the pass, I saw Jake sink to his knees, his hands covering his face, and tried not to think about what he might do next.

With the help of two other trekkers, we had to get Alex down to Muktinath. One of them had a set of ski poles and guided Alex's hands through the straps on the handles. They accompanied him on either side, and walked him like a drunkard down the mountain. After half an hour, Alex gradually regained his balance, and talked a little more coherently.

I, on the other hand, was still feeling miserable and sick, and it was nothing to do with the altitude.

THIRTY-FOUR

AFTER ALL THAT time, after staying out of your way, letting you continue to do your own thing and discover your own worlds, you wait until this place, one of the highest trails on the planet, to break my heart. Thorung La Pass is way more challenging than anything we scaled in New Zealand. I thought you would be so happy to receive my gift of a bar of candy along with the ring. It seemed like the perfect opportunity. The dream proposal. It was even more poignant to come to your rescue when you were feeling vulnerable and weak.

After our little game on the airplane, I made sure not to invade your space for the two weeks since. I was careful to maintain distance and made doubly sure you wouldn't catch my face in the crowds on Durbar Square or at the temples. The tables had turned since the flight. It was time for *me* to play hard-to-get.

I thought you would see me with different eyes. I wanted you to look at me like you did at Ranger Jerk or Hippy Boy. The last thing I expected was this inexplicable anger, the hate in your eyes. I figured you might be surprised, but not this. I thought you'd be ready for me.

It hits me like the slap of a prayer flag. There, at almost eighteen thousand feet. It rips through me. As you leave, all I can do is stand and stare.

'You all right?' Tenzing asks, shouldering my pack.

My chest is about to explode, and my heart feels like it's going to beat right out from between my ribs. It's as though I'm rushing down a steep canyon with nowhere to land. This thing I thought was divine. I was mistaken all the time. I've gone about it all the wrong way. I realise it was still too soon.

I stand there in the Himalayan wind, icy tears whipping from my eyes. I watch you and your friends hobble down the pass towards Muktinath, and my heart breaks in two.

I'll see you safely back to Pokhara. The mountain danger isn't over yet. But as you walk away, something gives way inside me. I bend over double but can't relieve the pain in my gut. My legs collapse, and my knees crush against the Himalayan shale hidden under a layer of snow.

All those times I wish I could have done things differently. I should have picked you up on the Golden Gate Bridge. I should have offered to carry your pack to the airport. We should have shared a taxi. All the things I should have done. Things I've now seen other people do on the familiar traveller's trail. What a hopeless jerk I've been.

And I realise, if you don't want me, I don't want this life any more.

THIRTY-FIVE

'WHAT WAS THAT all about back up there?' Anne asked when we were sitting on the wooden veranda of our Muktinath guesthouse.

I told her about Jake. About the coincidences of seeing him throughout my travels from as far back as New Zealand and Australia, and maybe even Hawaii. That dog, some of the unexplained incidents along the way. Anne said it was entirely possible for travellers to keep seeing each other. A group of girls she and Alex had met in Bali turned up in Java, and again in Singapore. Their story brought to mind the comments of the American couple in Chiang Mai.

'But we've crossed paths more than four or even five times, and not on the most frequently travelled roads,' I said.

'It does sound a little uncanny.'

'I don't even *know* this guy. Aren't stalkers supposed to know their victims? It makes me sick to think he's been following me, watching me all this time.'

I held my stomach, recalling New Zealand. Now I was sure it was him.

'Are you okay, Sandy? You still look a little green.'

After a fifteen-hundred-metre descent from the pass, Alex had made a miraculous recovery. He was currently on the search for a couple of bottles of beer in the village.

'I don't think this is altitude sickness,' I said. 'I haven't been feeling great for a few days. I think I might have picked up a bug.'

'Better keep an eye on that,' Anne said.

'I had dengue fever in Thailand. I thought I might be having a recurrence, but this is nothing like that. I don't think I have a fever.'

The next day's trekking became easier. We descended to yet lower altitudes, and I did feel a little better, at least less tired. I woke up groggy in the mornings, but put it down to the hard, straw mattresses and disturbed sleep with others snoring around me through the thin walls of the guesthouses. It didn't help that we were woken before dawn every day by roosters, braying donkeys and sherpas going about their work.

IT WASN'T UNTIL we reached Pokhara and checked in to a guesthouse that a girl mentioned one of their group had picked up a bout of giardia, a sickness caused by an intestinal parasite with several of the symptoms I'd been experiencing.

I went to the doctor to get it checked out. He palpated my stomach, asked about my bowel movements, took my temperature, and asked me to pee into a cup.

'You don't need a stool sample?' I asked. 'I thought you'd need to check for parasites.'

The doctor shook his head.

'No, Mrs… Ms… Bavaud,' he said, looking down at the form I had filled in earlier. 'That won't be necessary. Is your husband travelling with you?' I shook my head, now worried I had some life-threatening sickness and needed a next-of-kin present.

'I'm travelling alone,' I said.

'Well, not any more,' said the doctor. 'You're pregnant.'

Right on cue, my stomach gurgled and I placed my palm on my abdomen. Tears sprang to my eyes. I was gripped by a sudden panic. As the wave of shock subsided, I conjured Kai's face in my memory. How could I have let this happen? What was I going to do now? The doctor allowed me a few moments to compose myself.

'I'll never be able to find him,' I whispered.

I didn't even know Kai's last name, didn't know where he lived, didn't even know if he would still be on Koh Pha Ngan.

'How many weeks?' I asked.

'Hard to tell without a scan, your HCG – hormone level – is not so high, so I'd say not more than twelve.'

But I already knew. A quick calculation took me back to Koh Pha Ngan. The doctor told me he wasn't sure without a scan. I desperately wished I could see Kai, have him put his strong suntanned arms around me, stroke the hair from my face and tell me everything would be all right.

I didn't have enough money to return to Thailand to go and look for him. I certainly didn't have money to pay for an abortion, and even if I had, things could go horribly wrong. I was thousands of miles from home. Whatever my future, I had to get home. I couldn't stay in Asia. I still had the flight leg back to Delhi on my ticket, but the thought of travelling through India now, especially after having felt so delicate over the past couple of weeks, was something I was not looking forward to. My world had suddenly been thrown upside down. The only people I really wanted to see were Pierre and Papa and Marianne.

I didn't tell Alex or Anne. I would enjoy their company for the next few days and then quietly disappear back to Kathmandu before arranging my flight home. We hadn't really discussed our respective plans after the trek had finished, but they would be heading to Everest base camp.

After the discovery of my little inconvenience, I began to think about the miracle in my belly. I couldn't forget that there was a tiny human being in there. With funds running dangerously low, I only had the last sections of my onward ticket left to my name. I couldn't afford to go back to Thailand. Home soil was where I needed to be to consider our future.

THIRTY-SIX

I WAS SORTING our recently laundered clothes into piles when there was a knock on the door of our guest house room. A scrawny lad I'd seen working in the kitchen thrust an envelope at me with my name on it. Curious, I tore it open and read the note.

Sandrine my love,

We could have been invincible together, the perfect union. I have been protecting you on your journey in the certainty that one day you would see the strength in our relationship. Instead you have destroyed me. My world has imploded knowing you'll never be mine. I can't live without you.

Please remember me as a man who adored you from the moment he saw you until his dying breath. I'm doing this one last thing for you. They say drowning is the most comfortable way to die, that I'll feel no pain.

I love you so much.

Yours forever,
Jake

The paper fell from my hand. As the footsteps of the messenger boy thumped back down the stairs of the guesthouse, I thought I was going to faint. Suicide! A suicide note.

'Oh my God!'

Alex looked up from his open backpack on the bunk.

'He says he's going to kill himself,' I said. 'He can't be serious, can he? Is this some kind of horrible joke?'

Alex and Anne were due to fly the next day to Lukla. Alex was calculating how they could get everything into their backpacks. He stopped, looked questioningly across the bunks at me.

'It's Jake,' I said. 'The guy who's been following me. Oh God, Alex, he says in this note he's going to drown himself. No, no, no! I didn't want this. I've done nothing to attract this guy. I had no idea… He's mad, but I never imagined he would do anything like this!'

Alex came over, picked up the note. As he read it, I pulled my boots on.

'Shit, Sandy, this is wild.'

'What should I do? I can't believe this! I've got to tell someone… the police. Maybe he hasn't gone through with it. Maybe this is a cry for help. I didn't realise this guy was so desperate. I didn't realise I… Oh my God Alex. I just thought he was a bit of a creep, I never…'

Alex put his arm around my shoulder as I sat down on the bunk, sobbing. I put my hands over my face.

'But it's not your fault!'

'I feel so… I don't know. Am I responsible? This is so weird. I think he's been following me for months. I didn't know how to shake him. He made me feel so uncomfortable. Maybe he's harmless. All this time he must have been very sick. He seemed so… pathetic, I guess… *Was* harmless.' I went cold with the realisation that Jake could be dead, and I might have unwittingly had a hand in it.

Anne came in from the shower down the hall, rubbing her hair with a towel.

'What's wrong?' she asked. Alex showed her the note.

I bent down to tie my bootlaces.

'I have to tell someone. The police. Get them to check. God, I hope this isn't for real. I don't know what to do.'

'Did you ever speak to him? Did you ever tell him to leave you alone?' Alex asked.

'Of course! Several times. I told Anne about it after I saw him on the pass. I didn't want to bother you, because you were so sick, but yes, we had words. He must have overtaken us somehow. He must have known I was going to be there. I don't remember him in Phedi.'

'Why didn't you say anything before the pass? All that time trekking together. I had no idea. If he was following you, he was following us too. I could have confronted the asshole. That was nothing short of harassment, Sandy.'

'I didn't know, Alex. I thought I'd lost him. I saw him on the plane, but I thought I'd shaken him off. This is just crazy. It never occurred to me that he would follow us over the pass.' I shuddered. 'How close was he tracking everything I did?'

I squeezed my eyes shut.

'Oh, God.'

Alex looked down at the note again.

'I think he's trying to make you feel guilty. Sandy, you shouldn't feel responsible for one tiny second.'

'Alex, how can you say that? He might really have killed himself!'

'I'll go find out from the people downstairs who we should tell about this. You're right, the police, I guess,' he said.

Alex left and I pulled on a fleece, part of me wishing I could walk out of the guesthouse and see Jake standing across the street staring at me. I had never wished him dead.

'We should go to the lakeside,' I said to Anne. 'He wrote about drowning. Do you really think he's thrown himself into the water? God, this is a nightmare. I can't just sit around! Maybe he's still down there. On the shores of Phewa. We've got to stop him.'

I followed Alex to the reception where he was talking to the boy sitting on an upturned drinks crate, a tattered magazine in his hand.

'When was this delivered?' I asked, grabbing Jake's note from Alex's hand. I waved it in front of the boy.

'And who delivered it?' demanded Alex before he could answer.

The boy was alarmed by the two of us raising our voices. He looked from me to Alex and back again.

'Another boy. Don't know. He come yesterday. I forgot to give to you. Sorry.'

I raised my hands.

'Oh, shit! It might be too late! We've got to call the police. We've got to get to the lake!'

As soon as I mentioned the police, the boy's eyes widened. Following Alex's earlier instructions he ran off to find a policeman. I left the building and ran down the busy streets towards the water.

Beyond the portable barber stands and the tacky trinket shops, I stopped at the grassy bank leading down to the promenade along the shore. I put my hand to my brow and scanned the surface of the lake. It was a large body of water, perhaps a mile across, with forested hills on the far shore. The sun sparkled off the wind-rippled surface. The only living things I could see were a few ducks and a pair of cormorants.

I ran along the shore towards the pier. As I approached I saw the lad from the guesthouse pointing two policemen in my direction. I still had Jake's note in my hand. Alex caught up with me and ran ahead to intercept the policemen. One of them held out his hand.

'The letter? The one he say…' he pointed to Alex. '… a man take his life?'

I held out the note. He took it from me, read it slowly.

'This a joke?' he asked. 'This Jake. He boyfriend? Many boys fall in love in Pokhara. Don't know how to leave their girlfriends.'

'No!' I wailed. 'I hardly know him. It's someone who's…'

Who's what? I didn't know how to explain Jake. Would a Nepalese policeman seriously believe that someone had followed me halfway round the world?

The policemen headed down to the line of brightly painted rowing boats moored along the promenade.

The old man in charge of the rental boats began an animated conversation with one of the officers. His arthritic hands could barely tie a bowline, but they flew around in the air as he explained and nodded out to the lake. He pointed to one of the boats tied close to us. My heart began to thump.

The rental boat man spit a red line of betel juice on the quayside before retrieving something from the box on the back of his rickshaw.

'He say they found boat yesterday morning alone on lake,' said one of the policemen. 'Nobody on board. Boy had to row out to get it, then tow it in with rope. He thought it had broken free from the chain, but when he reached boat, he said he found something.'

The rental boat man came back from the rickshaw holding a bundle of clothes.

'When boy bring boat back, only these things in bottom,' he said.

He pulled the bundle of clothes apart between his hands. A hiking boot fell to the ground. I stared at the boot, then back at the clothes. The red plaid shirt in his hands. I was sure I had seen it before, way back in Thailand. And it came to me. Jake had been wearing it the day I went on my jungle tour, the day I had seen him across the road from my guesthouse.

'Why didn't you tell the police?' I asked the rental boat man.

As a rapid Nepali conversation ensued between him and one of the policemen, my stomach churned. The harsh shards of sunlight on the lake spun in front of my eyes. My face broke into a cold sweat, despite the midday heat. I swallowed several times, there was a ringing in my ears, and I knew I was going to faint. I reached out uselessly for Alex as my knees buckled and I collapsed to the quayside.

'Bloody hell, Sandy. Are you okay?' Alex asked as I came around.

I had no idea how much time I had been out, but I felt stupid. I also still felt sick. The back of my head was pounding. Bile burned in my throat. Alex passed me a bottle of water.

'They're talking about getting someone out there to look. But the cop says there's no chance he'd survive. The water is too cold.'

There was still much chatter and gesturing, mostly from the boat man, who raised both hands repeatedly towards the middle of the lake then slapped them down at his side. The second policeman came over to me.

'This boy, this man you say gave you letter. He friend of yours? Boyfriend maybe? This man boyfriend?' He pointed at Alex.

'No, no one is my boyfriend. I have no boyfriend. Will you stop thinking that he was anything to do with me? I met him once, maybe twice, but I don't know him. He's…'

How could I explain to these people that Jake was simply someone who was obsessed with me? The note trembled between the fingers in the policeman's hands.

'This is not America. What you say is, how you say, a fantasy.'

'I'm not American! I'm Swiss! This needs to be taken seriously. Those clothes, I've seen the shirt before. I'm sure it belongs to him.'

Alex turned to me with a wary look on his face.

'Sandy, why don't we just let the policemen do their job? They have the letter now. Let's go back to the guesthouse.'

'This is awful.' I turned to the policemen. 'You must believe this! At least check it out. I haven't been "joking" about this person.'

'We start with stolen boat. We hope you had nothing to do with it.'

I saw the look Alex threw at me. I'd said enough.

'You know which guest house this Jake stay in?' asked the policeman.

I shook my head. He sighed. His colleague approached with a basket. He stuffed the clothes and boots the rental boat man had been holding into it. They spoke rapidly together. The colleague took the basket and left.

'What are you going to do?' I asked, unable to follow their conversation.

'Many tourists go missing in our country. Some have stupidity for trying to climb our tallest mountains, some take our sherpas with them into the crevasses. Some, like your friend, freeze to death in our rivers and lakes. Most of the time, it is choice. This no different.'

'I had nothing to do with his decision, if he really has... drowned.' I said the last word on a sob.

'Where Mr Dhilani says he found boat, the lake is more than twenty metres deep. And very cold. It is not long since the spring melt came down the Harpan and Pirkhe Kola Rivers. You feel summer now, but three weeks ago, it was still snowing.' He paused. 'You must come to police station in Pardi Kaski to file report for your missing friend.'

'He's not my friend, I told you. I don't even know his full name. Only his first name, Jake.'

'I don't understand how you can know him and not know him.'

I wished I could have understood that as well.

I SPENT THE remainder of the morning staring out at the lake. A couple of other tourists hired boats from the old man and rowed towards the Barahi Temple on a little island to the south of town. The boat where Jake's clothes had been found was hauled out of the water and left on the lakeside. I found it hard to believe that in the wilds of the Himalaya a forensics team was going to turn up to investigate if he had been in the boat, but I guess they had to be seen to be doing something.

Later that afternoon at the guesthouse, a boy arrived with a message asking me to go to the police station. Alex agreed to come with me. I paid for a bicycle rickshaw to take us there.

The gated building hosted a labyrinth of rooms that could have been offices or cells. I was taken into one of them. Alex was asked to wait in the hallway. Sitting at a desk, one of the policemen I'd seen in the morning was fanning a passport between his thumb and forefinger. The name on his desk said Dipesh Bhandari.

'Your friend has indeed… gone. We found where he stayed. The guesthouse owner wanted to let another tourist have his room as he had not paid. When he opened the door, he found your friend's things. No one there. But at least we now have his details. This is his passport.'

'Which guest house was it?' I asked, feeling miserable.

'You must know, Sandrine-Ji. It was the Sawadee. Right behind yours. The buildings share the same garden. The rooms overlook your guesthouse.'

I thought I might faint again. I leaned forward and grabbed the edge of his desk.

'I honestly had no idea,' I said, and drew my fingers through the perspiration on my brow.

Bhandari looked at me with an expression of sympathy.

'We can issue a death certificate from this precinct. Then you will be able to leave.'

'How can you do that without a body?' I asked, shocked.

'It is a regular occurrence here Sandrine-Ji. The tourism ministry has to deal with careless climbers whose bodies cannot be retrieved out of crevasses almost every week of the year. He has drowned. His embassy will probably not put pressure on our external affairs to recover the body. They will issue a Consular Report of Death to settle his estate in the US. He is not the first American to die in our country and stay here for eternity.'

I rubbed my eyes, gritty with exhaustion. Detective Bhandari went out to the hallway. In order to get the death certificate issued, he wanted Alex to give a final statement to say I'd been with him and Anne for the past two days.

As Alex and I walked out into the late afternoon sun, I placed my hand on my belly. Hot dust from passing rickshaws and motorbikes clogged my nose. The air was suffocating. All I wanted to do was go home.

THIRTY-SEVEN

I DIDN'T KNOW if there would be any flights out of Nepal because of the fuel strikes. The city was eerily silent due to the cuts in bus travel and public transport. The only positive was a blissful reduction in tuk-tuks and ill-tuned trucks, which made for a less stressful walk around town.

I managed to find the last seat on a bus heading back to Kathmandu. On arrival I was relieved to learn that international flights were first in line for the rationed aviation fuel. I flew home on a series of back-to-back flights. A bumpy prop-engined plane from Kathmandu to Delhi, then a transfer from the international terminal to the domestic one across town, vice versa at Bombay, then home. I had cut short my trip, missed out India, but wasn't able to get a direct flight to Geneva from Delhi. Instead I added fifteen hours to the journey. All I saw of India were rows of filthy slum dwellings between the domestic and international airports of both cities. Grubby but beautiful scampering children, women bent over cooking pots, a criss-cross patchwork of corrugated iron, cardboard boxes and wooden pallets, all enhanced by the ever-pervasive smell of a nearby open sewer. These weren't the memories of India I had hoped to take home.

'HOW'S PAPA?' I asked, after my brother had thrown my pack in the back of the car and I settled into the passenger seat.

Pierre had met me at the airport. It was an effort to hold back tears when I came through the arrivals hall and saw him waiting at the barrier. He was on his own, which was good, because I wasn't sure how Marianne would take my news.

'Not great. He has his days,' he said.

I bit my lip. How would he react to the prospect of another little person living on the farm? The future would be uncertain with my dwindling finances and no prospect of a job for the next few months. I felt bad imposing myself on them when I was the one who had been free to take off on a round-the-world trip.

'But Marianne's coping. Now we've decided to get a nurse to come in every other day, she doesn't feel overloaded. She's become fond of the old man. There's something endearing to her about his helplessness.' Pierre paused. 'It's sad though, Sandrine, he's not Papa any more. He's been replaced with an old man who can't remember anything from one minute to the next. It's like he's already... gone.' Pierre's voice cracked, and he cleared his throat.

As he said the word 'gone' my mind turned to the reason I had cut my travels short. Unable to control my emotions, tears filled my eyes and spilled down my cheeks. My chest shook with silent sobs. Pierre glanced at me, looked away, then stared back.

'Shit, Sandrine, I didn't mean to upset you.'

I held up my hand and shook my head, not trusting myself to speak until I had gathered my emotions.

'What happened, Sandrine? Why did you come home early?'

I took two deep breaths, surprised at my own reaction to being home. *Must be the hormones.*

'A terrible thing happened in Nepal,' I began. 'I was followed by a guy, an American called Jake.'

Pierre huffed. 'A guy…'

'It wasn't like that.'

And I told Pierre the whole story.

'He followed you all the way up a Himalayan pass? Determined.'

'I can't exactly remember what I said to him then, but I was really angry. I think I told him he should stop following me. That I thought he was a creep…'

'Sounds like he deserved it,' Pierre said.

I sniffed, remembering the pathetic drop of Jake's thin shoulders, his body a display of absolute despair.

'Oh don't… Pierre. The thing is. This Jake. He… he took his life. In Pokhara.'

'My God, Sandrine, suicide! That's terrible.'

Pierre slowed down on the motorway as he listened to the rest of my story, eyes wide and mouth open.

'It was horrible. I felt responsible. I feel like I put him in that lake.'

I couldn't speak any more, and let the tears flow. I hadn't cried like this since learning of Jake's suicide. I hardly even remembered the journey back from Asia. I realised it wasn't until I saw Pierre that my emotions got the better of me. I sobbed into a tissue I found in the glove compartment. Pierre laid his hand on my shoulder.

'It's okay, Sis, we'll look after you now. You mustn't blame yourself for his death. He was obviously unstable. Fuck him for making you feel guilty. It's not your fault. Please don't cry, Sandrine. Christ.'

Pierre drove on in silence, slowly shaking his head as he digested all I had told him. I wanted to tell him the rest, before we arrived back at the farm. Before I had to face Marianne, or

Papa. Not that Papa would have a clue who I was, or that my pregnancy would have any influence on him whatsoever.

'How's the farm going?' I asked through a stuffed nose, but feeling a little better. 'Have you been able to balance the books?' His answer would affect how I delivered my next bombshell.

'Farm's doing well actually. We managed to get a good price for the last lot of heifers, and milk production's steady. Marianne's set up a side business selling wooden garden furniture and kiddies play equipment. It's really taken off. She's earning almost as much as the farm.'

He glanced at me. I looked out of the window as Pierre exited the motorway. We drove through the familiar landscape above the lake. Worried about a knee-jerk reaction, I waited until we had passed a cattle truck and the road ahead was clear.

'There's something else, Pierre.' I paused. 'I'm pregnant.'

The Land Rover drifted briefly against the grassy bank at the side of the lane. Pierre's head rocked back as he carefully turned the steering wheel to straighten the vehicle.

'Shit, Sandrine! How the hell did that happen? You went away for a few months and forgot to take your fucking condoms? How far along are you?'

'Pierre, it's okay. I don't want to go into details, but yes, I was careless. A little too much alcohol. A little too much holiday romance.'

Pierre was speechless. Seconds passed.

'I've decided to keep it,' I said, my words releasing Pierre's tongue.

'Bloody hell, Sandrine. How are you going to survive? I'm guessing you've come back with no money.'

I put my hand protectively against my belly, determined not to let my brother talk me out of keeping the baby.

'Who's the father? Does he know?' Pierre asked.

I told him about Kai. As I described our brief relationship minus the actual night together, the memory of him grew more romantic in my mind. I missed him terribly.

'You need a plan,' he continued more gently, seeing my distress. 'There's no problem you staying on the farm, Sandrine. It's still your home. Your room with all your stuff is still there. We'll find a way later to sort the food and bills.'

I was at least grateful he hadn't tried to convince me to terminate the pregnancy.

'I can work until the baby's born. I'm not intending to dump on you and Marianne. I haven't had the time or emotion to work it out, but I promise I will.'

'It's okay, Sis, I'm sure you will. Here we go then,' he said, turning into the driveway that led to the farm. 'Better go see how the news goes down at home. Will be interesting to see whether you get any reaction out of Papa.'

'*GRANDPÈRE*, EH? Isn't that a little soon?'

Papa was thrilled, and so was I. That was until it became apparent he didn't think it was me, but Pierre and Marianne who were expecting. When we'd arrived at the farm, I went straight to Papa sitting in his armchair by the fireplace. I'd given him a hug and was pleased to see a smile on his face. But he didn't know I was his daughter. 'Sandrine' was suddenly one of his cousins. I had hoped that by some miracle, my time away would mean he remembered me saying goodbye as though it was yesterday. But that was not to be. Pierre had warned me, but he'd been living with Papa during my absence and his deterioration would have seemed like a gradual decline. My shock at how little Papa remembered, and the difficulty I could see he had forming his words, made me incredibly sad.

I wondered if Marianne thought a new baby in the house might put Pierre off wanting a family. I knew she was waiting for a proposal from my brother. I imagined my impending motherhood might hinder her case. But she was warm and welcoming.

As I fussed around Papa, Pierre quietly explained to Marianne that I had come home early because of Jake's suicide. I thought she might have negative feelings about the news of me expecting a baby. But she was more concerned about whether I might be suffering psychological repercussions after Jake's death. I knew she was right when she said I had to wipe any dregs of guilt I might have from my slate so I could concentrate my positive energies on taking care of my baby. Deep down inside, relief was buried somewhere, but I couldn't admit it. As Marianne gently coaxed me into talking about the whole Jake thing, I realised she was as close to a sister I was ever going to get. I was grateful for her support.

She helped me unpack. As she emptied the side pockets of my backpack, she took out my passport and held up a thin plastic zip-lock bag with a querying look.

'Oh, they're my old ticket stubs, Nepalese visa, and hiking permit. The police kept everything for a couple of days when they questioned me at the station. At one point, I think they were trying to work out whether I was implicated in any way in Jake's death. They gave everything back like that with the passport when I left.'

'Is that your hiking permit?' she asked, shuffling the papers out and opening a yellow folded card. I nodded. 'Wow. Look at this script. I love the writing. So beautiful.'

As Marianne closed the hiking permit, shuffling the pile of documents together, a piece of folded paper fell from between them and slithered onto the table.

I gasped.

'It's his letter! The suicide note! The police in Pokhara must have filed it with my documents.'

'Incredible,' said Marianne.

'They didn't seem to know what the hell they were doing. When I told them I planned to come home, they simply handed me the bag, no questions asked. I never knew his note was still in there. I'm pretty sure they didn't mean to give it back to me. This is evidence.'

'Evidence of what?' asked Marianne. 'Since when do they need to keep evidence for someone who's taken his own life? It's not like you'd want to keep it as a souvenir, but still…'

I shook my head.

'I don't know. For his relatives, maybe? God, I just want to forget that whole thing ever happened. Please throw that note out. I never want to set eyes on it again.'

I took my passport to the office to put it in with the family's official documents. As I closed the desk draw I wondered if I'd ever have any good memories to cherish from my world travels when I reflected on them years later. I wished I'd listened to my mother, and could hear her voice in my head. *I told you so. You should have gone to college. What a waste.*

I went back to the kitchen where Marianne had cleared the table.

'The irony is, Maman would have loved to see me settle and supply her with a string of grandchildren,' I said, placing my hand on my still flat belly. 'It may not be in the order she would have liked, but she would have been excited about the baby.'

Marianne gave me a hug.

'If the baby is a girl,' I told her, 'I've decided to call her Elise, after Maman.'

THIRTY-EIGHT

BUT IT WASN'T to be a girl. As soon as the doctor announced I was having a boy at what ended up being my sixteen-week check-up, I knew I would name him Kai. I had almost forgotten that Kai senior had effectively abandoned me, but he was still the baby's father and I still held a romantic notion about him. So I figured I may as well give the baby the one thing I knew about his paternity – his father's name.

It was a wonderful pregnancy after what I realised had been morning sickness in Nepal had petered out. The first tiring trimester was over by the time I arrived back in Switzerland, and I was infused with energy. I didn't start to show until five months. The doctor said the baby was small for the number of weeks I'd calculated, but his development was normal. I was worried the alcohol I'd consumed on the night of conception might have affected him, but he said I was healthy and that it wasn't unusual for fit young mothers not to show. He wasn't concerned. Baby would soon catch up.

I didn't regret my decision to keep Kai. As the weeks flew by, I fell more in love with the idea of him. I kept Kai senior's image alive in my mind and began to write down things I thought I could tell baby Kai later. I wanted to keep every memory of his father fresh.

I found a Tai Chi centre in Lausanne and contacted them to ask whether they knew about the retreat on Haad Rin. They were able to supply me with an address, and said they were expecting to receive some brochures at some stage, but they didn't have any other information. I wrote to the address anyway, and asked whether they could send me any news of Kai's whereabouts. I didn't believe my letter would reach Haad Rin, so I didn't expect an answer.

I thought about writing to Mimu at Haad Khontee, but I knew she could barely read or write Thai, let alone any other language. I didn't know anyone I could ask to translate for her. I figured if the Tai Chi centre couldn't help me, then no one could.

I took on some work looking after an art gallery in Vevey for a man who was going on holiday for two weeks. It was a boring job, sitting waiting for the occasional customer who came in to browse. I didn't make a single sale during the fortnight, but it gave me a chance to look in the papers for other employment to tide me over until Kai was born.

The longest job I held was waiting tables in a Parisienne-style café on the lakefront. The café was a narrow room wedged between a barber shop and a clothes store, with tightly-packed round tables. Once my bump became too large, I could no longer squeeze between them, and I had to give up.

The last job was helping out the old couple at the local *laiterie*. Work began at six in the morning when the first deliveries of milk and cheese came in. This was no trouble for someone who'd woken every day on a farm for the past twenty-two years for the first milking of the day, even if it was never me who had to get up and trudge out to the barn.

I kept fit with a lot of walking, and re-established a weekly cinema outing with Valérie. I prepared a corner of my room at the farm for the arrival of little Kai.

I WAS SITTING in the Café Tivoli with Valérie when the first contractions started.

'Oh my God, Sandrine, what should I do, get my car?'

'No. You're panicking. Your driving scares me anyway. And I don't want my waters to break in the front seat of your car. I'd never forgive myself. It's not far to the hospital. I feel like walking.'

'You're shitting me. You're going to walk there?'

'It's not far, just down the road. It helps with the contractions, getting the head to engage. All that crap.'

'I can't believe you're so cool about this.'

'Well I'm going to finish my tea first,' I said, surprising myself at my own nonchalance.

Valérie stared at me wide-eyed. I laughed. I was a little scared about the discomfort and pain I knew I would soon experience. Now I'd reminded myself about waters breaking, I wanted to be out of the café too.

'Come on, Val. Women have been giving birth since Eve took the bite of that apple. It's not an extraordinary event. Besides, it could just be a twinge. I've read too many stories about women going in and out of the labour ward with umpteen false alarms. Better wait until we know it's the real thing.'

I leaned back in my chair to shift the weight of my belly. My lower back had started to ache. Perhaps I had been sitting too long.

Valérie took a forkful of her apricot tart.

'Did you find any more information about the father? The guy on the beach?'

I shook my head sadly. I thought I was over the fact that Kai senior wouldn't be at the birth. He didn't even know the baby existed. I would just have to remember to tell little Kai the best things about his father when he grew up.

'I had a letter from the Tai Chi retreat where he used to teach on the island. They've re-marketed themselves as a yoga centre, said the Tai Chi thing was too niche. They remembered Kai, but said he suddenly left before the start of the rainy season. They didn't know his home address in Canada. They didn't even know his last name – he was always known as "Mr Kai." He was paid in cash and didn't have a contract.'

'That's so sad, Sandrine.'

'I figured if we never really declared our love for each other back then, I could at least stay in love with the idea of him now. At some stage, I'll have a child who will be curious to know about his origins. I shall make the stories as romantic as possible.'

I knew I'd have to embellish what I would eventually tell baby Kai, as I didn't know that much about his father. Perhaps the adult Kai would be a hard-working philanthropist forever travelling from one charitable foundation to another. He could be spreading his humanitarian generosity around the world. I wanted my little Kai to grow up happy, believing his father was a good person.

We left the café and Valérie ran to her car to drive and fetch Pierre who hadn't answered the phone at the farm. He must have been in the barn. She wanted to come with me, but I needed Pierre to bring my things. I continued on my own for the short walk to the hospital.

I hadn't even reached the other side of the *Place d'Armes* when my waters broke. It was almost a relief. The anticipation had preoccupied me as I surveyed the passing traffic for Pierre's car. I was surprised to see I was outside the *laiterie* where I had worked for a couple of weeks. I didn't feel a thing. At first there was the vague sensation that something warm was rushing down my leg. Then I heard a splat like a water balloon on the pavement. I held my low-slung belly, looked down at the puddle, before stepping over it and walking on quickly as though nothing had happened.

Pierre met me at the hospital and we checked in together.

'You the father then?' the receptionist asked when Pierre arrived with my overnight bag. 'Got him well organised already,' she said, looking at me with eyebrows raised.

She perked up when I explained Pierre was my brother. I half expected her to ask him if he was married, as his caring interest in his sister seemed to have impressed her. I didn't have the heart to tell her he was taken.

According to the midwife, the birth was uneventful, though six hours of labour with a lot of grunting and pushing on my part seemed eventful enough to me. But something miraculous happened the moment I reached for my baby.

'He has all his fingers and toes, everything in the right place. A beautiful baby boy,' declared the midwife, as I took Kai in my arms.

Looking into his tiny, gorgeous, scrunched-up face, I realised nature had a built-in security mechanism. Something that makes sure all helpless new born babies receive the care and attention they need. Instead of falling in love with the idea of my baby, I could now fall in love with the reality of him. Kai was perfect.

His face didn't resemble me, or anyone I knew. Pierre had seen plenty of new born animals in his life, but wonder was still apparent on his face. We cooed over him. I repeated his name over and over 'Kai, Kai, Kai, my beautiful little soldier.'

My joy eclipsed a lingering regret that I hadn't been able to find his father. My time on those islands in the South China Sea seemed like a dream to me now. It was another life, playing back occasionally in my mind like a favourite film. The dancing flames of the fire on the beach, the silky warmth of the gently breaking ocean on the soft sand.

Any mistakes I had made were now buried in the back of my mind.

PIERRE DROVE ME home after three days in hospital. Pierre and Marianne now slept in our parents' revamped and renovated room. Papa had been moved downstairs to one of the larger living rooms. I decided to keep Kai in my room with me for as long as he needed to be there. But I wasn't sure of our future at the farm, so we hadn't decorated the room with fancy nursery furniture. I used the old crib that both Pierre and I had slept in, and set up a changing table on the top of a chest of drawers.

For the first few days the crib looked too big. Rather than put Kai in bed with me, ever the restless sleeper, I tucked him into a bottom drawer, padding it with baby quilts and blankets to give him a sense of security as he slept.

Pierre thought this was hilarious and called me the baby box lady.

I wanted Kai to feel safe and cocooned in a world full of warmth, that even when he wasn't in my arms, he would have the sensation of being held very close in a devoted family. Everyone loved him, and the family was part of the circle of protection I wanted to build as a single parent.

Then I met Scott and everything changed.

THIRTY-NINE

March 1988

I CAN'T PLACE where I am at first as I awake. But, as I feel a hot pulse streaking from my breasts to my lower belly, I remember: Paris!

Scott is still asleep next to me, so I don't move, contemplating the spark my body produces from the memory of our lovemaking. I must be the luckiest woman alive. The future for Kai and me is no longer uncertain. I've had my fair share of disappointment. It's time to simply be content, after Maman's death, Papa's illness, my travels gone wrong because of one person's insane obsession.

I smile, remembering the excitement when Scott told me he wanted to take me to Paris for this weekend. I didn't think things could get any more exhilarating. Valérie and I joked about it. *We'll always have Paris*. I close my eyes in half-wakefulness and let my thoughts wander.

I sensed before we even reached Paris that Scott might ask me to move in with him. I think of his house, perhaps soon to be *our* house, the dream kitchen, the stunning view, the spare blue room crying out for a little boy like Kai. The colour schemes in all the rooms mirroring my own tastes. To a tee. I remember his thoughtfulness borrowing the Maxi Cosi car seat, always considerate of Kai's needs.

There are other little things we have in common that are surely signs we should be together. We visited Maman's grave a few days before we came on this trip. Scott had asked to see it, after I told him her ashes were buried in the local churchyard. I knelt to show him Maman's plaque on the lower level of the columbarium wall. Removing an old posy of dried marguerites, I placed a bunch of her favourite orange tulips in the jar in the niche.

'When we buried Maman, Papa was already in the foggy zone of dementia,' I told him. 'It was a shock to us all. Pierre was already pretty much running the farm single-handedly. Maman complained of pains in her midriff one week and couldn't keep any food down. We thought it was a bout of food-poisoning, but when they took blood tests at the hospital and didn't let her come home, we realised it was more serious. Liver cancer.'

'Two motherless children meeting in this crazy world. We were meant to be,' Scott said, clearing his throat before continuing. 'My mother died of cancer too.' Scott put his hand on my shoulder, encouraging me to continue my story.

I thought this was so incredible, this deep common emotion. I wanted to share my feelings with him, to secure that connection.

'Maman was dead within two weeks after the initial diagnosis. I wish you could have met her. I know she would have loved you and Kai.'

'I never really knew my mom,' he had said, his voice suddenly distant. 'I was too young. I still miss her though. I look for signs of her everywhere.'

His voice faltered. I hugged him and said it was okay, that I wanted to make him feel better when he was sad.

'What about your dad?' I'd asked, and instantly felt the atmosphere change.

'I don't want to talk about him. We didn't have a… healthy relationship.'

'Is he still alive?'

'I don't know. I don't care.'

I was shocked at first, thinking of Papa, unable to imagine feeling such neglect, despite his dementia. Rather than questioning this sudden indifference, I felt a deep sympathy for Scott.

He had knelt back down in a moment of silence, placing his palm flat against the carved granite plaque, as though honouring Maman. I'd put my hand on the back of his neck where he crouched next to the wall, wanting to feed him my compassion, my empathy. As I stroked his head with my fingers, I was distracted by the barely perceptible dark roots on his scalp. Through the melancholic thoughts of our respective mothers, I was surprised that the sun-bleached highlights in his hair were growing out.

I recall the lotions and creams in the bathroom cabinet in his apartment, his touch of vanity I had swept aside when we first met. Something else my eye had been drawn to that day on the top shelf. A Maori bone fishhook that resembled the one Kai senior always wore. I'd forgotten to ask Scott why he'd never mentioned visiting New Zealand, especially as he knew I'd been there on my travels.

As I lie in the strengthening light of the Paris hotel room, the whirl of the last few weeks quashes a nagging feeling at the back of my mind, another memory trying to get through the fog of morning sleepiness. Before I can put my finger on it, I hear a snuffle from Kai in his travel cot in the sitting-room of the suite. He'll be waking soon for his breakfast.

Aware of our lovemaking still tingling between my legs, I stare at Scott's sleeping face. I notice the shadow of a beard darkening his tanned jaw, and something flickers again in my subconscious.

I can see Kai through the crack in the door. I make out his silky dark hair through the mesh on the side of his travel cot. I sit up to check his little round chest is still rising and falling, the ever-anxious habit of a new mother. One little fist lying next to his head twitches in infant salute.

I look around our room. Through the Regency curtains a sliver of morning sunlight is cast across one of Scott's muscular arms next to the pillow. I narrow my eyes, remembering the first time I saw him in the Café Tivoli, thinking I'd seen him on television or the cinema screen, thinking he might be someone famous. The joy of finding someone whose tastes so mirror my own, the feeling that we'd known each other all our lives and were just waiting to meet that day. Perfect partners.

I get out of bed, making as little noise as possible, and head towards the room next door where Kai is beginning to stir. On the way past the dressing room, I glimpse Scott's travel bag half open on the floor of the wardrobe. The bright red cover of my Swiss passport catches my eye through the partially open zip. He'd taken it to show the ticket inspector while I was occupied with Kai on the train. On impulse, I reach in to grab it, intending to pop it into my handbag. My hand closes around two passports. I'm about to drop his blue American one back in the bag when curiosity gets the better of me, and I open it.

At first, I think he must have accidentally been handed someone else's passport by the border officials on the train. The photo doesn't resemble Scott at all. I look a little closer. The hair is darker, and this person has a beard, but there is something familiar about the face. My head buzzes and a chill runs down my spine. I look down to his name, and my stomach does a flip.

JACOB SCOTT SPENCER

Jacob.

Jake.

I put my hand to my mouth to suppress a gasp. I feel like I've been punched in the gut as I realise this person lying in our hotel bed is no stranger.

Scott is Jake.

FORTY

THE BARELY PERCEPTIBLE swish of the door across the carpet and your feet padding across the floor next door wake me. You must be going to feed the baby. I don't move, not wanting to make any noise so I can gauge your mood before you discover I'm awake. As I remember my possession of you the night before, I get an erection, and hope I can take advantage of you again this morning.

I reflect on the journey we've both been on to get here. I'm on a high now, but it's a long way from the one I was expecting on that Himalayan pass. I'm working on forgetting the hurt I experienced when you wouldn't take the ring. I'd planned for us to look back on that proposal, remember it as our special day, and laugh about finding each other on top of the world. I still can't believe I got it all wrong then, thinking you were playing hard-to-get, thinking you were hiding the fact that you really wanted me. In some ways, it's even more satisfying to know I've been successful by using my initiative and my wealth to make something good out of it all.

There was nowhere easier than Nepal to disappear, to melt into the crowd. The chaos of humanity in that poverty-stricken region provided the ideal cover. Americans like me usually stick out like a sore thumb in Asia, especially when we open our mouths, but Pokhara is one of those places where tourists are as numerous as locals, the former to pour their cash into the pockets of the latter. The Nepalese pounced on every opportunity to make a buck out of me, and if I couldn't easily disappear, I knew I could pay someone to make me disappear. But in the end, I didn't even need to do that.

I purposely didn't tell the gimp at the guesthouse I was checking out. It was important the cops found my stuff there. My new life couldn't start until the authorities had officially reported my death. I tried my second name out a few times on other travellers I met. It sounded good on my tongue. Tough, capable Scott. Stronger than wimpy Jake who wanted to leave his old life behind.

It took two days for them to work out I'd drowned. For a while I didn't think you'd received the note. I cursed the kid at the reception of your guesthouse for not delivering it. I sneaked in during the night. The next day he found it sticking out from between the Himalayan Times and his Indian Bollywood magazine.

I'd rowed the boat into the middle of Lake Phewa under the light of the moon, then almost passed out on the cold swim back to shore. I imagined the chill waters peeling away my old Jake skin, birthing me into a new person. The cleansing reminded me of my baptism in Lake Wakatipu in Queenstown. This was another new start. By the time I got out, my fingers and toes had lost all feeling, and my eyes were aching from the cold. I'd left sweat pants and a thick fleece on shore, but it still took a couple of hours to stop shivering. Anticipation was the thing that helped warm me.

The new guesthouse I found on the edge of town was happy to take double my money rather than make me hand over any ID. I gave a different name for the register, knowing I already looked nothing like the bearded, scruffy backpacker who had trekked into town only days before.

My pack, my clothes, wallet, money and my old passport were all still in the room at the other guesthouse, so I bought a small sports bag from one of the busy markets. Apart from one of my credit cards, a wad of cash and the clothes I was wearing, the only thing I took with me was the new passport I was issued in Hawaii. I'd given my financial advisor strict instructions to keep my assets active, no matter what news he heard.

I only needed *you* to believe I was dead.

All hell broke loose when you read my note. Your reaction lifted my spirits; a reversal of the disappointment on Thorung La Pass. I saw your tears, and at that point my plan faltered. Should I have saved you the grief and come forward? You were genuinely sorry I'd killed myself. It gave me confidence for my new plan. I knew I had to give myself every possible chance in my mission to become someone completely new.

The reaction of the police was predictable: Confusion as to protocol, a lot of shouting, not much action, and a general feeling of helplessness, despite short fat men in uniforms throwing around orders to look busy.

When you decided to head home to Europe, Scott Spencer's life truly started the moment I booked a ticket on your flight to Geneva.

And it's all been worth it. Because now I know you need me more than I want you.

FORTY-ONE

JAKE'S SUPPOSED TO be dead! How can this be him? He drowned in Nepal. The police were so certain. But they never found the body, even though I expected them to after I'd gone. Now I know they never will. Oh, dear God.

I reach into the travel cot, lift Kai and put him to my breast before he's fully awake to prevent him making too much noise. My heart pounds. I look around the room, wondering what clothes I can gather, how I can pack Kai's changing bag as quickly as possible and get the hell out of this hotel suite. I'm only wearing my night shift. Most of my clothes are in the wardrobe in the bedroom next door. If I sneak through, maybe I can grab a pair of jeans, a sweater, my handbag.

Then I remember I don't have any money, or at least only a few francs. Where would I go? I don't know anyone in Paris. Perhaps I should go to the police. But why would they care? I have no idea where our train tickets are – probably in his wallet.

Biting my lip, I sit by the window to stare out at the morning traffic on the Champs Elysées. Kai begins to make little humming noises as he tucks into his first meal of the day. Think! I have to think! The slow uncoiling of horror slithers around my gut. I hope anxiety doesn't sour my milk.

How could I have missed this? How did I not see Scott was really Jake? Maybe because in my mind Jake was irrefutably dead.

I once read an article about the human brain's capacity for recognition with only the flash of an eye, the set of a nose, or the twitch of a lip. There are things our brains store away in the far reaches of our cranial filing cabinets that jump out as soon as we see facial features even decades later. I've been blind to it all. But not just the visual triggers. His voice didn't fire any synapses either, although I can't think if I'd ever had a normal conversation when I knew him as Jake. I've been so over-awed by the prospect of the perfect match, wrapped up in the gold ribbon of this man's financial support. Some survival instinct has blinded me.

He must have been working out, had some advice on the way he looks and behaves. He's so much more muscular than the scrawny Jake I remember. Is it possible he's had some kind of cosmetic surgery? To think until five minutes ago I thought he was so hot, the way he made me feel... I swallow, suppress a sob, and begin rocking back and forth, my hands prevented from trembling by holding Kai tightly without causing him discomfort.

Oh God, oh God, oh God.

FORTY-TWO

MY EYES FLICKER open to see my tanned bicep on my pillow, the muscle accentuated by a narrow seam of sunlight shining through a gap in the drapes. I smile with gratefulness for the people who helped me become Scott. The personal trainer at the gym in Lausanne. His girlfriend the hair stylist, who in a reversal of the old Samson tale infused me with an underlying strength when she snipped away my lanky hair. Her friend the beautician who also owns a tanning salon. The nutritionist. The optician for the perfect tinted lenses. The commission-paid shop assistants in the chic boutiques of Lausanne and Geneva. The dermatologist at the clinic in Montreux where movie stars and rich bankers go to make themselves beautiful. The pills, the injections, the treatments to improve my skin.

Despite the pain, I'm thankful for the doctor who recommended some reconstructive surgery for the acne scarring that no amount of lotions and creams could improve. He achieved some skilful skin grafting which took months to heal before I became the final version of Scott Spencer. When I first heard the idea I was hesitant. I was so impatient to begin my campaign for you.

But in the end the delay suited me. Because I found out you were pregnant.

I close my eyes and recall how, over the months I transformed into the man I knew you'd want, you began to change too. When you packed on some weight around your stomach and waist, I was a little worried. You could have benefitted from some advice from my personal trainer. Perhaps you were enjoying too much home-cooked comfort after your low-cost eating habits. It felt wrong that you were letting yourself go when I was making such an effort for you.

In November, I followed you into Lausanne on a shopping trip with your friend. I watched you come out of a baby store with armfuls of boxes and bags. And it clicked. The swell in your belly, the weight gain. You were pregnant! I was incredulous. How the fuck did that happen without me knowing?

I thought baby bumps show after a few weeks. Who the hell was the father? Who had you slept with under my fucking nose?

I figured my whole plan was in ruins. But after a couple more weeks, my anger turned to bewilderment. There were no clandestine meetings with a new boyfriend, no one turning up on your doorstep to declare their undying love. You continued as though everything was perfectly normal, getting bigger, and settling into life with your family on the farm. I wondered if you'd planned this, been to a sperm bank, had been artificially inseminated. You wanted a baby! Could it be possible you regretted my suicide so much, you needed to replace my senseless loss with another life?

As your pregnancy progressed and my scars healed, it was a race in time to see who would be born first. But I relaxed when I realised your pregnancy was a kind of insurance for me. Who would want you now, with a kid?

I want to laugh out loud as I remember my naivety, but I hold my voice so you don't know I'm awake. Because you need to finish feeding that baby. You need to give him the best you've got. It wasn't until the day he was born that I did a little research and re-worked my calculations.

FORTY-THREE

I CONTINUE TO connect the pieces of the puzzle. His contact lenses. They must be tinted. I don't remember Jake having such blue eyes. His sun-bleached hair? From a bottle. These things should have been big clues. But I ignored them all. I bite my lip until the taste of iron mingles with salt from my tears.

I stare down at Kai's beautiful little face, clinging on to him as though he is my life raft in a turbulent storm. I study his dark lashes, the silky black hair that has been thickening over the past weeks. With a lump in my throat I lean down to kiss the top of his head.

I reflect on the strangeness of running into a foreigner in our isolated village. I realise now it was all a convoluted plan. This thing Jake wants from me. It has been longer than a few months in the making. It has taken more than a year. Since the faked suicide. These changes in his appearance. But for what? Just so he could sleep with me? Where did he think our relationship would go? With someone else's baby.

I shudder now to think of it. To think that he's fooled me. Thinking of the sex last night, my heart pounds. He has finally fulfilled his sick dream. The sex. I swallow. My lower body burns as I remember him touching me.

And a memory rises from the depths of my mind with explosive fire.

Finally we are together.

Flashes of the beach in Thailand flicker behind my lids when I squeeze my eyes shut with horror. My nightmare isn't over. Bile rises in my throat.

That taser of memory is now a vice at my temples.

It was his fingers on my collar bone, his tongue on my neck, his breath on my ear, his whisper. The electric reaction through my body. I've felt that once before. After the Full-Moon Party.

Finally we are together.

It was Jake who had sex with me on that beach in Thailand. It was Jake who took advantage of me in my drunken or drugged state. His actions… that was rape. Oh, God.

I was raped. By Jake.

Oh, my God.

It means Jake is Kai's father.

FORTY-FOUR

AFTER A COUPLE of glasses of champagne last night, I could see I turned you on. It was such a kick to have your full response, rather than those sluggish reactions when you were drugged in Thailand. This time I get to sleep next to you in this massive bed with its soft luxury sheets. A far cry from the night on the beach. Although I still get a thrill thinking about our first time.

When I pushed open the door to your hut that night, moonlight shone on your body sprawled in the middle of your bed. You were on your back and you hadn't tucked the mosquito net around your mattress. I worried the insects would be feasting on your golden skin. I didn't light the candle for fear of attracting more bugs, but I propped open the wooden window shutter a few inches before closing the door and leaning your pack against it.

I sat on the edge of your bed and ran my hand down the length of your thigh. You made a little whimpering sound, and I was as hard as I am now. I pulled the ties at the waist of your wrap-around skirt and opened you like a birthday package. Hooking my fingers round your panties, I worked them down your hips and thighs, moving your legs together so I could pull them off over your ankles. As I moved your legs apart, you obliged by widening your knees and raising your hips, as though you'd just realised what I was doing.

I hastily removed my shorts and climbed on top of you. I kissed your mouth, because I knew that's what I was supposed to do first, but you tasted of sour whisky. Before you got the chance to kiss me back, I pulled away. I pushed your blouse up and touched your breasts. When I leaned down to kiss your nipple, it hardened in my mouth and a streak of pleasure ripped through my groin. I was very close to losing control. I stroked away the glossy hair of your mound and worked my way between the soft insides of your upper thighs. It took a couple of goes to find my way in, mainly because you felt a little dry. I had to use some spit in my palm to guide myself into you. I never imagined you would be so soft, so enveloping. It was as though you were folding yourself around me. It was heaven. I supported myself with arms locked either side of your body on the mattress. As my hips moved against yours, you groaned with pleasure and lifted your arms as though to embrace me. Your face rose, your eyes closed, the vee of cords in your neck straining in ecstasy. Then your head fell back to your pillow on a puff of your hair. I leaned down and nuzzled your neck, moved my lips to the shell of your ear, and gently pulled the lobe with my teeth. I whispered in your ear and you made that whimpering sound again, a little like you did last night. I now know that's what makes me come.

I didn't hang around that night. I wiped myself on your sheet, hauled up my shorts and left you to sleep off what would surely be a monumental hangover.

KAI... HMM, YES, we'll have to do something about changing that name. Although I haven't yet had proof that he's mine, I've been pretty sure since his face changed from infancy. The realisation happened the morning after I had a dream, a flashback from my childhood.

There used to be a photo of me as a baby on the shelf above the fireplace at the Kansas farm. I remember one of the old man's poker-playing friends bringing Pa home one night after a session, drunk and surly. Too drunk to be bothered with me, but irritable enough to keep me awake with his ranting. The wife had accompanied the two of them into the house. She stank of booze too and noticed me crouching beside one of the armchairs near the fireplace.

'You gonna be okay, son?' I remember her asking.

I wished I could have told her I was never okay. But I knew the old man would freak out. Our strange need for each other kept me silent. At that point in my youth, I didn't know whether another life would be any better than this one. Her gaze fell on the photo.

'Aw. You were a cute baby, Jacob Spencer. Look at those cheekbones. Same as your daddy's. Though one of his might be a little blue now. Sam Baker socked him after the game tonight. Accused him of cheatin'. He'll be hurtin' in the morning. You look after him, son.'

And with that she was gone, with her equally drunken husband and any hope of me sneaking out with them.

That morning I met you to walk around the market in Vevey, I kept staring at the kid in the pram. Those high cheekbones. The tufts of dark hair. About as far from Hippy Boy's blond dreadlocks as you could get. But I still need proof.

I'VE BEEN LIVING in a kind of dream since then, imagining our future. The thrill now instils itself in me every time I look at his little face. It has begun to grow into a fierce need to protect my offspring. There are suddenly so many things I want for this little person. He will become my little Jacob. That's it! His name will be Jacob. We'll find a way to change it. You'll have to learn sooner or later that Hippy Boy isn't the father of this boy.

Jacob needs a second life. I need to be compensated for all the shit that went down when I was a kid. This will be a way of replaying my early years. I'm determined to give him the perfect start.

I used to wonder why anyone ever wanted to be a father. Why would someone go through the theatrics of a relationship with another woman, pretend it's all down to love, to produce such a dependent little person, then do those terrible things, and treat them so badly?

I now realise what has been the underlying purpose of my journey to you. It isn't about my mother, though for a while I thought it might be. I doubt she would have had the strength to protect me from my father's body if she'd been around anyway all those years ago. I can see that now. Some mighty power has made me fall hard for you for one reason only. You are the vessel. This has been the subconscious goal all along. You were the one destined to carry my child.

When I had you in Koh Pha Ngan, my desire was a blind need. I hadn't realised until I met you as Scott that you were convinced you'd slept with Hippy Boy. I was shocked when you told me Baby Jacob's name that first day in the café. Then I realised you'd probably slept with everyone at that beach. I should have told you straight away who I was. Should have revealed my identity. But at the time I didn't know it would result in this. In him. In my baby.

What kind of life do you think you can offer my boy? On a hobby farm in the middle of postcard Switzerland in a two-hundred-year-old farmhouse in need of major renovation, miles away from anywhere. A country whose inhabitants' heads are so far up their asses, it'd take a quart of bourbon to muster a smile.

I want Jacob to grow up strong, with opinions that count for something. I want him to grow up speaking a normal language.

I want him to be a part of the greatest nation in the world. I want to take him to the US.

No one is going to tell me how I should raise my child, how he should dress, where he should go to school or college, what he's going to be when he grows up. These things are the job of a father. Although my father never did this for me, I can now relate to what he was supposed to have been doing all that time when I'd felt so abandoned on those windswept plains of Kansas.

We'll move to New York City. The cultural capital of the world. I'll educate myself about the things that matter, and in turn educate him. I don't want my son staying in some hokey cheese-making community, speaking some slow version of a language no one else uses.

I want to give my son the best chance to live the life I couldn't have. That won't happen in Switzerland where the important things in life don't go much beyond keeping things clean and being on time. With the skills I've learned over the past year, plus the results of a DNA test, I'm sure I'll be able to get papers, issue a US passport.

But I can't be sure that passing a few coins across the palm of a Swiss judge will get me custody. This is the eighties. Shit like that probably doesn't happen anymore.

I know you don't have any money. Are you thinking I could support you, along with my son? Do you think you have a right to decide any of these things? The more I think about it, the more I wonder if you were faking it last night, to get what *you* want.

You've served your purpose, I see that now. We need to do this on our own, Jacob and I.

The one thing standing in our way is you.

FORTY-FIVE

MY BREATH SHORTENS to quiet sobs as the tears continue. I stare at the hotel phone on the sideboard, wondering if I should call Pierre. Making a call would wake *him* up in the next room. I'm not sure I want him to know I know. Not until I can work out what his game is.

I look back down at Kai. I want to hate him, want to hate my baby for who he is, but when he suddenly releases my nipple and stares up at me with a curious look that says *What's up Mama, why the tears?* my heart melts. I know I will love him whoever he is. I try not to imagine the combination of these two seeds, Jake's and mine. I envision instead the total absorption of cells, a transferral of all identity to my own. I smile and stroke Kai's cheek. He carries on drinking, his little hand pressing into my breast to encourage more breakfast. Kai is *my* baby. One hundred percent mine. He is formed from my flesh and blood.

I wipe my nose quietly on his spit cloth and suppress a sniff. I must not let the imposter in the next room know I'm crying. I finish feeding Kai and lay him down in the cot with two of his favourite toys. I beg him silently to go back to sleep so I can figure out what to do.

I need the bathroom. As I creep back through the bedroom, I stare with revulsion at Scott-who-is-really-Jake asleep in the bed we have shared. His fake blond hair is splayed on the pillow and his face is turned towards the wall. I detect a crease in his cheek and imagine a smug smile on his face.

I move into the bathroom and grip the sink with both hands. Staring at my reflection in the mirror, I gulp for air and clench my jaws. I hear a limb move under the covers in the bedroom. Jake is waking up. My heart beats with renewed panic.

My natural reaction is to fly in rage at this man in the bed next door, scratch his eyes, spit on his face, make him leave, call the police, have him arrested for... what? False identity? He is who he said he was. It's not false identity. I never knew his last name before. How was I to know Scott Spencer was using his second name? He's allowed to do that. But it has been a despicable deception.

What will the police think if I turn up at the station with my baby, who is also his baby, calmly announce I was possibly drugged and definitely raped on a beach in Thailand by Jake Spencer over a year ago?

How could I possibly make the police understand the magnitude of theatre this man has gone through over the past eighteen months to ensure he could have me? But more's the point, what are his intentions now?

Jake's plan has been so calculated, so cleverly plotted, he must have a lot more on his drawing board than I am aware of. My fairy tale has turned into a horror story. I am the young maiden who was lost in the forest, and my Prince Charming has turned into some stinking, fire-breathing gorgon. He has wormed his way into my worst nightmare.

And then I wonder whether Jake has any idea he is Kai's father.

The covers swish again next door. I wipe the tears quickly from my cheeks, forcing my jaw to un-clench. For now, at least, I have to carry on as if nothing has happened, as if the world hasn't just come crashing down around me. Until I can figure out exactly what it is Jake wants, and what I need to do. I have to find a way of protecting myself and protecting my baby.

Jake softly calls my name. The first sparks of fear ignite. What a deception!

I think back to those products in his bathroom cabinet. And something else I saw that day on the top shelf.

It's possible Jake's never been to New Zealand. But if he was on that beach in Thailand, I wonder where he obtained the bone fish hook that looks exactly the same as the one Kai senior wore.

FORTY-SIX

SINCE CROSSING THE border back into Switzerland on the train, I've tried my hardest to maintain a neutral attitude towards Scott-who-is-really-Jake. He seems distracted. Perhaps that's only my paranoia. But I've noticed he's becoming a little obsessed with Kai. Does he suspect?

I have a sick feeling in my gut every time the realisation hits me: *I am sitting opposite my rapist.* It's difficult to appear unfazed, to appear loving. I have to work out what I'm going to do about my revelations.

'It was such a romantic weekend,' I tell him somewhere around Yverdon, my hand casually resting on his thigh, my palm burning.

'Yes. Yes, it was,' he says, putting his hand over mine.

I swallow, and force my hand to stay, though I want to tear it away from under his touch. I close my eyes and feign sleep for the rest of the journey. I feel like my heart has been racing for almost twenty-four hours.

The TGV slows on its approach to Lausanne. I must have truly fallen asleep as I wake up to the noise of people gathering their bags together, putting on their coats. Jake has picked up Kai and is bouncing him on his thighs. I want to snatch my baby back from him. I don't want this man's hands on my son.

They're both looking out of the window at the passing buildings. The light shines across Jake's face, and his irises flick back and forth as they track the view. His contact lenses float on the fluid of his eye. I wonder again why I've never noticed they're coloured. I now see a tint of blue on their viscous curves.

In the taxi back to the farm, Kai squirms himself awake in his car seat and Jake's eyes are drawn to him. A genuine smile lights up his face as their eyes connect, and my stomach drops. They must not bond.

He must know.

I desperately want to be home. I want time to work out what I should do. I want to talk to someone. Pierre, Marianne, Valérie – anyone – to put my crazy feelings into perspective. Until I know the extent of Jake's intentions, if no one else knows Kai's true paternity, then it will be easier to defend my case if it's my word against his. No one else knows I didn't sleep with Kai senior before that night in Thailand.

My first priority is to protect the two of us – Kai and myself – as much as I can.

AFTER THE TAXI drops us off, I carry Kai straight upstairs to my room.

'I'll be down in a moment. I'll just put him in his crib,' I say, as Jake takes the baby travel bag to the kitchen with instructions to empty out the rubbish and put on the kettle.

Pierre is outside somewhere, probably in the barn with the cows. Marianne must be out, as her car wasn't in the garage as we came up the driveway. I want to take Kai away from Jake. It's way past the baby's bed time. I should see Papa, but I want to get Jake out of the house first. Then I'll unpack, and let Pierre know we're home. After I've changed Kai and put on his pyjamas, I take his soiled baby vest to the laundry basket in the bathroom.

'What are you doing?' I squeal as I come back into the bedroom and glance at the crib.

I haven't intended my voice to rise so sharply. I bite my lip as I stare in panic at Jake, kneeling next to the crib. The one thing I swore to myself on that train on the way back from Paris was that I would never leave Kai alone with him. I've only left the room for half a minute. I realise even that was an error.

As I stand staring at Jake, a few seconds of guilty silence stretch out. The voice of a television quizmaster is muffled beyond the door of Papa's room downstairs, between brassy jingles and rounds of applause.

Jake stands up and turns towards me, hiding something behind his back.

'What's that? What are you doing?' I ask again.

His presence sends a shiver of alarm through me, but I force a smile to my face. Jake shows me his hands, palms up. They're empty.

'Why are you so jumpy, Sandy. What's up? You've been acting strange since yesterday. I was on my way to the bathroom and wanted to make sure the little guy was still sleeping. I might not see him for a couple of days. You didn't let me say goodbye. I just wanted to check.'

My heart pounds. Jake's only been to the house a couple of times. I try to remember whether he's ever used the bathroom upstairs, or if he even knows where it is. There's no reason for him not to use the one downstairs off the hallway. If he either suspects something isn't right or has plans to harm Kai, I have to do something as soon as possible. I'm not sure whether that involves exposing him for the stalker he is. Who will believe my claim that he raped me in Thailand?

'He's perfect, isn't he?' Jake suddenly says. 'His gorgeous brown eyes, his hair now growing thicker.'

I look at Kai, his fist pressed to his mouth, sucking it gently as his eyes droop sleepily. Jake might have been studying them. Does he think they look like his own, underneath that tinted layer of contact lens?

'Do you think he looks like you, Sandrine?'

My brows crease. His voice lacks warmth, and I resent his use of my full name. I wonder what he's getting at. Is this going to be confession time? I make my voice light, don't want to let on that I think he knows that I know. He's suddenly behaving out of character.

'Not really. I think he looks more like Papa. Or my Uncle Jean. Especially when he was a boy. That side of the family is all dark. Are you...?'

'He's just so perfect,' Jake interrupts. 'That's all. Shh. We must let him get some sleep.'

He walks out of the room and down the stairs, leaving me to gaze at Kai with my heart still thumping. This turnaround, this adoration of Kai must mean only one thing. I shake my head, close the door quietly and follow Jake downstairs.

He does know.

And if he doesn't know, then why am I so uneasy about him being in Kai's presence? Does he intend to do something horrible to him? If Jake is that obsessed with me, and thinks Kai senior is the baby's father, then it's also possible he'll do something unspeakable to Kai. I already know he has a sick mind. He might not want him to be part of our lives.

I can never leave Kai in the company of this man again. Ever.

It's time for this to end.

FORTY-SEVEN

I CHOOSE THE neutrality of Sherlock's Pub in Vevey to meet Jake. I tell him I have the car, but am not sure exactly when I can get away, so we agree to meet directly there. I don't want to risk Pierre and Marianne inviting him in if he picks me up from home.

Kai feeds early and goes to sleep, so I arrive at the pub before Jake. It's early evening. A few people are gathered at a table by the window, an end-of-week works do. I reserved a table a few days ago and I sit nervously with my back to the wall, so I can see him come in. I order a spritzer and wait nervously. A cool breeze around my ankles accompanies his entrance through the door, sending a shiver up my spine. One of the women in the corner turns and checks him out. He's a handsome guy. It makes his intentions all the uglier.

But it isn't just the looks. The waitress comes up to him and her face asks without words whether she can help. I didn't get the same treatment when I came in, and it takes me a while to realise what it is that Scott has that Jake didn't have before. He has somehow created charisma, developed his looks so they comfortably carry this false persona. I still don't recognise Jake from the geeky, thin, nervous guy I saw those few times on my travels.

He smiles and points in my direction. Disappointment flits briefly across the waitress's face. He shrugs out of his jacket and holds it out to her, still looking at me. She reaches for it wordlessly. I secretly want her to let it drop to the floor between them, but she takes it and hangs it up. Charisma.

But he's not fooling me anymore.

Another waitress brings my spritzer as Jake approaches the table. He orders a glass of Rioja, and I wonder whether he went to wine-tasting lessons while I was pregnant. I would never have imagined the word 'Rioja' rolling so comfortably off old Jake's tongue.

I fiddle with my glass as he settles into his chair. He seems genuinely happy to see me and I'm less certain about the scenarios I've run through. If I were still unaware of who he was, I might have fallen for him completely by now. I remind myself that this person has followed me for more than a year. He withheld his true identity to seduce me. He raped me.

It is unforgiveable.

'Scott, I think things are moving too quickly. I think we should take a little break from each other.'

I don't want to tell him point blank I don't want to see him anymore. I think he might get suspicious. His investigative skills are already honed. I don't want him learning about my own discovery.

I watch his face. He looks genuinely hurt, then his eye twitches. A spark of either anger or impatience flashes momentarily before he presses his lips together and looks down at his hands.

I think of what he might have expected of the evening. Perhaps he thought we would have a couple of glasses of wine, a simple meal, and drive back to his Perfect-for-Sandy home, take me to his Sandy-designed bedroom, feed me my favourite foods, pamper to my every carefully-studied need.

'How long do you think you'll need, Sandy?'

He speaks with a coldness I haven't heard before. I know his controlled voice is hiding hotter emotions. A shiver runs down my spine.

'I don't know, Scott. I just know I'm not ready, especially for the... intimacy. I'm not physically ready.'

His eyebrows raise.

'Wow. I didn't get that impression in Paris. You were...'

My throat closes. *I know. I was hot for you.* Rage and shame fight for a place in my head that I allowed myself to feel that way.

'You don't need to get hung up about the sex. It's okay,' he says, almost sulkily. He can't possibly mean that.

'It's not the same for every woman. I tore a little... down there, during the birth, and there were a couple of stitches. It's different for every new mother. Some take longer than others to feel okay. Think how different people's injuries heal at different rates...' I'm waffling. 'Look, I just think things are going too fast. Give me a few weeks...'

His eyebrows crease, probably trying to recover from going a little green at hearing the physical details, and right there, I see the old Jake. The one who is insecure and unstable. I see the person who hung on to my every word in a trampers' hut in the New Zealand wilderness. I see the person who pushed his bicycle across a busy Sydney street. I see the person who hid in the shadows of a tree across the road from a Chiang Mai guesthouse. I see the creep who has been following me for months. But most of all, I see the disturbed obsessive person who raped me on that beach in Thailand.

'Yes, Scott,' I say a little more forcefully than I had intended. 'It will take time. I'll call you. Please, you must do this thing for me. Give me time.'

'Can I still see you… as a friend? No strings, and all that. I've grown real fond of the little guy. I'd like to be able to see him too.'

It's not the first time I realise he never calls Kai by his name.

I panic. What can I say, without making it sound like I've uncovered his game? Without making it sound like there's no way back. What would he do then?

'We'll see,' I say, mustering control of my voice.

I try not to clench my jaw, to avoid letting him see how tense I am.

That tension, which is now churning my stomach into a very real fear. He isn't simply going to disappear.

I might need to do something more drastic.

FORTY-EIGHT

A FEW DAYS later I tell everyone I have a dental appointment. Kai is in the safe hands of Marianne. As I sit on the train from Châtel-St-Denis to Fribourg I think back to all those times Jake said he had an important all-day meeting in Geneva. I called J P Morgan two days ago, asking to speak to Scott Spencer, told them I was his fiancée. There is no one in the Geneva office with that name.

Those meetings, all fabricated. He's more likely getting his roots done. Or having a shirt tailor-made. He must be on a rigorous programme in a gym or fitness centre to get his body that well-toned. Where the hell has he secured seemingly endless funds to do all this, even after he's taken the time to follow me half way round the world? The Jake I met back then was no J P Morgan employee material.

THE *FREE SPORT* shop assistant is dressed in traditional hunting green, as though he might melt into the woods on the outskirts of town at any moment. He's surprisingly young, mid-thirties. I expected an old fellow, closer to the age of my father. He looks like a wannabe army recruit rather than the hunters I've seen Papa disappear into the forests with during the autumn months looking for wild boar or chamois.

I glance around the shop. Shelves stacked with sturdy hiking shoes and steel-toed boots stand next to racks of forest green jackets and hats with comic camouflage paraphernalia sticking out of their bands. Hooks up the wall hold backpacks and bags designed for the hunter who might spend several days and nights in the alpine forests. A glass case in the middle of the store displays high-tech binoculars, telescopes and sighting equipment.

Behind the counter, ammunition is stacked in various coloured boxes in a glass cabinet like provisions in a grocery store. On the back wall stand racks of rifles. Under the glass cover of the counter where my damp palms are now resting, is a collection of short firearms displaying price tags I now realise I might not be able to afford. I feel the first heated sting behind my eyes.

'What do you need a pistol for?' asks the assistant with raised eyebrows.

Because I want to protect my child against the man who raped me.

'We have a marten. In our roof. It's ruining our insulation, leaving droppings in our attic. The bait we laid hasn't worked. He's got to go.'

I thought hard about a legitimate purpose for needing the gun. I know we have a genuine case, living on the farm. Papa would have stood in this very same spot when this young assistant's father was running the shop. I had thought about saying I wanted to purchase the arm as a gift. Papa is still a member of the local shooting club, though he hasn't attended for at least a decade. Pierre has taken over his locker in the changing rooms there. Almost every young man we know is still obliged to attend the range once a year to practise their skills in their post-military years.

And then I remembered one of the many tasks on the farm when we were children to use as an excuse. Pest control. It's hard to believe we had such free access to firearms. It wouldn't happen today. Papa's weapons are locked up in a cabinet and Pierre is the only one allowed to touch them.

'It's not as easy as you think,' says the assistant.

He looks at me dubiously, and I wonder what he's about to say next. I try to remain calm. My eyes are hot and itchy, tears never far away.

'Do you have a license?' he continues.

'No, but my father does. We live on a farm. He has a shotgun, a .22 rifle, and another gun for putting down cattle in an emergency, if they're injured or...'

'Your father should come. Or he should ask at the local shooting club. It's not worth purchasing a new pistol for the sake of one pest. You should use your .22 for that. But I did say it's not as easy as you think, and it's nothing to do with acquiring a firearm.'

My heart beats hard. Is my real intention written on my face?

'My father's incapacitated. He's ill. He's...'

'That's not what I meant. My cousin once had two martens living in the roof above his bedroom. Kept him awake all night. Drove him half mad. Listen, I know why you need the weapon.'

I stare at him, thinking he's guessed my purpose. My face reddens with the same flush I feel every time I think about the security of my son. I no longer even consider myself in danger. Judging by Jake's recent swings in character, it isn't me who's now the centre of his attention.

'... I know it's hard to understand, because of the sleepless nights...'

I draw in my breath, put my hand to my chest. *He knows?*

'… but the marten is still a protected animal in Switzerland. You cannot shoot them. Live traps are still the only permitted means of extraction. I can give you the name of an expert trapper. He costs a bit, but he'll get rid of your marten. Laws have not yet changed. You should know it's illegal to kill one.'

I swallow, shocked to hear the pests Papa cursed on the farm when I was a child are now protected. I take the card he holds out with a cantonal fauna expert's details, mouth a strained '*merci*' and leave the shop.

The tears I've held back for the past hour now dampen my cheeks.

FORTY-NINE

I PUT PAPA to bed after a tough day with no recognition. His room looks out onto the garden, and his only words are about a blackbird singing from the top of a tree down by the river, inciting promises of the summer to come.

'Every verse is different,' he says.

I pour him a fresh glass of water and pat the covers around his frail, pyjama-clad arms. There are some days when he chooses to stay in them all day, tying his dressing gown around his thin waist in the chill of morning and shedding it by the warmth of midday.

I'm tempted to talk to Papa about Scott-who-is-really-Jake. He won't understand what's going on, but his hearing it might at least give some small comfort to a daughter who simply wants to get the thing off her chest.

He's been having more bad days recently. Some of his medication has reacted adversely, manifesting itself in angry outbursts. He's no longer the placid, aging man I returned to from my travels. His personality is erratic, and I no longer take Kai into his room. Even if he did understand what I might tell him, his reaction to my problem could be unpredictable.

Instead I ask Pierre and Marianne to meet me in the kitchen to 'discuss something' after Pierre has overseen the milking in the barn.

The kitchen window is open when they join me, and the blackbird is still singing. The river has swelled with spring rains. The sound of gurgling around the set of rocks where Papa dug out the swimming hole for us all those years ago should be soothing, like a meditation tape. But the noise of the high water does nothing to calm me.

It's an unseasonably warm evening. I don't know if Jake is still spying on me, so I ask if we can sit inside in the mugginess of the farm kitchen, just in case. It all makes so much sense now, that *he* knew so much about me, my tastes, my habits. It freaks me out just thinking about it. How closely he's been stalking me all the time.

I close the window. Pierre complains about the airlessness of the kitchen, and I placate him with my hand. He glances curiously at the window and opens the bottle of wine he's brought from the boot room. As I look at Marianne sitting across the table from me, Pierre pours me a glass, and the three of us clink a toast to each other. The wine gives me courage. The bottle sits between us as I deliver my confession about Scott-who-is-really-Jake.

'Why didn't you tell us before?' says Pierre. 'This is unbelievable, and pretty bloody complicated.'

'This is so hard to believe,' says Marianne. 'How could you not know they were the same person?'

'There's no one more bewildered than me, Marianne. I feel so stupid. I was duped into thinking he was a different person. I can't explain it, except that I crossed paths with so many travellers along the way, I never really saw him close up. You cannot possibly begin to know how different he looks today from back then. I'm still having a hard time accepting it.'

'Christ, Sandrine. I thought you were going to suggest it was about time we put Papa in a home,' Pierre says, glancing at

Marianne. She puts her hand over his and gives him a smile. 'That's a conversation we'll have another time. Shit, this is bloody huge. A gun, Sandrine! If you wanted one, you only needed to ask.'

Pierre says this with sarcasm, and I feel like a fool for thinking I could get hold of one so easily.

'I have a shotgun in the cabinet that would make the fucking creep's backside burn.'

I can't tell whether or not Pierre is joking. My intention to obtain a handgun was really only protection, but now I think about it, why does anyone buy a gun if they never intend to use it? I shudder.

'Pierre, I realise now it was stupid. I can't expect to get rid of him by shooting him… But I do need to get rid of him. I'm just not quite sure how to go about it. Do you think the police would believe my story if I went to them? Is there something like a restraining order we can get on someone like that?'

'He had sex with you without your consent!' Marianne says. 'Surely that's grounds for arrest.'

'Sandrine's right, though Mari. Do you think the police would believe her? It happened months ago on a beach in Thailand. You know how sceptical they are at the moment about provocation and young girls "asking for it." They'll probably accuse her of dabbling in drugs or something, leading the arsehole on.'

'Aside from that,' Marianne says gently. 'I can't imagine the psychological affects this is having on you, Sandrine. How the hell are you dealing with all this? It was bad enough when you thought you were coping with his suicide.'

I look from Marianne to Pierre, my lovely brother, who has always helped me out of scraps and tall trees as a kid. Then I have a vision of Jake saying, *'this is a totally different ball game'* in his twangy American accent, wiping the half smile from my face.

'Sandrine, you have to find a way to get him to leave you alone. Permanently. It might help he's a foreigner. I don't know. I'd like to think the police and the authorities would look after us first. I don't want him in this house anymore.'

Pierre scratches the stubble on his chin, the two-day growth testament to his stress about Papa's deterioration. He stops and widens his eyes, looks straight at me.

'Christ, Sandrine, have you thought about what he might do if he finds out he's Kai's father?'

'That's why I thought I should protect myself and Kai. Pierre, I'm so scared. I'm worried about what his intentions are. He seems to have changed his attitude towards me since we got back from Paris. He's dropped the romantic stuff. The simplest things irritate him. I thought it was because so much of my attention has been taken with the baby, but now I'm not so sure.'

'Are you absolutely certain Kai is his?'

I bite my lip, and nod as tears fill my eyes.

'I didn't have sex with Kai senior, though not through lack of wanting to. It was never the right moment. But I believed for so long that Kai and I had slept together after the Full Moon Party on Koh Pha Ngan. Now I know for sure it was Jake. My memory is coming back in pieces. Paris sealed it for me. I knew then it was definitely him. He must have drugged me. How horrible is that?'

'My God, Sandrine, that's evil,' says Marianne. 'The bastard raped you!'

'And he might want to claim Kai as his own. It was so long ago, and with so little evidence it could go terribly wrong in court,' said Pierre.

A tear trickled down my cheek and I swiped at it with my sleeve.

'Oh God, I don't want to have to fight for Kai in court. Can you imagine? He can probably afford to pay a celebrity barrister a fortune to make sure he keeps his son and takes him out of the country. I cannot lose Kai. He's the most important thing in my life.'

Marianne's eyebrows remain creased.

'He doesn't deserve to bring a little human being into this world. He doesn't deserve to be part of our life.' My fist clenches as I speak. *He will not take my son.*

Silence surrounds us momentarily. Through the closed window the blackbird faintly picks up a new shrilling tune on the top of his tree.

Pierre stands up, his chair scraping a discordant shriek on the kitchen tiles. He takes the empty wine bottle and walks into the utility room to clink it into the recycling box. He comes back and grips the back of his chair, his knuckles showing white.

'Whatever your crazy intention was at the gun shop,' he says to me. 'That arsehole needs to be taught a lesson.'

FIFTY

THE HARDEST PART is swallowing my disgust and calling Scott-who-is-really-Jake to invite him to the farm for dinner. At this stage in the deception I need to be convincing.

'I've been thinking about things. About us,' I tell him on the phone. 'Are you free on Saturday evening? Pierre and Marianne are going out. I thought you could come over, we could talk, focus on what's important for both of us.'

'Next Saturday. At your place.' he says hesitantly. Not a question.

He doesn't believe me.

'I figure it's a good time for us, without Pierre and Marianne around. We won't be disturbed. I need to be here for Papa, in case he needs anything. It'll be quiet. An opportunity for us to talk.'

My voice catches in my throat as I say the word 'talk.'

'Will Kai already be asleep?' he asks.

I'm not sure what I'm feeling at that moment. Why would he ask that? I can't work out whether it's disappointment I hear. I feel giddy with apprehension.

'Probably.'

Jake clears his throat. I imagine his face and try to guess what he's thinking through the phone. The unspoken promise of what might happen between us on Saturday night. Perhaps he thinks I'm going to give sex another go. I swallow.

'I'll be there at seven,' he says.

HE ARRIVES A few minutes before seven. The treads of his wide tyres crunch on the gravel driveway before the roar of his engine silences in front of the house.

I open the door with a tea towel thrown across my shoulder. It's taken the place of Kai's usual cloth. Jake eyes it suspiciously as he steps across the threshold. I laugh, trying to appear relaxed, and pull it from my shoulder.

'Bechemel sauce, not baby spit,' I say.

I lean towards him, not knowing whether or not I should brush a kiss to his cheek, but end up pouting at the air as he draws back slightly. He looks surprised, and I turn swiftly away. My face flushes furiously, and I pretend a saucepan on the stove needs my attention.

'I'm glad you could come,' I say. 'It makes things easier not having to worry about Kai or Papa when we're out.'

'I'm glad you changed your mind… I'm a little surprised it happened so quickly.'

'I could hardly expect you to wait forever. You'll soon be swept off your feet by someone with less baggage than me.'

'The baby is *not* baggage,' Jake says with certitude, and I draw in my breath.

'I didn't mean just Kai. I meant my Papa, the fact I don't have a permanent job…'

'You know I have enough money to take care of you, Sandy,' he says, then bites his lip. 'I didn't mean to make that sound materialistic. I know how much you value your independence.'

I shudder inside, knowing he's watched me work things out, take care of myself on my travels. But there was that one time when I didn't have control, when he took over and made sure I gave him what he wanted, even if I hadn't given him my consent.

I turn back to the stove so he can't see the anger in my eyes. I wish I'd been more aware of his delusion all along. It's hard to believe that the odd, self-conscious traveller I first met almost two years ago has turned into this cold, calculating monster.

'I think it's important we get to know more about each other, too. I know you've only met Papa and Pierre a couple of times, but I need you to know how important they are in my life. Why is it we've never talked about your family?'

I'm not following the script. Pierre suggested I don't mention anything that might put Jake in a dark mood. But I have to ask. My curiosity about what's made him into this monster has grown over the days since our return from Paris.

'Is that what your issues are, Sandy? That you don't know anything about my family? My family is nothing like yours. But I'd like to think I could replace the one I never really had with yours. Your brother seems like a decent guy. I can see he cares for you. And your father... How's he doing?'

I'm nonplussed by his sudden concern for my father when my thoughts have been spinning around protecting Kai, but I answer without missing a beat.

'He's sleeping too. He sleeps a lot. The youngest and the oldest in this household have ended up with the same waking patterns.' I swallow. 'Kai is upstairs, in the office, so he won't be disturbed if...'

Our eyes lock, and the sexual tension on his face shines. I flush with anger, but hope he'll interpret the colour on my cheeks as the heat of passion.

I prepare the scene for dinner in our rustic farm kitchen. I have no idea what his favourite meal is. I've only ever seen him eating my favourite foods. He says they're his favourite foods too, but I don't know if he's been telling the truth.

A *sauté de boeuf* bubbles on the stove, next to a colander of French beans about to go into the steamer, and a potato gratin in the oven. Good, wholesome farm food. I wonder who cooked his meals for him as a child. I don't want to ask him about his history, what his father might have done to make him hate him so. Is that what this is about? Jake transmogrifying into his father? My heart clenches as I think of Kai. I don't want to wait any longer to find out.

A bottle of *Humagne* stands on the counter next to the stove, already opened.

'To let it breathe,' I explain.

I pour wine into both our glasses on the table beside our place settings and pick mine up. I wait for him to do the same.

'Here's to us,' I say, forcing a smile.

We clink glasses and both take a sip.

'What challenges have you faced this week in the wonderful world of finance?' I ask.

'Oh, not much. I received some endowments on some investments I made. Money makes the world go round.'

That sounds so crass.

'Investments for J P Morgan, you mean?'

'Well, yes, I work for the bank's clients. Hey, I don't want to talk about work. It's boring. Tell me what you and the little guy have been doing this week.'

It irks me that I've still never heard him say Kai's name.

He sounds so credible, but when I called the bank and learned they didn't have a record of a Scott Spencer working there, it made me doubt that Jake is capable of working for anyone. I can't imagine where all his money has come from. It didn't sound like he was rich when he was growing up in some little-known back-water of the Mid-West. Did he obtain his money illegally? What other lies has he told me? What else can this creep be hiding?

'Kai had another check-up, another weigh-in at the doctor. The gynaecologist also checked me out. I'd experienced some soreness after...' I was going to say 'Paris,' but have to control my nausea as the vision of Jake having sex with me on that hotel bed comes unbidden. I smile uneasily and turn to take two plates from the warming rack above the stove.

I put them on the table, pushing the cutlery apart with the rim of china, the noise emphasising the sudden silence between us. I imagine Jake hoping for his prize, with me dreading the inevitability. But I know that's not going to happen. I have other plans.

Pierre hasn't wanted me to go through with this but Marianne agreed it would make things more authentic. And Pierre needs time to complete an important task.

I put the gratin and beans on the table, pick up each plate again and spoon the steaming stew onto each one directly from the pot on the stove.

'Smell's delicious, honey,' he says.

He's never called me 'honey' before. It sounds almost comical on his tongue. His hand at the small of my back is like a cattle brand. I hope he doesn't notice my shudder. It prepares me for the sickening feel of his lips on my cheek. My hair is pulled up into a scrunchie, and his breath moves the tiny loose strands curling around my ear. The gravy sloshes as I place the plates back on the table. I give myself a mental kick to keep things together.

Noises seem suddenly too loud. There's a ringing in my ears, and I pray I won't faint. I turn on the radio on the kitchen counter, not only to mask the silence but to fill the uncertain gaps between words. The radio is tuned to a classic station. I can't think who's been listening to it in our kitchen, but I leave it on. The heavy bars of some symphony, Mahler or Wagner, seem bizarrely appropriate. I pull back my chair to sit down.

He raises an eyebrow, probably about the music. I think again how different this person in front of me appears, a strange alter ego to his former shadowy self. I preferred the other one, actually. Jake rather than Scott. I think I read him better. But then if I *had* known him better, perhaps none of this would have happened. I would have dealt with this long ago. There is one thing I wouldn't have if things had been different. And that's Kai. I don't know how that makes me feel, wondering if I could have changed fate.

I take another sip of wine, smile disarmingly at Jake and raise my glass again.

'*Bon appétit!*' I say as I pick up my knife and fork to eat.

FIFTY-ONE

IT'S LIKE A well-practised school play. I have predicted the role my antagonist will take. I don't need to look at his script. But then it occurs to me that today *I* am actually the antagonist. On the day of the performance, the stage direction is now in my hands. Scott is the ignorant actor who has to improvise his lines.

Marianne, Pierre and I went over the plan earlier in the afternoon. I was nervous about the dinner. My worst fear was for the silences where I simply didn't know what to say to the person sitting opposite me. We discussed various topics of conversation I might cover. Marianne thought it was important not to ask him too many questions, so I agreed to ramble on about the mundane in my life.

The trouble is, I can't forget that I thought this exciting thing was happening to me. I was falling for this great guy who swept me off my feet. I can't forget it's all just been an illusion. The only thing I feel when I look back on the past few weeks is sick. Sick to my stomach. Sick for me. Sick for Kai. Sick for all of us. I don't want to talk about any of it.

I pick up on a bit of family history. I talk about growing up on the farm. Better memories for my own benefit rather than Jake's.

'Pierre's taken over the running of the business where Papa left off. Marianne seems to enjoy farm life. She's a great farmer's wife.'

'Like your mother was,' comes a voice from the door.

'Papa! You're... awake.'

My eyes and voice give away the panic of this unscheduled intrusion. I hope Jake reads my reaction as embarrassment.

'Do you need something? I can bring it to your room. You should have called.' I nod to the three-way baby-monitor on the counter which serves both Kai and my father.

He shuffles in to the kitchen, his hair in disarray, his dressing gown hanging off one shoulder. I stand to help him into the other chair.

'Mm, smells good.'

'You should try some, Monsieur Bavaud. Your daughter is a very good cook.'

'My daughter...? I should like that, smells like Elise's favourite casserole.'

I shake my head at Jake over the top of my father's head as I help him get comfortable in his seat.

'You already had some earlier, Papa. Aren't you full?'

He frowns, presses his hand to his stomach.

'When? I'd like a little food please, *madame.*'

He speaks as though addressing a waitress in a restaurant. I know today he doesn't remember who I am, though he knows who my mother was. He's compensating the oversight with an uncharacteristic friendly attitude and a revival of movement. I'm surprised he made it to the kitchen without knocking anything over. I serve him some of the stew in a bowl and give him a spoon. He dips it into the gravy.

'*Attention,* it might still be hot. *Chaud!*' I warn, too late.

The hot gravy touches his lip and he tips the spoon, leaving a beefy brown streak down the front of his pyjamas. Of all the scenarios I had imagined for this theatrical moment, having to change my father's clothes and put him back to bed was not on the list.

'I should have waited until it was cool,' I say, patting his shoulder.

He puts the spoon back in the bowl and looks up.

'I can wait,' he says with a rare smile.

He gazes across the table at Jake.

'You've changed your hair,' he says, and my heart just about explodes in my chest.

Jake's eyes open wide.

'This isn't Pierre, Papa, this is Scott.'

Jake leans back in his chair. I note a slow release of air through barely open lips. I grimace an apology across the table, the irony not lost on me.

'Pierre? Who's Pierre? This is J…' his stutter makes my eyes widen and I draw in my breath. '…Jean. This is Jean, you stupid woman. You think I don't recognise my own brother?'

Jake is concentrating so hard on my father's face, he hasn't seen my reaction. This is all turning into some terrible farce. I have to get Papa back to his room, or our plan for the evening will be in ruins.

'He thinks you're my Uncle Jean,' I explain to Jake, who nods.

'He's not your Uncle, young lady, he's my brother.'

Papa is tumbling further into confusion.

'You can eat the stew, Papa, it'll be cool enough now.'

I'm impatient to move Papa back to his room at the end of the hallway so I can get on with dinner with Jake. But as I watch my father eating a second serving of the meal, he is actually a welcome distraction, contrasting the dread that I don't want him witnessing anything he might later become confused by.

I go quickly to the living room where a handful of photo albums sit on the bookshelf. I pick up one from my childhood, carry them back to the kitchen, and lay them at the end of the table. Filling time.

'It's okay, Sandy, I know this stuff is confusing, what with his poor memory and all.'

'My memory is just fine, *jeune homme*,' quips my father.

I'm shocked he's understood Jake's English. Jake has a bemused look on his face. Papa's message is perfectly understood. I catch him looking from Papa to me. I wonder if he's comparing us, curious whether the same thing will befall me in my old age. I can't help it, I have to ask.

'Have you heard from your father since you settled in Switzerland?' I ask, before popping a morsel of beef into my mouth.

Jake's mouth flattens to a line, his eyebrows fall momentarily. I can see the cogs of his brain moving on from the study of my father.

'Sandy, it's not appropriate to talk about my father in front of your own. There are things… I can't tell you. Terrible things he did to me. I see a lot of love here between you.' Jake blushes, perhaps embarrassed to be saying the word *love*. 'I can't talk about it here.'

I wonder if Pierre is already outside in the yard and can hear what's going on, whether he knows we've gone off script. I told Jake when he arrived that Pierre was out with Marianne, but my brother has been on a mission. He will have sneaked into the hallway earlier and taken Jake's keys out of his jacket pocket hanging on the hook. He will have driven to Jake's apartment fifteen minutes' away and taken the fish hook from the cabinet in the bathroom. He was to return and wait for me outside in the farmyard. If any part of this plan has gone wrong, he would have come to the kitchen if he couldn't get the keys, or telephoned if he couldn't find the fish hook.

Papa's spoon clinks noisily back into his bowl.

'*Très bon,* Michelin standard,' he says, and I smile, remembering how he said that after every meal my mother ever put in front of him when I was a little girl. We always guessed how many stars it deserved. 'Filling, though.'

It's useless pointing out he ate only an hour ago.

'Shall I take you to bed now, Papa? Are you feeling sleepy?' I ask gently.

'Not really. Just full. But I'd like to lie down.'

He stands unsteadily, and I take his elbow.

'I won't be long. I'll just help him back to his room. Please eat, and help yourself to more. There's plenty.'

I wave my hand in the direction of the pot on the stove.

'Not saving any for your brother or his girlfriend?' Jake asks.

'No… They won't be back for dinner.'

I hate all these lies. They sting my tongue every time they slip off. I wonder if the weight of all this guilt will bring me down in the end.

FIFTY-TWO

I LEAVE MY father's door open as I take him back to his room, to keep an eye on the hallway. I don't want Jake going upstairs to look for Kai. I help Papa remove his dressing gown, change his pyjama top and pour him a glass of water from the jug by his bed as he climbs in. I'm relieved he's chosen his bed rather than the armchair near the television. Some nights he insists on sitting in front of the screen and falls asleep in the chair because he can't remember how or when he's supposed to get into bed.

I listen intently for a disturbance in the corridor as I move about the room, but the noises I hear are from the kitchen, the clink of a piece of cutlery and water running into the sink. If Jake attempts to go upstairs, I'm prepared to run and block his way.

I lied to him about Kai being asleep in the office. Marianne has taken the baby to her sister's place in Oron. We had to make sure he would be safe this evening. If something goes wrong, he's the one person who needs to be protected most from Jake.

Once Papa is settled, I go back to the kitchen. Jake has finished his food and has begun flicking through the album. I was going to show him a picture of Uncle Jean before Papa spilled his dinner, but the moment has passed and I let Jake thumb through without comment.

I pour us some more wine, glance out of the window at the darkening dusk, then pick up my plate and put it in the microwave, heating it for a half a minute.

'I'm sorry it's not really been the romantic dinner I was hoping for,' I say wearily, trying to muster a smile.

'Sandy, it's okay. It's nice. This is… comfortingly domestic. Hey…'

He reaches for my hand as the microwave pings. I jump up to fetch my plate, take it back to the table.

I force a smile and pick up my fork. I'm not hungry, and don't really know why I re-heated my meal, but it's a filler, a barrier to him touching me. I have to occupy my hands or they'll shake. The hot meat sticks in my throat and the coagulated gravy on the plate makes me feel sick.

I barely sip my wine, but I will Jake to drink more from his glass. It'll make my task a lot easier at the end of the evening. I look outside again. Almost dark. I calculate how much time has passed.

I POUR THE dregs of the bottle into Jake's glass.

'Woah, steady. You know, I might not be able to…'

I laugh nervously, and Jake flashes his fake blue-eyed smile.

'What with Papa and a busy few days, I need this,' I say, taking another mouthful of wine.

'The little guy's quiet tonight. Does he always sleep so soundly?' Jake asks.

'Pretty much. Remember Paris?' I silently beg him not to ask to see him.

'How could I forget?' he says.

He reaches into the back pocket of his jeans and pulls out an envelope.

'Go ahead, have a read. It's very good news for us, Sandy. And when you've seen this, I have a little story to tell.'

I swallow and pick up the envelope he's pushed across the table. The logo says *BioLaboSuisse* and is addressed to Scott Spencer at his Chardonne address. A creeping feeling of alarm raises the hair at the back of my neck. I slide the paper out of the envelope and unfold it. It takes a few seconds to register the confirmation of a DNA sample, matching it to a specimen from Scott Spencer. I remember him in my room after we'd returned from Paris. He took something, hidden behind his back. It must have been something from my son.

Kai is 99.999% his child.

My gaze remains downwards on the document, not wanting to believe what I'm reading, and not wanting Jake to know the confirmed horror in my mind. Why is he showing me this now? He's admitting his violation of me. What story is he about to share with me?

As my eyebrows crease in theatrical confusion, his hand reaches into another pocket and he places a gold ring next to the letter on the table. Tiny diamonds glitter out of a multitude of delicate filigree settings under the kitchen light. It's the same ring I saw in the palm of his hand on the top of Thorung La pass. He must have retrieved it from the snow.

This is madness, his obsession complete. The piece of paper makes things blatantly clear. I want to scream at him: *Are you completely deranged? You are admitting you raped me!* But I don't. Instead, I put my hand out and with a great effort rest it on his arm. I raise my eyes and force a wide smile. Genuine tears pool against my lower lids. I hope he'll see them as tears of joy. My cheeks ache from forcing my lips into the grin.

'I don't understand. What does this mean? How can this be? What kind of magic is this?' I try to sound surprised.

He's either finally coming clean, or he's going to give me some amazing story about having slept with me as Scott on that island in Thailand. Either way I find it so hard to believe he would now let me know his true identity. As he picks up the ring, I know he's going to try and put it on my finger. I jump up from the table.

'This calls for more wine!' I shout, and head towards to the boot room.

Jake's mouth hangs open, a perplexed look on his face. I rush past him before he can say anything. Whatever he was about to utter is frozen on his lips. He must wonder why I haven't mentioned one of two elephants in the room – either sex with me in Thailand, or his true identity.

I'm briefly out of his line of vision in the boot room and put my hands over my face as I approach the wine rack. I have no idea what he plans to say next. He doesn't realise that whatever his answer, Kai was conceived out of an act of rape. What is he expecting from me now? The sight of the ring makes me feel sick. I wish I hadn't seen the proof from the lab, but a determination fixes itself in my heart.

As I put my hand on another bottle of wine, I glance back at Jake through the kitchen door. He's still holding the ring, staring sightlessly at the photo album open at the end of the table. I know he's trying to re-think his story. Does he really expect me to throw my arms around him and declare us the perfect family? Accept the proposal he attempted to offer me on the Himalayan pass? So many questions to answer. The apprehension is unbearable.

As I come back into the kitchen with the bottle I will never open, I know I can't let this go on any longer. I glance at the clock on the wall, turn towards the dark night through the window.

It is time.

FIFTY-THREE

AS I PLACE the bottle on the table, I put my hand to my head and sigh.

'Woah, I'm a bit lightheaded,' I say. 'I'm feeling a little overwhelmed by all this. So much excitement in one day.'

'But... I haven't even begun to...'

I hold up one hand to silence him, the back of the other touching my forehead, like an actress playing a role in an old fifties movie.

Jake looks at me with a puzzled frown, followed by the clench of his jaw. I wonder if he thinks I'm making an excuse not to have sex with him. The clichéd headache scenario. But he still needs to deliver his explanation for Kai.

'I think I need a little air. You can tell me your story afterwards. Will you come out with me?'

He looks at me with confusion but stands up.

'Are you going to throw up?' he asks, disgust touching his voice.

'No!' I say crossly, looking at the ring now lying next to the lab's letter on the table. 'I just feel a little faint. I need some air.' *I just need you to step outside with me.*

I walk through the boot room towards the back door, close my eyes, and pray he will follow.

With my hand on the doorknob, my head suddenly feels hot and heavy, as though my deceit has come back to bite me. But remembering his own abominable actions, I take a deep breath. I stare through the glass panes to the dark farmyard outside. Jake's reflection in the glass sways. He's finally showing some effects of the wine.

Stepping out into the darkness, the soles of my slippered feet tap-tap on the step down to the yard. My hand reaches to the side of the door where a cattle feed sack is folded on a bench sheltered from the rain.

I shake out the sack in one quick movement as though it's a tablecloth and it makes a loud crack, like a gunshot. I turn as Jake steps through the door after me and the last thing I see as I pull the sack over his head are his eyes squinting into the night before he jerks with surprise.

'What the...?' he says.

As was my intention, he's disorientated. I pick up the rope that was coiled under the sack. I keep silent, hoping to confuse Jake before the onset of any physical anger. He stumbles and as I feel the weight of his body pulling away from me, I am a little uncertain about what I'm going to do. I should have waited for Pierre as was originally planned.

I tie the rope tightly around the sack, pinning Jake's arms to his body inside, but leaving a trailing lead. I check the knot. This isn't the first struggling animal I've had to deal with on the farm.

I push Jake forward so he has no choice but to stagger on. He coughs inside the bag. Grain dust must be catching in his throat. I hope he doesn't go to ground before we've made it across the yard.

'Sandy? What the fuck's going on?' he yells, voice slurring.

He stumbles sideways and knocks into the almost-empty giant grain silo next to the barn. A deep, hollow boom echoes around the farmyard.

'Sandy! What was that? Sandrine!' Jake calls. 'What the hell is going on? Are you there? Are you safe?'

I hate hearing him call my name. The desperation in his voice when he asks me if I'm safe pulls at my guilt. His concern for me sends doubt through my mind. But he needs to be taught a lesson. That's all I'm going to do.

It was Pierre who suggested we frighten Jake enough to make him go away and never come back. But Pierre isn't here; he must still be on his way. I realise it's not guilt I'm feeling, but fear.

Jake knows Kai is his baby.

Under the overhang of the barn sits a pair of rubber boots I placed there earlier. I kick my slippers off and they skid across the rain-soaked concrete yard. I pull the boots on, the line of rope coiled tightly around my arm.

Jake spins on the spot, trying to keep his balance. He begins to struggle, and I know he will soon fall over. Next to the gate leading to the field is a wheelbarrow. As Jake trips, I tip him towards the barrow. He shouts in pain as his legs catch the metal edge, but his backside sinks conveniently into the bucket. The barrow almost tips over and I reach out and grab a seam of the feed sack, pulling him around so I can lift the handles without his legs getting in the way. The wheelbarrow is far heavier than I imagined, and I know for sure I should have waited for Pierre. A sob escapes my mouth.

As I push the barrow through the field to the river, Jake must figure something bad is going to happen as he struggles harder. This is no longer the wimpy guy I remember from the hiking trails of New Zealand. This person has strength and power. But without use of his arms, he's trapped in the bucket of the barrow.

It wobbles from side to side and I pray I can make it through the boggy field sucking at the wheels.

It's now completely dark, which is what I have waited for, but I now realise I have put myself in danger. Despite the remoteness of the farm, we agreed to do this at night to avoid anyone out on an evening stroll seeing what's going on. Not that I imagine anyone would have been out in this rain. With panic pressing at my chest, I hope I can make it to the river.

Jake's voice is muffled from within the bag.

'Sandy! Are you there? Come on, answer me! Are you okay? What the fuck is going on?'

I had a speech prepared, but I'm finding it hard to form words. My jaw clenches against the cold.

'I'm not okay, as it happens. But I'm here to teach you a lesson, Jacob Scott Spencer.'

It's a relief to finally spill the words. Let him know that I know who he is. Simmering anger has built up since I told Pierre and Marianne about Jake's treatment of me, the deception, dishonesty and violation. But it's only now I realise it's the first time I've uttered his real name.

The rushing water of the swelling river at the end of the field roars between my words.

FIFTY-FOUR

I'M ALMOST AT the river when the barrow finally sticks in the mud. I tip it up and Jake slides onto the slick grass like a birthing calf. I take hold of the end of the rope and drag him the last few metres to the river. For that I am glad of the heavy rain.

He can't move his arms, but that doesn't stop him kicking and shouting. I'm glad there are no other houses in the vicinity. Having hindered my way here with the barrow, the rain now makes it easier for me to slide him in spurts to the bank, despite his struggling.

The rain increases, pelting us with heavy cold drops, almost as hard as hail. I hope it's only an April shower, short-lived. My thin sweater is soaked, and I shiver. I hadn't thought to leave any extra clothes for myself earlier outside the kitchen door.

The river is still running high. As we approach the bank, the sound of rushing water blocks out some of Jake's pleading. I tug and pull Jake over the edge of the bank into the river.

The biting cold water floods in over the top of my boots as I wade deeper. Jake's horizontal body floats in front of me at thigh level. His legs thrash uselessly. I think of the speech I'd prepared in my head, the things I discussed with Pierre and Marianne I was going to tell Jake. To make him leave us alone. To make him go away and never come back. All those words suddenly stick in my throat like a dry crust. Because he knows Kai is his.

'What the hell am I doing?' I whisper to myself.

I close my eyes and conjure up a vision of baby Kai. His trusting face. His loving smile. I turn Jake's body, and push his head under water. I count slowly in my head. When I reach five I haul out his head. Jake gasps inside the soggy bag.

'This is a warning to you to stay away from me and my family,' I yell next to the sack. 'I know what you did to Kai in Thailand. We have his necklace as evidence. If you don't stay away, we will go to the police!'

I wince as I say this. I'm quite sure the fish hook is Kai senior's, but there's a small chance I'm wrong. And there's also a chance Pierre couldn't find it in Jake's apartment. I push Jake's head under the water again, then pull him out. This time he coughs. He must have swallowed some water.

'You will leave here tonight and never come back, never see me again, or I will call the police and tell them not only have you threatened our lives, but that you must be a wanted man in Thailand. You're going to take yourself back to America, and never try to contact us again.'

The thick, layered paper of the feed sack is starting to disintegrate. The kicking of Jake's legs becomes feeble, but I am also weakening. I won't be able to hold him much longer. The water is icy, flowing straight from the pre-alpine slopes of the Dent de Lys. Jake coughs violently and speaks from his captive bubble for the first time since we entered the water.

'The boy needs a father! He's mine! The baby is mine. You have proof!'

I press my lips together and push Jake down again into the river. When I pull him back out, he speaks straight away.

'Sandy, you've seen the letter. The DNA results. You can't do this! I have rights.' His voice is hoarse.

'You raped me!' I shout. 'You're sick, Jake. You will not take my baby. Kai is mine, and no one else's. You are not entitled, you are an evil monster.'

'I know you thought he was Hippy Boy's baby; well, you got it wrong.' *Hippy Boy?* 'He can't dispute it, anyway. He won't be speaking again. I made sure of that!'

Kai senior. My suspicions are now confirmed. Hearing the truth makes it real. It makes the threat tangible. Kai, my love. Anger courses through me like an electric current. He did it. He *murdered* him. My head spins. It means he is capable of anything. The Maori fish hook, probably sitting in Pierre's car, flashes in my mind.

'I've come to take what's rightfully mine,' he says.

Oh no... oh no, he's talking about baby Kai. I have a vision of Jake abducting him to America. What would he do to him? The same things that were done to Jake as a child? For one blinding moment, I see no end to the nightmare for me or my son.

SHADOWS OF JAGGED pine trees rise like sentinels towards the rocky peak of the Dent de Lys above us in the night. The flow of water pulls at my legs, trying to sweep me off my feet. Together we edge towards the lip of the swimming hole Papa dug out for us when we were kids. In the pitch dark I know without looking where the slope leads sharply down to the depths. It's as familiar to me as my own bedroom.

With the rope wrapped around my upper arm, Jake tumbles against me and I push him away in the flood. While we are separated only by the rope, I reach down, tug off my boots, and throw them to the bank. With the river already up to my waist, I launch myself towards the water hole, yanking him with me. Rage fires through my body. I no longer feel the cold.

He gives the wretched cough of a choking man and his legs kick out spastically at all angles. Movement is slowed by the weight of water and when his foot meets my thigh, the impact is dulled. Grabbing a flap of shirt with my other hand, I take a deep breath, and dive head first into the depths of the swimming hole. My fingers skim the familiar contours of the stony riverbed. I push further, anger giving me strength. The bent root of the willow on the far bank meets the cup of my left hand like an old friend. I have anchored onto this smooth piece of wood a hundred times when we practised holding our breath as kids.

The current drags our bodies downstream, but I hook my elbow around the root and draw him towards me with my other hand, using as little energy as possible.

I count in my head, five, ten seconds, and his thrashing weakens. My lungs begin to burn. Despite the chill water swirling my hair, my head pounds with a searing heat. My nails, softened from the water, bend outwards as my determined clasp tightens. The joints of my fingers ache in their desperate grip. I will not let him go, and pray the river won't rip him away from me.

Fifteen seconds. Twenty.

My lungs are screaming for air. I swallow hard, pressing my throat closed to stop the inhale reflex. And just as I think I can no longer hold my breath, his hand reaches round and spiders against my face, a finger and a thumb gouge my eyes and instead of the darkness all I see is a burst of stars.

FIFTY-FIVE

HE'S BEEN CONSERVING his energy. I fight the urge to inhale. I'm beginning to lose consciousness. My limbs are numb. But I give one sharp toss of my head, loosening his palm from my face, and clamp my jaw has hard as I can, biting down onto two of his fingers. I taste his blood in my mouth.

He immediately lets go of my face, and I think I hear a cry of pain through the rushing water. Which means he must take a breath inwards. As deep as his cry of outrage was forced out, so the reverse must now happen. Tiny sparks are flashing behind my eyes, I am visualising a slowing of time in my brain. I have no more air left.

As I propel myself to the surface using the hidden tree root to push against, I force Jake's body underneath me with my feet, pushing him further down in the water for a few more seconds.

I break the surface, the taste of peaty soil in my mouth and gritty water strafing my eyes.

Coughing, I pull myself out of the river and heave myself onto the bank. Lying on my back I haul great wads of icy air into my oxygen-deprived lungs. Once my breath is under control, I sit up and bring the loose end of the rope to my mouth and kiss it, a sob of relief releasing a warm tear onto my cheek. The other end of the rope feeds through the hook of the tree root deep in the river, anchoring Jake under the water.

I pull my hair back from my face, wipe my eyes with the back my hand and look towards the farm.

A dot of light is bouncing towards me across the field.

Pierre is wearing a frontal head-lamp, the kind climbers often wear. He uses it when the cattle are calving in the fields at night. The sight of his shadowed face under the bright beam of light makes me cry with relief. He stands on the river bank, staring at me.

'Sandrine, are you okay? My God... Is he...?'

'Did you get it?' I ask, and Pierre nods, holding up the fish hook in his fist.

'Why didn't you wait for me?' he asks.

'I don't know. I was impatient, had to act. And I didn't want to implicate you. But I didn't know this would happen. Oh God, Pierre... He had a DNA test done on Kai. He's his.'

Pierre looks at me, his eyes wide. He's still confused.

'Don't say it. Don't say anything. With this high flow, the body won't stay in the hole if I let go,' I shout, fear at what I have done making me suddenly colder than the water.

'What do you mean, "the body"?' he yells back. 'I'm sorry I wasn't back in time. What the fuck's going on?'

Before I can answer, I dive back into the hole, easier this time with two free arms to guide me. In the blindness of the murky water, I feed the rope back through the root and rip at the feed sack, paper pulp coming away in my hands. I tear as much as I can and find the stringed seam near Jake's head. As I pull the sack, I realise his hair is caught in amongst the pulp, and I almost inhale water with horror.

I have no intention of saving him. But anyway I know he's already dead. I push myself to the surface again.

'I have to get the rope!' I say.

Comprehension fills Pierre's eyes. I must make this look as much like an accident as possible. I can barely feel my hands. I squeeze them to a fist and spread my fingers in front of my face. The pale bloodlessness of them ghosts in the dark.

I take a deep breath and dive for the last time back into the swimming hole. Jake's body has moved away and is being pulled downstream with the current. I grab the rope still tied round his waist, the feed sack now almost completely disintegrated from under its loops. This gives a little room for me to feel the knot, worry and loosen it enough to slip it off his body. In a bizarre last embrace, we move together towards the edge of the swimming hole. With my knees finding purchase in the shallows, I brace myself against the stony riverbed and pull the remainder of the rope from his body. It rolls, suspended, pulled slowly by the water. I'm glad I can't see his face.

IN THE IMMEDIATE aftermath, the river seems to calm, but it's still raining hard. I hug myself. Pierre and I watch Jake slowly moving away in the dark. He's not completely floating, but the current has been known to move boulders along this riverbed in a spring flood.

Twenty metres on, his shoulders appear out of the water and I hold my breath. The body is tugged upstream momentarily by the eddying water. Then he disappears again. The delayed horror comes to me in great flashing images. My gulping sobs remind me of the primal noises I made in the delivery room when I was giving birth to Kai.

I stare at Pierre. He drags the palms of his hands down his face. Rain and muck drip from his chin.

'What have you done, Sandrine?' he whispers.

The cold renders me mute. My shivering increases to a violent shuddering. My jaws hurt with clenching them so tightly. Snot and tears pour from my nose as my sobs quieten to a hyperventilated heavy breathing. I look for Jake's body in the distance, but it has ghosted under the brown water of the river. Instead I turn to Pierre who is also staring with his mouth open at where Jake's body has disappeared.

As we listen to the hiss of the deluge on the water's surface, Pierre looks up into the night sky, blinking against the sting of rain.

'I don't know whether this is a gift or a hindrance,' he says, and I wonder what he thinks of me in that moment.

We survey the mess of the riverbank, deep footprints and ruts from the barrow in the mud filling with water, and grass tussocks pulled from the unstable silt of the bank. I rub my arms where the muscles have strained to continually haul Jake in and out of the river.

'There's not a lot more we can do right now. We're both too cold. We need to get back to the farmhouse, get warm and dry, at least for the moment, then decide what we're going to do.'

Nothing makes sense right now. All I can do is nod dumbly. I faithfully follow my big brother towards the familiar glow shining from the farmhouse windows.

'I've got a horrible feeling this is going to look like a murder scene tomorrow morning.'

Is Pierre trying to be funny? Does he realise what he just said?

FIFTY-SIX

BY THE TIME we reach the farmhouse and enter the kitchen, it feels like hours since I was here. Everything is as I left it, except now there's water from my clothes and hair dripping all over the brick-tiled floor. Stripping down to my underwear, I throw the wet clothes in the utility room sink. As I pass the kitchen table, without thinking, I snatch the lab letter with the envelope, take a tea towel from the hook, use it to open the door of the wood burner under the stove, and throw them in.

On my way upstairs to find some dry clothes, I quietly open my father's door and check he's sleeping. His soft steady snore is the calming sound I need. I take a deep breath to try and stop the anxious flutter in my chest.

Upstairs in the bathroom, I'm still shivering, so I remove my underwear and climb into the shower. It's the only way I can get warm. But then I realise I must be shaking from shock. It's not long before I am nervous about being in the shower, the noise of rushing water blocking all my senses. I need to be able to hear what's going on. I keep expecting Jake to throw open the shower curtain and ask what the hell I've been playing at.

I turn off the water and dry myself vigorously, wrap the towel around me and go to my room. My heart is still beating hard, and all I can think is: *What have I done? What have I done?*

I touch Kai's crib, pick up the blanket and breathe in the smell of my reason for being. I've done this thing for him. For Kai. To protect my child from obsession, maybe abduction, and who knows, perhaps abuse. I keep justifying this thing to myself as I open my wardrobe, pull on a pair of jeans and a sweater.

When I come back down to the kitchen, Pierre is rinsing the mud off our clothes and boots in the sink in the utility room.

'Is it still raining?' I ask.

'Yes, but it's easing,' Pierre pauses. 'We have to go back out there, Sandrine. It's a mess around the riverbank. We don't know if anyone is going to come looking but we have to act as if they will. I don't quite know how we're going to make it appear 'normal' but we've got a give it a go.'

I nod, and grab Papa's old oilcloth coat from the hook by the door. I'll be better prepared for the weather this time, although the last thing I want to do is be outside, go anywhere near the river. As I open the door, one of the cows shakes its sleepy head in the barn, the clanging of her bell a comforting noise of normality.

'That's it! I'm going to let the cows out,' Pierre says.

They're usually let out after milking in the morning, but with the heavy rain and potential flooding, Pierre wouldn't normally let them into the field by the river at all. But having them cover our tracks is a logical solution. I pull my wet boots back onto my bare feet and my toes immediately feel cold.

'Don't you think they'll stay away from the river in this weather? Do you really think they'll cover our footprints?'

Pierre raises a finger.

'I'll put some hay down there.'

Together we go to the barn. Pierre hauls half a bale into the wheelbarrow we brought back from the river.

'I don't know how you managed to get Jake to the river in this,' Pierre says, lifting the handles of the barrow.

It's the first time since we came away from the river that either of us has mentioned his name. It brings on a bout of sobbing and retching. I'm glad we're outside in the dark.

'Christ, Sandrine,' whispers Pierre.

I'm unsure whether he's disgusted or sympathetic. I'm not helping him at all, while he seems to be so calm and cool about the whole thing. But he's not the one who's just committed murder. Before this, I hadn't killed so much as a spider my entire life. Pierre's been eliminating animals all the time on the farm: rats in the barn, calves that birth wrong, even once a trio of kittens who were born with awful deformities. Not that he can compare this situation to mercifully ending an animal's suffering. Well, maybe. There is no denying Jake was far worse than an animal. I wonder what's going on in Pierre's head. Although we have a strong relationship, I am in awe that he would help cover this up for me.

'I'm sorry.'

'Hey, Sis, it's okay. Don't apologise.'

Is he keeping it together for my sake? I envision Jake's body floating down the river towards the lake, as far away from the farm as possible.

Pierre slides the bolt on the barn and opens the metal-barred gate next to the milking stalls. The cows puff vapour through their noses and wiggle their ears. The familiar smell of hay and silage floats out of the barn on a warm gust. Pierre slaps one of them on her rump and the herd lumbers uncertainly out into the damp darkness, following him. We trudge across the field towards the river, the rain now lightening to a cold drizzle.

With the hay spread about, the cows tentatively take mouthfuls and their deep hoof-prints soon cover the shallower tracks of our boots and the ruts in the mud.

'I hope none of the girls get foot rot in this,' Pierre says as he coils up the rope that was tied around Jake's waist, and throws it into the wheelbarrow.

We collect the last pulpy torn pieces of the cattle meal sack that have washed up on the riverbank. Pierre throws the grey wet lumps into the barrow. They make a slapping sound against the metal sides.

'I'll be back at milking time after dawn to bring the girls in.' He pauses. 'I wonder how far he's been pulled downstream?'

Pierre gazes down the river in the dark. I shiver under the heavy oilcloth coat.

'It would be helpful if the river could carry him all the way down to the lake. Pierre, I don't know… What should we do?'

'We have to agree on what we're going to say if the police come to question us. I'm thinking, Sandrine.'

'Will you call them? The police?'

'No… I wouldn't do that. It's probably best we act innocently.' He pushes his fingers through his hair.

I think of the scenarios we might be able to invent. It's going to be harder to explain things with Jake's car parked in our driveway.

Back in the kitchen, I put the kettle on the stove to make tea for Pierre and me. It's 1:30 am. He calls Marianne, and she immediately answers. She's been sitting by the phone at her sister's place. She expected us to call earlier. I can clearly hear her voice squawking down the phone.

'I've been waiting for you to call. Is everything okay?'

Pierre carries the phone into the utility room, stretching the wire as far as it will go to continue his conversation with Marianne in there.

'Something went horribly wrong,' he says as the door swings closed, and his voice cracks for the first time. I follow him in, despite him waving me away with his hand.

'She doesn't need to know!' I mouth.

As he turns away I notice his bloodshot eyes.

'Is Kai okay?' I mouth again, and he nods.

'Later *chérie*,' he says, finishing his call to Marianne.

'She's bringing Kai back now.'

I'm glad, despite knowing he will wake when he's disturbed. I simply want him near me.

Oron is only a fifteen-minute drive away. Once the kitchen is clean, the utility room mopped and dried, I hear Marianne's car in the driveway.

'Will you be okay?' Pierre places a hand on my shoulder. I nod, my throat still raw from screaming at Jake, retching in the yard, and crying so hard.

Marianne comes in carrying Kai directly from the car seat. She brings him straight to my open arms. I sit at the table and put his mouth to my breast to feed, to send him back to sleep.

Together we recount the events of the evening to Marianne.

'I'm so, so sorry. What have I done? I'll go to prison!' I say.

'Not if we can help it, Sandrine,' says Pierre. 'You're my sister. Whatever mistakes you've made, I'll help protect you.'

'But they'll find him eventually. It will come back to us. God, I don't know what came over me. It seemed like the only answer. I couldn't see past the horror. I think he's done some awful things. Kai, the guy I met in Thailand who I thought was the father. What Jake said... He murdered him.'

Marianne puts her hand on my shoulder.

'It's okay Sandrine. Everything will be okay. Jake had it coming. I'm sure we can explain an accident. His car is still outside. Yes, they will trace him to us. Perhaps an argument, he went out into the dark, and slipped in the river. We'll work out a story.'

I sob quietly. My anger turns to dragging grief. If there was any initial doubt, I know now why no one could find Kai on those last few days in Thailand. Jake's comments confirmed that he must have killed him. He murdered the man I loved. The man I still desperately believe should have been the father of my baby.

But that's not an excuse for what I have done. I know that's not how the law works. I have intentionally killed a man. That's still murder.

I am now a murderer too.

FIFTY-SEVEN

HIS BODY DOESN'T get very far. Where the river flows onto the neighbour's land, another weeping willow grows on the bend. An angled root much like the one in our swimming hole was exposed from the unstable bank eroded during last year's flooding. Jake's leg has caught under it and he's held there, the flow of the water not quite strong enough to carry him further.

Marguerite Villard calls us first thing in the morning. She spotted the paleness of Jake's billowing shirt in the water from her bedroom window, thinking at first it was a piece of plastic torn from a silage bale. She tells us she's contacted the police.

I haven't slept well and feel exhaustion grabbing at my limbs. We sit at the table in the kitchen to try and hash out the story we are going to tell the police when they arrive, which they inevitably will. I have no idea whether Jake was carrying any ID, whether he had his wallet in his pocket, but the one thing that will connect him to the farm is his car parked in our driveway.

We start discussing what kind of accident could have happened. Jake's body would show a high level of alcohol. We could say we had a fight, that I was intending to break up with him, which was stretching the truth. But I couldn't see it working. They'd have known it was a deluge out there last night. Why would anyone in their right mind have been by the river?

'I'm doomed,' I say. 'They'll surely suspect me, charge me with his murder. Do you think they'll let me take Kai to prison? I know they have mother and baby cells in some institutions. What would I get for murder? Oh God, they won't let me keep Kai once he's a toddler.'

'Don't worry about that, Sandrine. Kai will always have family here to look after him. We can fight your case in court. If it comes to that, I'm sure yours would be considered a crime of passion,' Marianne says as she brings the Mocha coffee pot from the stove and pours each of us a cup of strong black brew.

'Let's not get ahead of ourselves,' Pierre says. 'Stop talking murder. You need to tell them he was completely upset by your doubts about the relationship and ran out into the night. We already did the groundwork to make this thing look like suicide.'

An ironic laugh puffs out of my nose.

'Suicide!' shrieks Marianne.

Pierre and I both look sharply at her.

'Wait right here, boys and girls. I have an idea,' she says as she scrapes her chair back and leaves the kitchen.

FIFTY-EIGHT

IT'S MARIANNE'S IDEA to use the tools Jake provided me with. It would never have occurred to me, but even if it had, I had no idea the instrument was still available.

Marianne comes back into the room holding a piece of paper. She places the sheet on the table and carefully smooths the creases. As she lifts her hand away, I look down at Jake's spidery handwriting. The sight of his looping signature makes me sway on the spot.

The suicide letter has been folded in four, just as it was when we found it amongst the tickets and permits months before.

'Marianne! I thought you'd thrown that thing away!'

'This is all we need, Sandrine. His motive.'

Pierre stares incredulously at his partner. Marianne's tone is one I haven't heard her use before. Her quiet confidence infiltrates the underlying nervousness pervading the kitchen.

'I know you'll think this is weird, but I kept the letter. I thought at some stage you'd need to discuss this. Maybe talk to a professional psychologist. I wanted to wait until after Kai was born, knowing how hormones could affect you during pregnancy. I thought you might eventually need a friendly ear. You know, woman-to-woman. When you arrived back from your travels, you weren't the same person you were before you left. Pierre was worried about you. Apart from being pregnant, he was worried about the way you were reacting, your ambivalence about showing photos, not really wanting to talk about your adventures.'

I stare at the letter on the table, not wanting to touch it. This fantastic lie Jake tricked me with.

'This letter can save you. We have to protect little Kai too, Sandrine. We have to protect both of you.'

Tears spring to my eyes. Pierre puts his hand over Marianne's on the table and smiles at her.

'Pierre worries about you, Sandrine. When you met Scott, we thought everything would work out. I forgot all about the letter. Until Pierre mentioned "suicide" just now.'

Marianne clears her throat. Her fingers resting on the letter begin to thrum repeatedly, as though playing scales on piano keys. The final details of the plan must still be forming in her mind.

'The bastard already wrote his future all those months ago, Sandrine. You've just given him a little help to finally fulfil his wishes.'

I stare at her open-mouthed, then look down at the letter.

'But it doesn't look like it was written yesterday. Surely anybody investigating a suicide can tell.'

'Look around you. You're living on a farm. How easy would it be for a shocked girlfriend to drop a note on a mucky kitchen floor?'

Marianne has worked it all out.

We go over it again. We need to refer to him as Jake now at all times. My story will be that I invited him to dinner to break things off with him. I'll say I arranged for Marianne to babysit Kai so he wouldn't be disturbed in case there were tears or angry words. I'll claim we shared a bottle of wine, and Jake was too drunk to drive. I offered to put him up on the sofa – most of these explanations are an extension of the truth. We need to stay as close to the events that unfolded as possible.

Pierre decides to call the police, pre-empting a visit that would surely come anyway sometime this morning. He tells them his sister has just found a note from her boyfriend saying he's going to kill himself.

And we wait for them to arrive.

FIFTY-NINE

ONCE THE AMBULANCE has taken Jake's body away from the Villards' land, Inspecteur Angéloz from the Fribourg Cantonal Police appears at our door. He clears his throat and asks us all to sit at our kitchen table. My heart is pounding. The suicide note lies between us. It's grubby, a tea stain seeps from one corner over a third of the letter and dust from the kitchen floor clings to it in patches.

'I'm sorry, I dropped it. I was so shocked,' I say, remembering the day I truly dropped it in horror in the dorm room of our guest house in Pokhara.

I can't read the expression on the policeman's face as he leans across to look at it with a frown. I'm sure I have guilt written all over my face. He reaches out and takes a tiny corner of the paper to spin the letter towards him so he can read the text. I wonder if he understands English.

'I will need to take this, madame... mademoiselle.'

The correction is not lost on me. It seems strange, considering I'm holding Kai. I feel very old at this moment. Kai is in my arms to give the impression of an anxious mother and a grieving fiancée. He's awake, practising his new gurgling language that only he understands. I vow never to tell him about what I have discovered over the past couple of weeks. When I picked him up from his crib this morning, I swore I would keep the idea alive that a handsome Canadian Tai Chi instructor was this little boy's father.

'And you will need to come to the morgue in Fribourg later to officially identify the bod... Monsieur Spencer. Do you know whether he has any family here?'

'I don't think so.'

'We will have to try and find a next of kin,' he says.

'His mother has died. I think he was an only child. He said he was estranged from his father. He grew up in the US – Kansas, I think. I don't know much about his family. He was very... secretive. You'd have to search his house. We were dating, then I... broke it off. Felt it wasn't fair to burden him with a baby.'

My voice is still genuinely shaky, knowing I have to stay as close to the truth as possible. I don't need to feign the trauma.

Kai wriggles in my arms. I rock him gently and reach for a teaspoon on the table for him to play with. He looks at me and smiles. I automatically smile back. He is my shield to the guilt. I stare at him to maintain a visual connection with anything other than the policeman sitting in front of me. When my heart calms, I kiss the top of Kai's head. The policeman nods towards Kai.

'So the victim isn't the father of the little one?' he asks.

'No!' I say, shaking my head.

My voice sounds suddenly too loud in the confines of our kitchen. The sharp *No* echoes in the space. The policeman's use of the word 'victim' sends panic through me. I can't work out if that's accusation in his tone. What do you call someone who's killed himself? I guess he must be a victim. But the policeman doesn't seem fazed. He touches the button on his radio slung near his shoulder as it hisses suddenly in the silence.

Pierre's eyelid ticks nervously as he stares at the table. I can tell he is worried someone will blurt the name Scott. Kai's amusement on my lap turns to a whine as he senses my tension.

'No, but they had been planning a life together... before,' says Pierre.

My eyebrows crease in alarm. I hope Angéloz hasn't seen the dagger look I give my brother. Then I sniff and pretend to let out a little sob. I force my gaze back to my baby. I don't want to look at either Pierre or Marianne, afraid I can be read like an open book.

'I am sorry,' says Angéloz, sounding genuinely sympathetic. 'Once we confirm his identity, we may need to question you again. You may be the only contact we have in Switzerland. Do you know where he was working?'

I think of the phone call I made to J P Morgan in Geneva. I shake my head.

'He was on some kind of sabbatical,' I say.

Angéloz rises from the table. Kai sits up and stares at him with his little mouth making an almost perfect 'O.'

'You have a cute son,' says Angéloz. I wonder whether he has children of his own. 'I'll need to take this,' he indicates the suicide note, 'And I'll send a car for you to go to the morgue this afternoon – what time would suit you best? Around the baby's timetable of course.' As though pampering to my every need, sympathy slips off his tongue.

We organise a time, and Angéloz leaves. I didn't realise his partner had been checking the area around the river where we'd taken Jake in the middle of the night. I wonder what they'll talk about on the way back to the station in the patrol car. I wonder how closely they'll examine the suicide note.

I don't yet feel I can breathe a sigh of relief.

SIXTY

JAKE'S BODY ON the gurney doesn't look human. He's like a dressmaker's mannequin that's been slathered in pale grey makeup for a horror film. I hardly recognise his face. He resembles more the old Jake, before his transformation. He looks so far from the Scott I fell for. There's a strange chemical smell in the viewing room, and I can't wait to leave. But before I do, I confirm to the physician on duty that this corpse is Jacob Scott Spencer.

It was Angéloz's assistant who drove me to the morgue, but it's Angéloz himself who drives me back to the farm.

'I don't want to upset you, but I would like to just have another little chat with your family,' he says. 'We have to write a report with all possible scenarios considered.'

'What scenarios?' I ask.

'It's pure formality, mademoiselle, those close to victims will always be interviewed. It's possible you also may need counselling, so we can see what the best way forward is, whether we need to assign anyone to you. With our approval, it will be covered by your health insurance.'

This is probably a standard procedure for my benefit, but I get the uneasy feeling he's fishing for something else.

'You're wearing it again,' he says, observing the filigree gold band on my left ring finger, emphasising the reason behind his concern.

We thought it would somehow help, to show I had regrets about Jake's death, signs of a grieving fiancée, lamenting the intention to break the relationship. The ring sears my finger like molten metal. I stare out of the window at the passing vines and mountains above.

When we reach the farm, the police talk to Pierre and Marianne. They put on an admirably good performance. Then they want to speak to Papa.

Pierre and I demand to be with him. Papa's responses will be unpredictable. The police agree to our presence. We can at least explain the random people Papa will talk about. He'll recount events that happened decades ago, members of his family who are either dead or haven't been seen for years. I wonder why they insist on talking to him. He can't help them. They say it's merely a formality.

'What's all the fuss? Have you been in trouble, Jean?' Papa asks Pierre as we crowd around his bed.

'It's my friend... Jake,' I explain to him. 'He's committed suicide.'

'Your young man? Wasn't he called something else?' Papa asks, looking at me. I hold my breath. In a moment of clarity, he turns to Monsieur Angéloz. 'Didn't seem particularly sad to me. They made such a lovely couple, had such adventures, creating a wonderful life on the other side of the world. Never had the desire to go to Australia myself. Shame. I suppose you never know. They say depression is such a secretive illness.'

My heart is pounding.

'He's mixing things up,' I say to Angéloz, thinking: *He's not the only one.* 'He's talking about my Uncle Jean. He thinks Jake was Uncle Jean. It was his reaction to me breaking off our relationship.'

'Jake? Jean?' says Papa. 'No no, I mean, what was his name? S… Stéphane.'

I almost faint when Papa utters the first S and hope my face hasn't drained of colour.

'That's our cousin in Australia,' Pierre says, his tight voice coming to me as though down a very long tunnel.

The police give up, and eventually leave, realising Papa is as incoherent as we'd explained.

THE NEXT ALARM bell rings when Valérie calls to tell me they've been round to see her. I had no idea they would do this. I wonder how they knew she was my friend. I also regret not having shared any of my secrets with her. Every time she's called since Paris, I've put her off, telling her Kai was under the weather, or that I've had so much going on and haven't had time to meet her. But now the police will be confused about the names.

'What did they ask you?'

'They called him Jacob. I said no, the man you were dating was called Scott. They seemed surprised, but then realised that was his second name. I didn't know what to tell them, Sand, what was I supposed to say?' I don't know what to tell her, but before I think of an explanation she continues. 'Was something going on between you guys? A rocky patch? Had you met someone new? I was confused when they talked about this Jacob. The police wouldn't tell me how he… died. They said it was an accident, but then something they said made me think he'd taken his life. Are you okay, Sandrine? This must really be terrible for you. I'm so, so sorry. What a horrible thing to happen, especially after that guy who drowned himself last year in Nepal.'

I draw in my breath.

'Did you tell the police about that?'

'No, I... I only thought of it after they left. I thought it was weird... a coincidence. It's nothing to do with what's happened... is it?

'No, no, it's not. Look, Val, I'm really sorry. This is such a mess. I promise I'll call you in a few days to catch up. There are a few things to sort out here, and then I'm sure I'll be needing a bit of a lift. It's been hard. But Pierre and Marianne have been so good to me.' *You'll never know how much.*

I sniff, to make it sound like I've been crying. She tells me to phone if I think there's anything she can do, and I end the call.

SIXTY-ONE

THE NEXT TIME they come back to the farm unannounced, the police act awkwardly, as though uncertain about procedures. There are three of them this time. We watch them through the kitchen window. One police officer looks around the yard, opening barn doors, lifting water butt lids, shifting farm tools.

Inspector Angéloz approaches the back door leading out of the utility room with a man in a white coat. Pierre puts his coffee mug down on the counter by the sink a little heavily and utters a quiet *merde* under his breath.

'What's the problem, officer?' Pierre asks as he opens the door.

I know Angéloz is going to mention talking to Valérie. I wonder who else they might have spoken to. I can't think how they discovered Val is my best friend.

'There are many unclear fingerprints on Monsieur Spencer's suicide note,' he tells Pierre. 'It is nothing to be alarmed about, but my director has asked that we check them all by taking the family's fingerprints. He is questioning the age of the note, when it might have been written.'

My heart beats hard. I'd been afraid of this, but hadn't thought it would happen.

'Are you kidding me?' I say, my voice a little higher than I had intended.

Pierre holds out his hand, patting the air between us.

'It's okay, Sandrine.'

He turns to the policeman, and I hope this brief exchange doesn't look like we're covering something up.

'What are you suggesting, Inspector?'

I admire his skill at keeping his voice steady, as though he's been practising his lines.

'It's a mere formality, Monsieur Bavaud, but there are so many prints. Most of them are not readable – the note is quite dirty. But there is one particularly prominent print on the letter which is not that of the victim. It is very clear due to the presence of an oil-based product. But the origin is vague. I'm just following instructions from forensics. I'm sorry, I know this is distressing for your sister.'

I immediately have a vision of Mr Bhandari, chief inspector at the Pokhara District Police Station, slicking back his dark oiled hair with his hand and picking up the letter. Do they think Jake might have penned the note under duress? That someone forced him to write it? Do they suspect we had a hand in his death?

'Your friend Mademoiselle Valérie Mermod told us it was her understanding that your partner was called Scott. We're wondering if there is something you haven't told us. Perhaps there is more to your breakup with Monsieur Spencer than you would first have us believe.'

'He... he introduced himself to me as Scott on the first day,' I say truthfully. 'He said he used his second name professionally, but very soon after we met, he wanted me to call him Jake.' The lie slipped easily off my tongue.

Angéloz doesn't say anything, but tips his head to one side.

'I don't understand how someone would want to use different names,' he says after a pause.

'I don't know either. It must have been something to do with his business… perhaps he thought we wouldn't see each other again after our first meeting. I knew him as Jake after that. I never asked him why.'

I pray they believe me. I imagine this isn't a common occurrence in rural Switzerland. A suicide, maybe, but a tiny seed of something that isn't quite right means they have to come back to question a woman they're feeling sorry for and were comforting a few days ago. This is beyond the stuff of television and films, but I'm still terrified they'll ask me to *assist them with their enquiries* down at the police station.

'We are going to need to take fingerprints,' Angéloz says.

His dark eyes flash with sympathy. I have the feeling he doesn't want me to be guilty of anything other than dating the wrong man. At the word 'fingerprints' the man in the white coat next to Angéloz lifts the bag he's holding.

They take prints from all four of us, including Papa. I wonder if they can tell it's not a Caucasian print on the suicide note. I wonder if they can tell where the paper comes from. And I wonder if they'll be taking prints at Jake's apartment. They'd find Pierre's would match a few on Jake's bathroom cabinet. I suck on my bottom lip.

'One last thing. I've been instructed to search the house,' says Angéloz and my shoulders drop as I take a deep sigh. 'I'm sorry, it's only instructions from my director,' he says.

'I can't imagine what you're looking for. Just because of one fingerprint? We have nothing to hide Monsieur Angéloz. Jake has been in the house several times.'

My story about offering to put Jake up on the sofa because he'd had too much to drink would hold. He'd sat there often enough, even though it might have been weeks ago. The sofa only gets a vacuuming once or twice a year, so some trace of him will still be present, a hair, a flake of his skin, Jacob Scott Spencer's DNA.

'What are you looking for?' asks Pierre, and as an afterthought. 'Don't you need a warrant for that kind of thing?'

'Pierre,' I blurt. 'You've been watching too many movies.'

The forensics man's mouth turns down at the corners and he shakes his head.

'We don't know what we're looking for. It's routine. We only want to check your rooms. It's nothing specific. Monsieur Spencer's apartment will be the focus of a more thorough examination.'

I swallow, glance at Pierre, and know he's had the same thought about his fingerprints.

'I hope you're not going to turn the place upside down,' says Pierre.

'Monsieur Bavaud, we won't take long. This isn't being treated as a crime scene,' says Inspector Angéloz.

His tone has wavered from sympathetic to impatient. He makes me want to add the word 'yet' to his sentence.

When Pierre shows them the gun safe, they ask to see where the keys are kept. I can't work out why they want to know, and wonder if they're merely filling time. Pierre pulls out the licenses for all three weapons in the cupboard. A shotgun, the gun bolt for putting down injured cattle, and the .22.

I think of *Free Sport* in Fribourg, and blush at my naivety of thinking I could just march into the shop like a US army surplus store to buy a gun to protect Kai and me.

I hope they don't find out I've been there. I hope they don't interview the man in the store.

SIXTY-TWO

THEY TURN UP again when we're all sitting in the kitchen late
on a Friday afternoon, a heavy spring shower hammering the
windows. Angry clouds scud above the Dent de Lys, dulling the
green of the beech forest across the river. I imagine the irritated
team wanting to sign off, a reluctant detective and his side-kick
hoping to tie up a case before the weekend.

The fingerprint on the suicide note remains unidentified.
They say it appears to be a primary print, but are vague about
their theories. It was only identifiable because of the oil residue.
Again, I envision the shiny oiled hair of Chief Inspector
Bhandari. They don't comment about the low-grade paper the
note is written on, which I guess Jake picked up from a stall in
Durbar Square. By the time the police took it away from the
farm for forensic inspection, the note had passed through the
hands of myself, Pierre and Marianne. It was scuffed from the
kitchen floor and spent a brief spell in a small puddle of tea on
the counter.

'We've been to Monsieur Spencer's apartment. As you know,
Mademoiselle, one of our issues has been the authenticity of his
suicide note, and for that I am so sorry to have put you through
so much anxiety.'

I take a sip of tea from my mug to stop my lips or hands trembling. They haven't been treating Pierre any differently this time, so I hope they didn't take prints in Jake's apartment.

'My colleagues found some documents, particularly an agenda showing Monsieur Spencer's work-out regime at *Fitness Equilibre*, the gym he was regularly attending in Lausanne – he had gold membership.'

Angéloz said this as though he was impressed. Even on the slab in the morgue it was obvious how well-toned Jake had been. 'We interviewed his personal trainer. He was also called Scott by everyone at the gym...' *Here we go, I am done for now* '... which reassures us that he did indeed use both his names in different situations.'

I let out a long silent breath.

'But the main thing is we were able to verify that Monsieur Spencer's handwriting in his agenda was the same as his suicide note.'

It's something I hadn't considered. All along they were trying to establish the authenticity of the suicide note, made all the more challenging by the use of different names. But they have matched his handwriting. I'm concentrating so hard on my own guilt, trying to avoid having murderer written all over my face, that I almost miss this vindication. I nod and Angéloz continues.

'Once we found his passport and papers, we confirmed his identity with the US embassy. They've come back to us with some information. Monsieur Spencer's father is recently deceased. He also took his own life.'

I cover my mouth with my hand. I'm sure I'm not the only one surprised by the symmetry.

'Depression may have been a family trait. We do not know if he had contact with his son before his own... death. Given your relationship with Monsieur Spencer, we have been instructed by the US consulate to have you sign this form as his... former partner, to expedite procedures. As there is currently no evidence of an immediate next-of-kin, they are suggesting that the body be cremated here to avoid repatriation. As his... partner you would have the choice of how to dispose of the remains.'

I'm determined not to look at the rubbish bin under our kitchen sink.

SIXTY-THREE

KAI SMILES WITH recognition when Angéloz returns a few days later with his assistant in tow. The policeman ruffles his hair. Kai giggles in return, before I sit him in his high chair.

'Please, take a seat.' I point to the chairs around kitchen table. 'Would you like a *briselet* with your coffee? This is becoming a regular thing. I feel like I should ask Papa to join us and get the cards out for a game of *jass*.' I let out a short laugh for the first time in days.

As Angéloz pulls a chair out to sit beside Kai, I open a glass jar and shake some of the biscuits Marianne made yesterday onto a plate. Angéloz's assistant approaches me at the sink as I begin filling the Mocha coffee pot, and speaks over my shoulder.

'It's okay, Madamemoiselle,' he says quietly enough so the others can't hear. 'I don't know why Monsieur Angéloz has insisted on coming. This should have been organised through Monsieur Spencer's bank. If I didn't know any better, he's making an excuse to call on you again.'

I recoil with surprise, which I cover by clattering mugs out of the cupboard one at a time. I hadn't considered the swarthy inspector as anything other than a policeman, even when he was being sympathetic. It was the last thing on my mind. The assistant takes the plate of biscuits to the table.

'We were wondering whether you intended to make a claim. Financially,' Angéloz explains when we are all seated.

I look at him, puzzled, as I pour coffee into their mugs.

'You are... were... Monsieur Spencer's fiancée,' he says as he slurps his coffee.

I try not to look at the ring I put on as I saw the patrol car pulling into the driveway. I wish he wouldn't keep referring to me as Jake's partner. Every time he says it, I feel sick.

'I am, but... I wouldn't have thought I had the right. We weren't living together.'

Angéloz sits back, his eyebrows raised.

'I thought I told you the baby isn't his,' I say.

'You did, but that doesn't mean he didn't want to be involved in the child's life. Now that we've finished searching Monsieur Spencer's apartment, we wondered if you wanted to pick up any of the things you left there. The rental company wants to clear the place as the contract runs out at the end of the month.'

I frown.

'What things?' I didn't want to be responsible for Jake's furnishings.

'This little chap's things, for example,' he said, putting a hand on Kai's shoulder. 'The clothing, changing bag and travel cot for a start. Surely these are things you will still need?'

I draw in my breath, and my heart begins to pound. Was Jake planning to take Kai with him so soon? Oh God.

'And I ask about the claim because Monsieur Spencer was rather well off. It's a bit complicated because we still haven't heard whether he has any living relatives, and he has no written will. But his financial advisor was told to keep his accounts active, whatever rumours he might hear about Monsieur Spencer. We can only assume it's because he might have been in the process of including you and your son on one of his accounts. Some of his credit cards linked to accounts in Las Vegas were cancelled some time ago when he was travelling.'

I swallowed, didn't trust myself to speak.

Angéloz smiled, sympathy apparent on his face.

'As a fiancée in this country, you might have a claim, but I'm not sure how the US will favour this. If you don't proceed, the Kansas court administering his probate case will appoint a personal representative for Monsieur Spencer's estate who will try to locate his distant heirs. If no one qualifies, I imagine they will exercise their doctrine of escheat, and the assets will go to the state. It would be a shame if this happened, especially… if you think you have any right to the assets.'

'What do you mean by "well off?"' I say, thinking about a snazzy modern jogging buggy I'd seen that I couldn't possibly afford, and wondered what other equipment Jake had acquired for Kai.

'His assets amount to several million.'

My eyes widen.

'Dollars,' he says.

This time my mouth gapes open.

I could have told them there and then we had intended to marry, to qualify the comment Pierre made during the first encounter with the police. That yes, to all intent and purposes, we were living together. A common-law relationship. That in an unusual deviation from the bureaucracy that makes Switzerland so efficient, I had never officially changed my address to his duplex in Chardonne.

But it made me sick to think I could claim anything that belonged to my aggressor, my rapist. I told myself I didn't need his filthy money. Not only because it was his, but because it would always remind me of my own guilt.

But then I think of Papa, how soon we will need to consider putting him in a home where professionals can take care of him better than us as his condition continues to deteriorate. The cost will be significant, and the profits from the farm business probably won't be able to cover them. Then I consider whose guilt I am thinking of. My mind flees back to Nepal.

I recall Chief Inspector Bhandari at the Pokhara District Police Station. I imagine his disorganisation, perhaps still trying to muster up a team of divers to look for a body on the bottom of Lake Phewa. I had no inkling of this whole deceit back then.

Bhandari will never find that body, but I send him silent thanks for inadvertently slipping the key to my freedom into the package of documents the day I left Pokhara to come home to the Alps.

I think of the lies, the horror, the real reason I couldn't find Kai senior on my last day in Thailand.

My eyes fill with tears and Angéloz presses his lips together. He must think I am grieving Jake's loss. Kai touches my face in a gesture beyond his age and practises a 'Mum-um-um-um' sound through his lips. I look away from the men sitting at the table. They're probably anticipating the headlines in *Le Matin*: "Local girl heartbroken after regretting break-up with suicidal boyfriend."

But I am grieving. It's true. I'm mourning the loss of someone else. I can't even begin to mentally reconstruct the brutal thing Jake did. My guilt finally runs out. The tears flowing are for Kai. For the lover I only ever knew on a spiritual level, for a true and beautiful soul. I cling to the image of the man I had already convinced myself for so many months was the father of my child.

Then the memory of the document from the lab slips into my mind. The proof of paternity is a feathery pile of burned ashes in the wood stove. But the lab office will have a record in their files. This will make the search for an immediate next-of-kin a whole lot easier for the Kansas court administering probate for Jacob Scott Spencer.

I realise now why Inspecteur Angéloz has come personally to tell me this. To give me this opportunity. And the more I think about it, the more I'm sure that I should take his advice and secure a future for my son.

ACKNOWLEDGMENTS

The Beaten Track formed the dissertation of my Masters in Crime Writing at UEA. For their wise tutelage I thank Julia Crouch, Tom Benn and Nathan Hughes. For their invaluable help at various stages of the manuscript: Antony Dunford, Elizabeth Saccente and the rest of the Crime Gang 17 cohort at UEA, Zoë Apostolides, Franca Bernatavicius, Christie Worrell, Diane Jeffrey and early beta readers in the Zug Book Club. Thank you Sean Coleman for being so enthusiastic about Sandrine and Jake's journey and offering the perfect publishing kennel at Red Dog Press. Thanks also to my parents who never once discouraged me from taking off around the world with my backpack or my bike in the days before mobile phones and internet. I wish you were here, Dad, to have witnessed my subsequent journey to publication. Lastly, thanks to my long-suffering husband and sons Chris, Max and Finn, who continue to put up with me tap-tapping away at our dining room table when we are not travelling to new lands and discovering new adventures.

ABOUT THE AUTHOR

Louise Mangos writes novels, short stories and flash fiction, which have won prizes, placed on shortlists, and have been read out on BBC radio. Her short fiction appears in more than twenty print anthologies. She holds an MA in crime writing from UEA for which *The Beaten Track* formed her dissertation.

You can connect with Louise on Facebook — /LouiseMangosBooks, or Twitter @LouiseMangos, and Instagram as @louisemangos, or visit her website www.louisemangos.com where there are links to some of her short fiction.

After travelling several times around the world on her own, Louise now lives in the Swiss Alps with her Kiwi husband and two sons.

CPSIA information can be obtained
at www.ICGtesting.com
Printed in the USA
LVHW090455240322
714211LV00001B/1

9 781914 480614